With Banners

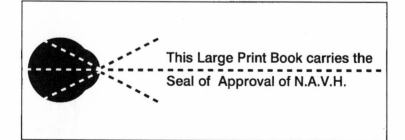

With Banners

Emilie Loring

Thorndike Press • Thorndike, Maine

Published in 1999 by arrangement with Little, Brown and Company, Inc.

Thorndike Large Print ® Candlelight Series.

The tree indicium is a trademark of Thorndike Press.

The text of this Large Print edition is unabridged.
Other aspects of the book may vary from the original edition.

Set in 16 pt. Plantin

Printed in the United States on permanent paper.

Library of Congress Cataloging-in-Publication Data

Loring, Emilie Baker.
    With banners / Emilie Loring.
        p.   cm.
    ISBN 0-7862-2195-X (lg. print : hc : alk. paper)
    1. Large type books.   I. Title.
    [PS3523.O645W58   1999]
    813'.52—dc21   99-41717

To
The Playwrights and Players
Past and Present
of My Family

I

With a nice sense of dramatic values, the heel of Brooke Reyburn's shoe turned sharply as she ran across the street. She went down on one knee just as the traffic light turned green. She had a confused sense of an automobile bearing down on her, the screech of brakes, of panting cars, of arms lifting her to the sidewalk.

"Hurt?" a voice demanded.

She was conscious of the sticky dampness of one knee even as she shook her head and dazedly looked about. The gold dome of the State House shone in the afternoon sun; boys were calling the headlines of the evening papers; an autogiro was crawling like a huge spider across the blue ceiling of the sky. She was still in the world. For one horrible instant she had thought she might be passing out of it; her heart beat like a tom-tom.

She looked up into the eyes blazing down at her. She must have had a narrow escape to have wiped the color from the man's face. It was chalky. Even the lips below his clipped dark mus-

7

tache were colorless.

"I'm all right, really I am. It was my silly heel that threw me," she assured breathlessly, even as she moved her knee experimentally. It worked. It wasn't broken.

"Why wear such fool heels? If you're not hurt, why did you wince?"

The man's voice was husky; his eyes had a third-degree intentness which roused a little demon of opposition. Brooke retorted crisply:

"If you insist upon probing the secrets of my young life, I think I've skinned my knee."

"Perhaps that skinned knee will teach you not to sprint across the street against the traffic light. I almost lost my mind when I saw you go down just as that car cut around the corner. Don't you know better than to try such a foolish stunt?"

Even making allowance for his fright and for the fact that a man usually roared at the nearest woman when frightened, he had no right to speak to her as if she were a dumbbell. Wasn't it maddening enough to fall in the middle of a city street without being lectured for it? Brooke's eyes flashed up to his.

"At least I know better than to stand on a street corner talking to a stranger," she

retorted in a voice which was fiercely satis-
fying to the tumult within her.

She thought the man spoke as she
merged in the stream of passers-by. She
passed the building to which she had been
hurrying to keep an appointment when she
crossed the street. She wouldn't go in yet,
she'd better wait till her still thumping
heart quieted before she entered the offices
of Stewart and Stewart, Attorneys at Law,
she had too much pride to appear there
breathless and shaken. That had been a
narrow escape, not only for her, but for the
man who had snatched her from the path
of that speeding car, and — horrible
thought — she hadn't even said "Thank
you!"

Her cheeks burned as she remembered
the risk he had taken for her and her
abrupt and ungracious departure. He had
made it clear enough when he had deposited her on her feet on the sidewalk that he
thought her brain quite devoid of gray
matter. Her apparent ingratitude wouldn't
send her stock up.

If only she knew who he was she could
write to him, but he might have been a
stranger passing through the city whom
she never would see again. In that case she
would have to bear always this pricking

sense of being ashamed of herself, it would bring her sitting straight up in bed when she thought of it at night.

She stopped at a flower shop. Its color and beauty were like a soothing hand on her smarting conscience. The air had but a hint of the crispness of early October. It was so mild that great pots of chrysanthemums, white, yellow, pink, rusty-orange, and browny-red, were massed under gay awnings. There was a flat dish of rosy japonicas in the window; gladioli, dozens of them; spikes of heavenly blue larkspur; violets, deeply purple, by the alluring bunch; unbelievably perfect Templar roses in crimson masses, and a tray of gardenias in waxy perfection.

Overhead a steeple clock chimed. The sound reminded Brooke of her engagement. She winced as she moved. The words of her rescuer flashed through her mind:

"Perhaps that skinned knee will teach you not to sprint across the street against the traffic light."

Dictator! She made a little disdainful face as his flashed on the screen of her mind. To shake off the memory she glanced again at the flower-shop window. The violets were ravishing. How she would like a bunch but — no "but" about it now, she could buy them. Hadn't she incredibly and miraculously acquired a fortune?

The fragrance of the purple flowers tucked into the green tweed jacket of her suit helped unbelievably to keep her mind off her smarting knee and pricking conscience as she entered the office of the junior partner of Stewart and Stewart. No one here?

After a furtive look about, she examined her knee. Skinned. She had known it. Shreds of her silk stocking clung to the raw flesh. She winced as her lowered skirt scraped it. Her unknown rescuer and dictator need not fear that she would forget that lesson in a hurry.

Where was Mr. Jed Stewart?

There was an open book on his large flat desk. The title fairly jumped at her.

UNDERWOOD ON WILLS

Brooke's heart did a nose-dive. Did that particular book on that particular desk mean that Stewart and Stewart were preparing to contest the will in which she had been named residuary legatee?

Silly, she derided herself, wasn't the firm executor of the estate of Mary Amanda

Dane? Hadn't Mr. Jed Stewart notified her that the will had been allowed, hadn't he asked her to be at his office today at four? It was her late shakeup and this gloomy room which had started her imagination on the rampage. Where it wasn't knotty pine it was walled with books impressively, if mustily, bound in calf. An Indian drugget, worn thin under the swivel chair at the desk, covered the floor. The brass top of a massive inkwell glowed red gold where a vagrant ray from the slanting sun struck it. Heavy rust-color hangings framed the windows. No wonder the electric lights were on at this time in the afternoon.

From outside came faint distant noises in the corridor: footsteps thudding, scuffing, springing past; the incessant clang of elevator doors. Inside, "Tick-tock! Tick-tock!" the wall clock marked time for the quick procession of the minutes.

And the minutes were marching along. Where was Mr. Stewart? Was it part of legal procedure to keep clients in suspense? The secretary in the outer office had shown her into this room, had said that she was expected, that the junior partner was in conference but would be at liberty in a few moments.

She compared her wrist watch with the clock. When she had dashed across the street, she had thought she was late for the appointment, she had been detained at the store. She had been in business long enough to realize what it meant to keep a person waiting, that time was money. The rumble of voices in an adjoining office drifted through an open transom. If only Jed Stewart would cut his conference short and tell her why he had sent for her. If the legacy was to be held up, she would like to know. She hated uncertainty.

Restlessly she crossed to the window. She slipped behind one of the hangings to shut off the electric light in the room behind her. What a view! Roofs. Tiers of roofs alive with pigeons. Patches of bright blue broke up the pattern of gray clouds. Weather vanes pointed to the north. Innumerable wires etched gigantic cobwebs against the sky. Skylights shone like sheets of molten brass as they reflected the sun. Flags were flying. Smoke from chimneys was blowing out as straight as the tails of kites in action. Huge signs glimmered with faint lights. Far away on the hazy violet horizon a white spire pointed the way to Heaven. The beat of drums, the shrill of a traffic whistle, the wail of a siren on a fire-

13

boat in the harbor pierced the muted roar and rattle, the rhythmic, vibrant throb of the city which rose from the street thirty floors below, pierced even the deafening thunder of the wings of the night mail as it passed overhead.

Her eyes lingered on the roofs. Beneath them business units were pitched together. Honesty and fraud; virtue and vice; ups and downs; efficiency and stupidity; ambition and lethargy; each unit moving in its own orbit and each thinking itself of supreme importance in the complicated pattern of the business world. She ought to know something of that world. She had been buffeting her way in it for five years.

Had been. Her throat tightened. Could she really use that tense? Was it possible that in future she need not squeeze every nickel until the buffalo on it bucked? Was it true that while everyone she knew was adapting expenses to meet a reduced income, a small fortune had dropped into her lap from an absolutely clear sky? It was a "Through the Looking-glass" reversal. It had a fairy-story quality, it belonged in Once upon a Time land — but — she touched the violets, it was true.

"Miss Reyburn ought to be here, Mark, but I suppose like the majority of women

14

she has no idea of the value of a man's time."

The annoyed comment in the room behind her snapped Brooke out of her reflections. How like a man to assume that she was at fault. She would make a dramatic entrance, and then —

"Glad she is late. I told you, Jed, that I didn't want to meet her. It was a *beau geste* for her to offer me half of the money, all of which should be mine by inheritance. I'll make my get-away before she comes. Let her move into Lookout House pronto. I'm the only person in the world with the right to contest Aunt Mary Amanda Dane's will, and, much as I would like to own the family heirlooms and add her part of the house to mine, I won't do that. I would have to prove 'undue influence' or 'unsound mind,' wouldn't I? How could I do that when under oath I would have to acknowledge that my aunt had said she would cut me out of her will? The fact that I didn't believe she would do it wouldn't cut any ice with the Court. Nothing doing. I've had publicity enough over my domestic casualty to last the rest of my life."

Brooke's hand dropped from the hanging. That must be Mark Trent's deep voice tinged with anger. By "her" did he mean

15

herself? So he thought her offer to share with him merely a *beau geste*. Should she have refused to take any of the legacy? This was hardly the tactful moment to make her entrance. He was going. As soon as the door closed, she would appear and explain to Mr. Stewart why she had been at the window; meantime she would be strictly honorable and not listen. She stuffed her fingers into her ears.

At the same moment on the other side of the hangings, Jed Stewart was saying:

"I never did understand why Lookout House was cut in two, Mark."

"It wasn't. Grandfather Trent had two houses built exactly alike, one for his daughter, Mary Amanda, and one for his son, my father; the Other House, the family called ours. Not satisfied with that, he had them set side by side on a rocky promontory — he intended them for summer homes only — with doors through the library downstairs and the hall on the second floor and connecting balconies; he was a glutton for balconies. Aunt Mary Amanda recently has lived there the year round. I inherited Father's house, but I haven't lived there since — well, for three years. It has been closed. I haven't rented it because I thought it might be unpleasant

16

for my aunt to have strangers near when she was wheeled into the garden which serves for both places. Now, see what she does to me. She picks up this girl and later, while I'm starting a branch office in South America, leaves her her half of the real estate and all her money. Well, I'll be off. I have a date."

"Don't go, Mark. I asked Miss Reyburn to come here this afternoon to tell her what financial arrangements have been made for her, but principally to get you two face to face so that we could straighten out this mess about the personal property in the house."

"Mess! Do you call a sound, unbreakable will a mess? Aunt Mary Amanda Dane warned me that if I married Lola she would cut me off with the proverbial shilling; then, when my divorce became necessary, she was more opposed to it than she had been to the marriage. Can you beat that for inconsistency? I've always had a hunch that the French man and wife who have worked for and worked Mary Amanda for years might hypnotize her into leaving all her property to them — I warned her against them and somehow they found out and have hated me ever since — but I didn't think she would leave it to a comparative stranger. In my opinion, Clotilde and Henri Jacques are no better than a couple of bandits; they'll bear watching. I don't trust the Reyburn female either, her fine Italian hand crops up all through that will, but I don't like the idea of a girl living in the same house with them. However, she'd probably think I had an axe to grind if I warned her. Why in heaven's name didn't you give me a hint how the property was going?"

"Yellow journals and hectic fiction to the contrary, lawyers don't talk about the affairs of a client, even to their best friend, fella."

"Don't blow up like a pouter pigeon, Jed. Of course I didn't expect you to tell me; equally, of course, I wouldn't try to upset that will. My aunt's High Church convictions wouldn't permit her to approve of my separation from a wife who had been sordidly unfaithful. I thought she might soften toward me when Lola married the third time, but evidently not. If she wanted to bequeath her house, her money, and her jewels to a girl she had picked up via radio, okay. But perhaps you can tell me where all the money she left came from? I knew that she inherited half of Grandfather Trent's property, but I hadn't supposed that her husband, Dane, left much. About five hundred thousand, you said?"

"Plus, and all in savings banks and gilt-edge securities, that is, as gilt-edge as any investment, these days. Can you beat that for a mild little crippled old lady who looked as if she didn't dare call her soul her own?"

"And who lived as if the big bad wolf of a moneyless future were forever sniffing at her door. I about laugh my head off when I think of the cheque I sent her each month with which to buy a few little luxuries, knowing how incomes had been cut — I thought it must take all of hers to keep her home going — the money was a long delayed return for the fun I had visiting her when I was a kid. Mother wouldn't live in our half of the house, but for years I spent Thanksgiving with Aunt Mary Amanda. I hadn't thought she had much of a sense of humor, but she must have crackled with it when she dropped my small cheques into her fat bank account."

"But she didn't drop them into her bank account, Mark. Have you forgotten her reference to that in the will?"

"Not a chance. I know it by heart. She kept the money in a separate deposit, which was to be paid to me with interest.

19

She had accepted it because she thought it good discipline for a youth in this wild generation to deny himself for someone else. Why didn't she tell me about the Reyburn female? Why not ask me to meet her before I went to South America? That's what makes me suspicious. The secrecy of their friendship. Was the girl afraid that if I knew I would try to influence my aunt against her? If I was so dense, how do you suppose she got wise to Mary Amanda's fortune? I understand that she had supper and spent a night with her once a week, the night the companion-nurse had off. She must have had a strong motive to commute twenty miles after business hours. She's a fashion adviser in one of the big shops, isn't she?"

"Yep. Worked up from a model. Mary Amanda Dane tuned in on the radio one morning just as Brooke Reyburn was giving her fashion talk. She fell in love with her voice, and wrote to the girl asking what the well-dressed invalid tied to a wheel chair was wearing. Miss Reyburn answered with such sympathetic understanding that your aunt invited her to Lookout House."

"It's a fairy story brought up to date. Only, for the spell of a witch, substitute the broadcast of a girl's voice. The little schemer got not only the money but Mary Amanda's jewels, many of which were my grandmother's."

Brooke dropped her hands from her ears after what seemed hours. Still talking? Perhaps Jed Stewart was talking to the office boy. She heard him say:

"Your aunt said in her will, remember, that if she left the jewels to you, you might — well, that Miss Reyburn would appreciate them. She relented toward you to the extent of naming you legatee should the girl die without children; she was canny enough to prevent her fortune from falling into the hands of her family. You wouldn't think Brooke Reyburn a schemer if you saw her; you'd know that she had a background of cultivated living. She has a vivid face with a deep dimple at one corner of her lovely mouth; her voice is sweet, spiced with daring. She came out of college to carry her whole darn family when her father died — he was one of the tragic twenty-niners whose investments were wiped out — now, I suppose, her brother, who is acting in a stock company, and her sister will chuck their jobs and settle down on her. Her hair is like copper with the sun on it; her eyes change from brown to amber, and when she smiles at me I feel as cocky as a drum major at the head of a regiment."

"Help! You're raving, Jed. Perhaps you're thinking of marrying her?"

"Marry her yourself, Mark, and keep the fortune in the family."

"I! Marry that girl who hypnotized an old woman into leaving her a fortune! You're crazy. Besides, I am married."

"You haven't caught your aunt's ideas on divorce, have you? You don't feel tied to that woman who ran away with that French Count, do you? You divorced her, didn't you? You —"

"Hold everything! We were talking of the Reyburn girl. You have nerve to make the suggestion that I marry her. Men have been put on the spot for less. I wouldn't marry that schemer if —"

Brooke flung back the hanging in a passion of rage.

"Nobody asked you to!" She cleared her voice of hoarseness, and flamed:

"Has it never occurred to you, Mark Trent —" She stopped, her eyes wide with amazement. Was this really the man who had pulled her from in front of that speeding car? After the first flash there was no recognition in his eyes, nor any concern, rather a quiet mockery, which, she felt, at

22

the first word of hers would turn into active dislike.

"You! You —" Her breath caught in a laugh that was half sob. "What a mean break for you that you didn't know who I was, that you didn't let that car hit me! Then you would have had the money."

She had never seen a face so colorless as Mark Trent's as his eyes met hers steadily.

"Lucky I didn't know who you were, wasn't it? I might have been tempted. Schemers somehow lead charmed lives."

For a split second Brooke thought that fury had paralyzed her tongue. She made two attempts to speak before she protested angrily:

"I'm not a schemer! I suppose it never has occurred to you that the 'Reyburn girl' may have loved Mary Amanda Dane? May have been glad to spend one evening a week in a homey old house away from her whole 'darn family' in a crowded city apartment?"

Failure of breath alone stopped Brooke's tirade. There was plenty more she could say, she was apt to be good when she started. A laugh twitched at her lips. The two men facing her couldn't have looked more stunned when she made her theatrical entrance had a hold-up man with leveled gun suddenly stepped from behind the hanging. So this was Mark Trent. She had been careful never to go to Lookout House when he was there, for fear that he might think she had planned to meet him, and then he had gone to South America. Mrs. Mary Amanda Dane had had no photographs of him about. Once she had spoken of his youth, of his prowess in football, tennis, and his election as Class Day marshal, and his promotion to head a large insurance business, and then bitterly of his marriage and divorce.

In reporting her Lookout House visits to the family upon her return, she had referred always to Mrs. Dane's nephew as Mark the Magnificent, with a spicy twist to her voice which had delighted her audience. But she had not realized that he would be so bronzed nor so tall, that his dark eyes were so uncompromising, nor that the set of his mouth and chin could be so indomitable. There was a fiery, strong quality of life in him which sent prickles of excitement like red-hot slivers shooting through her veins. She knew now that she should have appeared from behind that hanging at Jed Stewart's first word.

Stewart's always ruddy face was the color of a fully grown beet. He coughed apologetically.

"Sorry, Miss Reyburn. Didn't know you'd come. I'll slit the throat of that secretary of mine for not telling me. So you two have met before? That's a coincidence."

"No coincidence about it, Jed. Apparently we were both on the way to this office to keep an appointment with you, when we 'met' in the street almost in front of this building."

Brooke's anger flared again at Mark Trent's cool explanation. She met the terrier brightness of Jed Stewart's gray-green eyes. She had liked him when she had come to his office in response to the Court's amazing notification that she was residuary legatee under the will of Mary Amanda Dane. The black and white check of his suit accentuated the rotundity of his body. He puffed out his lips as he regarded her with boyish entreaty. She laughed.

"The present uncomfortable situation only goes to prove, doesn't it, Mr. Stewart, that listeners never hear any good of themselves? Though really I wasn't listening. I stepped behind the hanging to look at the marvelous view, and then —"

"You heard Jed say that your hair was like copper with the sun on it, and —"

"I stuffed my fingers in my ears for a while, but I heard a lot more, a whole lot more," Brooke cut in on Mark Trent's sarcastic reminder, "before I heard you refuse to marry me."

"But that was before I had seen you." The suavity of his voice brought hot tears of fury to her eyes. Before she could rally a caustic retort, he picked up his hat.

"That's a bully exit line. I'll be seeing you, Jed. Hope you'll enjoy the house and the fortune, Miss Reyburn. Happy landings!" He laughed. "I'd better say, 'Safe landings!' You're such a reckless person."

"Hi! Fella!"

With an impatient jerk, Mark Trent shook off the hand on his sleeve, rammed his soft hat over one eye, and closed the door smartly behind him. Stewart relieved his feelings in an explosive sigh and pulled forward a chair.

"That seems to be that. Sit down, Miss Reyburn, while I tell you about the allowance which will be made you while Mrs. Dane's estate is being settled."

II

From the lighted stage Brooke Reyburn looked into the auditorium of the department store in which she had worked for four years. She had begun by modeling sports clothes, and because she had loved her work and had given it all the enthusiasm and drive there was in her she had been promoted steadily. The first of this last year she had been made head fashion adviser and had been sent to Paris. She had made frequent trips to New York, but never before had she been abroad. Now she was talking for the last time to a hall full of women, many of whom she had come to know by sight. She had given her last radio talk. It was the end of her business career. What would the new life bring her?

Even as she thought these things, she told her audience that the silver frock the lovely blonde on the stage was modeling was a copy of Chanel, called attention to its touch of theatre; that the smart black tailleur she herself was wearing was from the Misses Better Dress Shop at $29.50;

that neither brown as a color nor gold jewelry should be worn by the gray-haired woman; that a questionnaire had brought out the amusing fact that the majority of married men liked to see their wives in blue; asked if the ravishing scent she was spraying from the atomizer was reaching them — one dollar a dram at the perfume bar — and said for the last time in closing:

"This concludes our fashion show. Thank you."

As she stepped from the stage, Madame Céleste, the autocratic head of the store's department of clothes for women, stopped her. Her figure was a restrained thirty-six; her black frock was as chic as only a Lanvin model could be; the pearls at her ears were the size of able-bodied marbles; her make-up would have done marvelous things for a younger woman, for her it achieved nothing short of a miracle. A hint of emotion warmed the hard blue of her eyes as she caught Brooke's hands.

"Cherie," her French was slightly denatured by a downeast twang, "I shall lose my right hand when you go. Why did that meddlesome old party want to butt in and leave you money? You were on the way to making it here."

"I shall miss you, Madame Céleste."

Brooke's voice was none too steady.

"Perhaps you won't have to long. In this here-today-and-gone-tomorrow age, money doesn't stay in one pocket. Remember, *cherie,* whenever you want a job, come to me. You'll be needing one. *Au revoir!*"

"Cheering thought that I may lose the fortune," Brooke reflected, as she approached her office across the hall. Suddenly the black letters:

MISS REYBURN

on the ground-glass panel of the door jiggled fantastically.

She blinked moisture from her lashes — she hadn't supposed she would feel choky about leaving. She opened the door, closed it quickly behind her, and backed against it as a man slid to his feet from the corner of her desk. His black hair shone like the coat of a sleek well-brushed pony; his dark eyes were quizzically amused as they met hers; his teeth were beautifully white; he was correctly turned out in spic and span business clothes. He was likable, but there was something missing — rather curious that never before had she felt it. He lacked — he lacked salt, Brooke decided, and then reproached herself for being critical. He

29

had been marvelously kind to her, and she was quite outside his social circle — now, she would not have been during her father's lifetime.

"How's tricks?" he inquired gaily.

"How did you get in here, Jerry Field?"

"Easy as rolling off a log. A taxi, an elevator, a few strides on shanks mare, and here I am."

"I've told you time and again not to come to my office."

"While you were on the job, you said, sweet thing. I've stayed away and all the time the old wolf jealousy gnawed at my heart. I've imagined you here entertaining the male heads of departments and letting them, or stopping them, make love to you."

"You've been seeing too many movies. I shall drop fathoms in your estimation when I tell you that no man in the organization has ever been otherwise than friendly and helpful. Perhaps I'm not a glamorous person, perhaps I haven't the divine spark which touches off the male imagination."

"Perhaps it's because they know that those corking eyes of yours look straight into their minds. We're wasting time. You are through, and here I am all in a dither to take you teaing and stepping and dining to celebrate your entrance into the land of the free."

"Nice of you but — I wonder how free I shall be."

Brooke crossed her arms on the back of a chair and looked about the office. She would miss it, miss even the display figure in the corner with its red polka dotted cheeks and staring eyes. There had been hectic moments when she had talked out her problems to its wax immobility. Her glance came back to the man watching her.

"How long is it since you and I first met, Jerry?"

He drew a memoranda book from his pocket and consulted its pages.

"Six months, one week, and six days."

"Foolish! Pretending you have it in black and white."

He tapped the closely lined page. "Believe it or not, there it is, the date when you and I spent an hour trapped in an elevator which wouldn't move. You were coming from a radio talk and I from a conference with my broker who had informed me that my account was figuring exclusively in the red. Fate, sweet thing, fate."

"Fate! The starter told me it was a balky cog. It was an experience I hope never to repeat, even if it brought you and me together. I was frightened."

"But you laughed. That's what got me, your sportsmanship, and when you clutched at my coat it was like fingers on my heart."

Brooke turned quickly to the closet. She must switch him from that track. As she took down her short lapin jacket and slipped into it, she said lightly:

"How you dramatize life. You have been miscast. Instead of being born a rich man's son and spending your days dabbling in paint and the stock market, you should be on the stage. With your flair for good theatre, you'd be packing them in. Perhaps Sam can get you a chance in his company. Have you seen the play in which he is acting?" she asked with a quick change from lightness to gravity.

"Yes. Your brother's good."

"But you don't like the play?"

"I can't hand it much."

"Neither can I. It's a dummy with not a breath of life, not a drop of red blood, just clever epigrams and stuffed-shirt characters. I wish Sam hadn't been cast in it."

"Don't worry. It won't last long. What's the next play on the stock list?"

"The Tempest. The apartment rings with, 'Bestir! Bestir! Heigh my hearts! Cheerily, cheerily my hearts!' "

"You're not bad yourself, Brooke. Why didn't you take to acting?"

"I ought to be good. We children were raised on dramatics and quotations. It was Father's habit to orate when he was shaving, and we could spout Shakespeare before we could spell. Besides being a publisher, he was a playwright for amateurs, but Sam is ambitious to write for the professional stage; he has one three-act comedy finished, that is, as finished as a play can be until it is put into rehearsal. That is why he is acting, that he may know all there is to know of stage technic. I've had theatre enough in my late job. Late! I can't believe that I'm through. Come on, Jerry, before I sob on the shoulder of that display figure."

"Lot you'll sob on that when I'm here." He patted his shoulder and grinned engagingly. "This one is warranted sound, kind, and a corking tear-absorber."

"I'll wager my next week's salary that it is damp from constant use. Let's go. I asked the girls not to come to say good-bye as if I were going away forever. They gave me a grand farewell party last night, and I have perfume, hosiery, and bags enough to last the rest of my natural life. Go ahead. I want to snap out the light myself."

As she stopped on the threshold, Jerry Field caught her arm.

"Hey, no looking back. Remember what happened to Lot's wife. I'd make a hit, wouldn't I, tugging a pillar of salt round the dance floor." He shut the door smartly behind them.

Brooke blinked and swallowed. "Okay, Jerry, from now on I go straight ahead like an army with banners, but straight ahead doesn't mean teaing and dancing with you tonight."

When they reached the already darkening street, Jerry Field demanded:

"Why won't you go stepping with me now?"

"Because I am going home to plan with the family about moving, and to plot the curve of our domestic future."

"Look here, Brooke, don't persist in that silly idea of living in the house Mrs. Dane left you. It's all right for spring and summer, but what will you do marooned on a rocky point of land almost entirely surrounded by water when the days get short, in a place where the residents dig in and nothing ever happens? The causeway which connects the peninsula with the mainland sometimes is submerged in a storm. Suppose we have one of our typical

New England winters?"

Brooke had thought of that. She loved living in the city, loved this time of day and this time of year when the shops glittered with lights, when the smell of roasting chestnuts seeped from glowing braziers on corners, when the streets were jammed with traffic and every person in the crowd hurried as if he or she had somewhere to go and were on the way. She drew a long breath of the keen October air and let it go in a sigh.

"It is a charming old house, Jerry. I shall love it. I'm a business woman on the outside and a home-maker at heart. I hear that many of the residents who usually summer there are planning to keep their homes open and live in them this winter — it's a trend — so perhaps something will happen, something exciting, on that peninsula of land you scorn. These are the melodramatic thirties, remember. It will be rather thrilling to go into an absolutely new environment; an adventure in living. One never can tell what's waiting to pounce as one turns the corner. Twenty miles isn't far from town."

"It's twenty miles too far. If you were here in the city, I could pick you up in a minute and we could go places. To date

35

you've handed out the excuse that you were too busy. People are planning to winter there, are they? That's an idea. You won't lose the fortune if you don't live in the old place, will you? It wasn't a condition?"

They were walking toward the crimson and jade sunset against which a huge electric clock seemed colorless.

"No. Mrs. Dane merely left a note with her lawyer, in which she wrote that she wished I would live there for two years, or at least until I had cleared the house of her belongings, that she knew that I would not laugh at her treasures, that I would understand, and that I would care for her parrot, Mr. Micawber. That parrot leaves me cold, Jerry. So you see, I must live in the house for a while — now that the lordly Mark Trent has given permission. I —"

"What has Mark Trent to say about it?"

Brooke looked up in surprise as they waited for the traffic light at the corner to change to red and yellow.

"Don't bite. Do you know him, Jerry?"

"Sure, I know him."

"Why haven't you told me?"

"Why should I? I'd forgotten that he was Mrs. Dane's nephew who had been cut off with a shilling or less."

She caught his arm. "Look out! Wait for the light! I had that lesson seared into my mind last week — and ground into my knee," she added to herself.

"Now we can go. You must have been excited to start to walk in front of a car. Why do you dislike Mark Trent?"

"Don't dislike him. Just don't want to think about the man, that's all. My sister Daphne went cockeyed about him and he turned her down hard. Like a perfect gentleman, of course, but it got my goat."

Brooke visualized Mark Trent as he had glared down at her on the street, and later as she had seen him in Jed Stewart's office. She couldn't imagine him changing his mind when once he had determined on a line of action. He looked like a man who knew exactly what he wanted and was out to get it. Even the memory of him sent little prickles along her veins.

"Are you sure he turned her down?"

"Sure. I'm not blaming him, I'm ashamed for her, that's all. He was probably fed up with her type. His ex-wife was never quite sober, I've heard. Daphne fell for him the minute she saw him, she had worried me by her crazy ideas of freedom for a girl, she'd picked up a post-war germ somewhere — all talk of course — and when Trent came along, she stopped drinking and staying out till morning at Night Clubs. I was relieved. Then he sidestepped. Forget it. I don't know why I told you. Nice street this, isn't it?"

Brooke nodded assent as they passed houses whose polished windows, violet-paned some of them, screened by laces of unbelievable fineness, regarded her with inscrutable calm. Thoroughbred dogs, proudly conscious of their gay collars and smart breast-straps, decorously escorted their young masters. Shining limousines waited before charming old doors. In the distance rose the faint, far sound of traffic, murmurous as a mighty flood which never rolled nearer.

"Here we are at your door. Sure you won't change your mind and go stepping?" The boyish quality was back in Field's voice. "Grand old house. Pity it was turned into apartments. Do you realize that you never have invited me to meet the family? What's wrong? Ashamed of your home — or me?"

"Neither. What a beastly suggestion, Jerry. If you must know, I haven't told them about our friendship. I have the finest family in the world, but their bump of humor is over-developed, it isn't a bump, it's a coconut."

"What is there about me that's a joke?"

"Nothing; don't be so touchy. I decided to be a little mysterious, that's all. Sam resents it if I ask him a question about his friends, thinks I am treating him like a boy when he is almost two years older than I; and since I got Lucette the chance to model and she is financially independent, she scorns my interest."

"Is your mother like that?"

"No, Mother's a dear, but she is so bound up in her children that she has no real life of her own. It's a pity because she is a comparatively young woman."

"She sounds old-fashioned and motherly to me. Grade A in mothers. I like that kind. Can't I come in and meet her? I had planned to celebrate with you. Now that you've turned me down, I haven't any place to go."

"You carry off that aggrieved, little-boy pose well, Jerry, but it leaves me cold. You, with your Crowd — capital C —, having nowhere to go! That's the funniest thing I ever heard. I intend to devote the next two hours to making plans with the family. It's hard to get hold of Sam, but he promised to stay at home until he had to go to the theatre."

"How soon do you take to the sticks?"

"I'm going down tomorrow to look over the house, my half of it, though it isn't a half, it's a whole twin. A week ago Mr. Stewart told me what I might spend to make it livable — it's a dangerous concession, he doesn't know my spending capacity. It has been on leash so long that I tremble to think what will happen when I loose it. I'll take one gorgeous crack at extravagance."

"Is that guy doling out money to you? Isn't it yours?"

"Not for a year. He could hold it up if he wanted to, but, as Mark the Magnificent — that's what we call him in the family councils — is the only legal heir and as he won't contest the will, — I wanted him to take half of the property or a third even, but he turned me down hard — it is safe to give me an allowance. When we are settled, I will invite you to Lookout House. Goodnight, Jerry."

As she waited in the hall for the elevator to descend, Brooke thought of Jerry Field's question:

"Ashamed of your home — or of me?"

She certainly was not ashamed of her home. The apartment might be small and crowded, but there were many fine pieces of maple and mahogany and the family portraits were choice, but no choicer than the family itself. This change of fortune would change her outwardly. It would free her real self, the impetuous self whose impulse was to help, to be hospitable. She had had so little money since her father's death that the old bogey, FUTURE, had jogged her elbow whenever her fingers started toward her purse. She must remember always what it meant to have little. People were so apt to forget when they became prosperous, so apt to become slightly contemptuous of those who were struggling to make ends meet. She had seen it happen a number of times. She would be much happier if Mark Trent had a share of the money, but he must know how bitter his aunt had been about him. Probably that was the reason he wouldn't touch it.

The front door slammed with a force which shook the house. Sam, of course. The atmosphere tingled when he appeared. He was whistling as usual. Good-looking boy! His horn-rimmed spectacles added a touch of distinction. She patted his sleeve as he stopped beside her.

"Had a nice day, Sammy?"

"Not too good. They're taking off the

play tomorrow. Our dear public wouldn't see it."

He pulled open the elevator door. "Hop in." As it clanged shut, he asked:

"All through being a working girl?"

Brooke swallowed a lump in her throat and nodded.

"It will seem queer being a lady of leisure."

"Leisure! You don't know the first letter of the word. I can see you wondering what you'll do next. Leisure isn't your line. You'll plunge into classes and sports. There won't be hours enough in a day for you."

The elevator stopped. A voice seeped through the cracks around the apartment door. Sam Reyburn grinned.

"Say, listen! Lucette's on the air — and how."

"Oh dear, what's her grievance now?" Brooke whispered, and put her key into the lock.

She tried to appraise with the eyes of a stranger the high-ceilinged, large living-room she entered. A connoisseur of portraits would know that Grandfather Reyburn over the mantel had been painted by a great artist; that the portrait of his daughter on the opposite wall was a choice bit of work; that the Duchess of Argyle in her sables, green satin, and emeralds was a masterpiece. Always she had wanted to decorate a room as a background for the picture. Now she could. The Duchess was hers. The mahogany and maple was sadly in need of rubbing up, but no amount of wear and tear could disguise its period and value.

Her eyes lingered on her mother perched on the arm of a couch. She did young things like that. Her hair was a sheeny platinum; her eyes were dark; her skin was clear and smooth; her figure in the amethyst crepe frock was round without in the least suggesting fat. There was a quizzical twist to her lovely mouth as she looked at her younger daughter, who, with legs thrust straight out before her, was slumped in a chair. Her red beret, which matched the belt of her slim green plaid frock, was on the floor. Her hair was black and wavy; her eyes were brilliantly dark; her painted lips drooped at the corners. Brooke recognized the symptoms. Sam had been right, Lucette was on the air. She said as she slipped out of her lapin coat:

"In the Valley of Despond again, Lucette? Had a nice day, Mother?"

Mrs. Reyburn smiled and nodded. She would make her home-coming children think she had had a nice day, if the heavens had fallen. She was like that. Lucette answered her question.

"You'd be in the Valley of Despond, if you had had the day I've had, Brooke Reyburn. I'm dead to the world. A woman came into the sports shop with three daughters, and kept me showing clothes all the afternoon. Gosh! My feet ache like teeth gone nervy."

"Did she buy much?"

"Not that baby. She bought that little blue number only. For Pete's sake, why does Sam have to whistle when he's under the shower? The walls of this apartment are regular sounding boards."

"Bear up, Lucette, you will be out of it soon. If we can't sublet this apartment, we'll shut it up."

"Spoken like a lady and a multi, Brooke darling. And after that what?"

"You won't have to model for fussy women and you'll have a dressing room of your very own. Mr. Stewart has told me that I may take possession of Lookout House as soon as I like. Mark the Magnificent has given the Jovian nod. He won't contest the will. I'm going there tomorrow with a plumber. A bath for every bed will be my battle-cry."

44

Silence followed her words, a silence fraught with significance. Brooke caught her sister's look at her mother before she sat up straight and tense. She knew that posture, she was preparing for a skirmish. Lucette said defiantly:

"Glad you brought up that subject, Brooke. News flash! I'm not going to the sticks with you, not if you offer me a gold tub with diamond settings. I spent one night at the home of the late Mary Amanda Dane, and, so far as I am concerned, the name means look out and not go there again. That sealed door in her living-room gave me the creeps. I kept thinking, 'What's on the other side?' for all the world like Alice when she wonders what goes on in Looking-Glass house. There might be bodies concealed there or loot, it has been shut up so long. No thanks! I'm all for the city. 800,000 residents can't be wrong. Sam isn't —"

She dashed to the hall as the telephone rang.

"Lucette Reyburn speaking," she answered eagerly.

"Yes — yes — he is. I'll call him." Her voice was as flat as de-bubbled champagne. She pounded on the bath-room door.

45

"Phone for you, Sam. — How do I know? It's the girl who always calls just as you've stepped under the shower. — All right."

She returned to the phone. "Hold the line. He'll be here in a minute."

Back in the living-room she dropped into a chair. With elbows propped on her knees, chin in her palms, she stared at the floor.

What had Lucette meant by "Sam isn't —" Brooke wondered. She watched her brother as, knotting the cord of a striped bathrobe about his waist, he scuffed to the telephone in slippers several sizes too large for him. He leaned against the side of the doorway as he talked. Stunning boy. No wonder girls called him at all hours. His hair, with a tinge of red in it, stood out from his head like a curly wet mop. His shortsighted blue eyes were clear and forthright, wonderful eyes. He was a tease and a torment and dictatorial, but a rock of dependability, and she adored him. Who was the girl calling? He was frowning, and his voice was brittle as he refused:

"Can't make it — No. It's not another girl, it's a family confab. Sam Reyburn signing off. Good-bye!"

He slammed down the receiver. "And I

know of no reason why I should explain to you what I'm doing," he growled under his breath.

"Hi! Sammy! What's the shower-dame's name?" Lucette called.

Her brother scowled at her. "There's about as much privacy in this apartment as there is in the bandstand on the Common."

"Cheerio, darling. You'll have privacy, and how, if you live with Brooke. She's going house-owner in a big way. If there's to be a bath for every bed, of course there will be a sound-proof telephone booth with every room. What did you say the girl friend's name was?"

"It's none of your business, kiddo, who calls me." Hands deep in the pockets of his hectic bathrobe, Sam paced the living-room floor.

"Darned ungrateful, I calls it," Lucette persisted impishly. "But it's a man's world. Don't I break my neck to answer the phone? Don't your fans ring you at all hours? Before you are up in the morning, while you're shaving — sometime you'll cut off an ear in your excitement — lucky television isn't attached to the phone yet, but I'm betting on the shower-dame. Usually your voice goes kind of mushy when you answer her. You'll be the proud possessor of a daughter-in-law before you know it, Mother."

Sam Reyburn frowned at his younger sister.

"Get this, Lucette. No girl is going to invade my life. I've seen too many of my friends dragging a ball and chain. No marriage in mine."

His mother laughed softly. As he glared at her, she patted the couch.

"Stop walking the floor like a hungry lion and sit down, Sam. Lucette started something just before the phone rang. She should have known better than to start anything in the Reyburn family before it has been fed, but now that she has, you'd better finish it."

"What d'you mean by started, Mother?"

Brooke perched on the arm of a chair at the desk. She faced them all. Most of the time she could tell quite well what they were thinking. She answered her brother's question before her mother could.

"She means that Lucette announced that she did not intend to live at Lookout House with me, and that you —"

"Were not going either, Sam," Lucette finished triumphantly.

"Aren't you, Sam?"

"Say listen, Brooke. Don't you see how it is? I have to be at the theatre early; I'm late when I get through; rehearsing all the morning. Twenty miles is a long way to commute."

"I had planned to buy you the snappiest convertible coupe on the market."

"Don't make me feel like a brute. Don't you see —"

"Of course I see, Sammy. You want to be on your own. I do understand."

"Don't worry about his being on his own, darling," Lucette cut in bitterly. "No one can be on his own in this family. The Great Adviser intends to stay right here to look after his little sister."

Brooke's eyes met her brother's; he nodded. Lucette flamed on:

"And Mother's going to stay to look after both of us."

"Mother!" Brooke echoed the word with shocked incredulity. "But I've planned the most wonderful things for Mother. Is it true?"

Celia Reyburn's eyes shone through a mist as they met her elder daughter's. Her lips curved in a lovely, trembly smile.

"When you say Mother, Brooke, I think it the most beautiful word in the world. But I will not make my home with you —

at present. First, because Lookout House is yours and you should assume the responsibility and direction of it. You will do it more easily if I am not there. Second, I want to stay in the city, not so much because of the children, but because now that your financial future is assured, I shall feel that I may use a little of the money your father left me. I want — I want to be in the heart of things. I'll have an experienced maid, I'll have the right clothes, and — and I'll go places, I'm dying to go places."

Her impassioned voice broke. "Perhaps I'm selfish, perhaps you children think I'm a silly old woman."

Sam flung his arm about his mother. "Hooray for the Spirit of '56! Sorry; I shouldn't have mentioned your age, Celia Reyburn. Don't worry that you won't get enough of your family, Brooke. I'll have to drag these two giddy girls off to the country for rest occasionally. When Lucette quits work —"

"Who says I'm going to quit. I'm not. I'm going to work as Brooke worked till I get her job and hit the airlanes. Why the chuckle? What is there about that so funny?"

Brooke shook her head. "I wasn't laughing at what you said, Lucette."

She couldn't tell them that Jed Stewart's words had echoed in her mind:

"Now I suppose the brother and sister will chuck their jobs and settle down on her."

How little he knew them. How like Sam, much as he would love being on his own, to stand by Lucette. She wasn't old enough yet to live alone, and she was much too pretty and daring. And her mother — how cheerfully she had kept on the treadmill of housework while all the time she had ached for a certain amount of freedom. They were all looking at her. What did they expect her to say? She met Sam's anxious eyes.

"Aren't sore at us, are you, Brooke? Don't feel that we have let you down to go on alone?"

"Of course I don't, you old dear. Why shouldn't each one of us do as we like, now that there is some money back of us? Because I feel that I must carry out Mrs. Dane's wishes is no reason for dragging the rest of you into the country. It is like Through the Looking-glass though, isn't it?"

"What do you mean?" Lucette demanded. "Don't talk riddles."

"Nothing, except everything is reversed, not as one expected things would happen."

"What did you think would happen? That we'd all stop work and live on you?" Sam accused testily.

Brooke laughed. "I didn't think that. Let's get busy planning. If you are all sold on staying in the city, we'll have a bigger apartment. I may want to spend a weekend away from the sticks myself."

III

Through the open transom above the office door came the hum of typewriters. Mark Trent, behind his desk, scowled in the direction of the sound. He had paid good money for those machines on the understanding that they were noiseless. Curious that he never had been annoyed by them before. Must be this confounded note in his hands. He read again:

DEAR MR. TRENT —
Many times your aunt has told me of the Thanksgivings you spent with her at Lookout House. Won't you dine here on the coming holiday? My mother, sister and brother will be with me. There are many family treasures which you should have. I would like to go over them with you, and more than all, I want to thank you for pulling me out from under that car. I really wasn't so ungrateful as I sounded. This is a late invitation because I have been bolstering up my courage to ask you. Please come. Bury the hatchet, or accept the

olive branch, or however peace between enemies — though I am not for a moment your enemy — is being accomplished now.

Sincerely yours,

Lookout House   BROOKE REYBURN

He dropped the note and frowned at the red carnations in a crystal vase on his desk. He lived over the instant he had seen a girl go down in the street, had seen a speeding car almost upon her. How had he managed to save her? Colorless and dazed as she was, he had thought her the loveliest thing he ever had seen as she looked up at him. As for a second he had steadied her in his arms, his brain had fought against her attraction and the live warmth of her body had prompted him to growl at her. No wonder she had been angry, and no wonder — he admitted honestly — Mary Amanda Dane had been taken in by her. Well, one victim in the family was enough. She shouldn't hypnotize him.

He drew letter paper toward him and picked up a pen. He'd settle this question of friendship between them for good and all. Little schemer! Now that she had the property she wanted to appear friendly with him. Probably thought it would help her socially in the community in which she had taken up her residence. If what he had heard was true, the conservative old-timers there had held an indignation meeting, and because he had been cut out of the property, had turned thumbs down on the legatee. They would freeze her out, and they could do it, he had seen the method applied to one girl. It must not be done. If only Aunt Mary Amanda's old friend Anne Gregory were on this side of the water, he would appeal to her to be decent to Brooke Reyburn. The Empress, as her friends called her, was the social arbiter of the community. Meanwhile the invitation must be answered.

Dear Miss Reyburn, he wrote.

As he hesitated as to how to word his regrets, another picture of the girl as she had appeared between the hangings in Stewart's office flashed in his mind with startling clarity. Brown eyes blazing with amber lights, lovely scornful mouth, glints of gold in the copper bronze of her hair, red spots which were not rouge in her cheeks, and her slender body rigid with rage. He seemed destined to make her angry. Had her pose been acting? Her brother was on the stage. Why be unjust? She wouldn't have been human had she not been furious. Hadn't she heard him refuse to marry her?

He must get along with that note. His frowning regard of the opening door changed to a welcoming smile as a head poked in.

"Come in, Jed. What's on the little mind now?"

Jed Stewart perched on a corner of the flat desk. He pulled one of the red carnations from the vase and drew the stem through the buttonhole of the lapel of his checked coat.

"I'm taking a lady to tea, need a posy to make me look like a million, so combined utility with business and came here. Knew you always had them."

"What's the business? If you've been sent again to ask me to take half of that —"

"Hold everything; that's all washed up. The matter has not been mentioned to me since the day you and Brooke Reyburn met in my office. I guess you killed her interest in you by your infernal sarcasm:

" 'Hope you'll enjoy the house and fortune, Miss Reyburn. Happy landings! Perhaps I'd better say, safe landings,' sez you."

"Oh, you think so? Read that."

Jed frowned over the note Mark Trent tossed to him. He read it through, reread it. Looked at his friend.

"Going?"

"Going! What do you think?" Mark answered a buzzer. "Who? Mrs. Gregory. Of course I'll see her."

He explained hurriedly to Stewart. "It's an old friend of Aunt Mary Amanda's. She sailed for France a week before my aunt died. She's a martinet, one of those terrible women who don't care where the lash of their tongue falls, and a confirmed matchmaker. They call her The Empress. I always got on with her, though she resented it because I did not marry a girl she had picked out for me. Don't go, Jed. I've been wishing I could see her. I hear that the social registerites are planning to freeze out —

"This is mighty good of you, Mrs. Gregory, and it's a clear case of thought transference; not ten minutes ago I was thinking of you."

A wave of feeling menaced the clarity of Mark's voice as he bent over the white-gloved hand of the woman who had entered the office. She had been a vital part of the life at Lookout House which now seemed so irretrievably far behind him. A smile tugged at his lips as he observed that the floppy wide-brimmed picture hat was

57

the model she had worn since as a boy he had admired the deeply waved blonde hair it shadowed. The hair was still faultlessly marcelled, but it was snow white. He thought now, as he had thought then, that the large hat needed only streamers to make it go Bo-Peep, and that if her tall ebony cane had a crook, it would be the last perfect touch. In spite of changes the years had wrought in her, there was still a hint of exceptional charm.

She settled into a chair with the same rustle of taffeta he remembered, and adjusted a diamond brooch of a size and brilliance to make a discriminating thief avidly flex supple fingers. She peered up at him through a jeweled lorgnette, with eyes once a brilliant blue, now the color of faded larkspur.

"Handsome as ever, aren't you, Mark, in spite of the way those two women let you down. First that wife, with a *grande amoureuse* complex, and then Mary Amanda. I don't wonder that your hair at the temples looks as if it had been touched by frosty fingers, if you are only thirty. Who's he?"

She waved her lorgnette toward Stewart, who, back to the room, apparently had been absorbed in a study of the calf-bound books on the shelf.

"Stewart, of the firm of Stewart and Stewart, attorneys. Jed, come here. I want to present you to Mrs. Gregory, my first love."

"Hmp! Flatterer! You always could coax my heart out of my breast with your wonderful smile and your voice, Mark. They haven't changed. Whenever I see you I want to hit the ceiling because you won't represent our district in the Great and General Court." She peered through her lorgnette as Jed Stewart took the hand she extended with the air of a sovereign.

"Stewart and Stewart! You were Mary Amanda Dane's lawyer, weren't you?"

The contempt in her voice deepened the color of Jed Stewart's already sufficiently ruddy face.

"I had that honor."

"Honor! Do you call it an honor to help cheat her nephew out of his inheritance?"

"Really, Mrs. Gregory, Jed can't be held responsible —"

"Hold your tongue, Mark. I've started, and now I intend to get rid of a few things that have been boiling and sizzling inside me since the day I heard that Mary Amanda had cut you out in favor of that fashion adviser she'd gone crazy about.

59

When they heard of her will, I'll wager my step-daughters hugged themselves to think that their father left his money in a trust fund which I couldn't will away if I happened to have a brain storm."

The shortness of her breath, the feverish light in her eyes, the spots on her cheeks which glowed like red traffic lights frightened Mark. He had been half angry, half amused at her outburst at first, but people had suffered strokes under less excitement. He said soothingly:

"Forget it, Mrs. Gregory. I don't need the money —"

"Of course you need it. No one has money enough now because no one has a sense of financial security. Didn't you take over all the lame ducks as your share of your grandfather's property so that your aunt wouldn't be worried by them? Aren't you making that ex-wife of yours an allowance? Mary Amanda told me. What's she been doing since she left you for that French Count? It was a French Count year, wasn't it? They were buzzing round rich girls thick as wasps about a broiled live lobster."

"She has married, I understand."

"Married! After she divorced the Count! The third time! Getting to be a habit, isn't it? She isn't entitled to a penny. I don't wonder your aunt was furious when she found out that you were giving her money. Perhaps that's the real reason she cut you off, though I thought it was because she didn't believe in divorce; on that subject she was stuck back in the eighties. However, that wasn't what I came here to talk about. I just wanted to tell you that if I had known what was in that will I witnessed two days before I sailed for Europe — it was just a week before she died — now, Stewart, don't look at me with your jaw dropped as if I were a moron with a Medusa complex — of course, I know that a person isn't supposed to know the contents of the will she witnesses, but I still say that had I known that your aunt was leaving her money away from you, Mark, I would have cut off my hand before I signed."

Mark Trent's heart stopped and galloped furiously on. A will witnessed a week before Mary Amanda's death! The will which had been probated was of a date two months prior. As he opened suddenly stiffened lips to reply, he met Jed Stewart's warning eyes, eyes which seemed like flames in a chalky face. Jed was as amazed as he.

In the second of silence which followed Mrs. Gregory's angry declaration, Mark wondered if he were in a dream. He listened. Typewriters were purring in the outer office; a whistle, shrill but faint, rose from the street, the traffic cop was on his job; a plane roared overhead; the four lights in the room, the spicy scent of red carnations were real. He was awake.

Jed Stewart stepped hard on his foot as he passed to offer a cigarette to the woman in the chair. She sniffed.

"You ought to know by looking at me, young man, that I wouldn't take one of those. Lawyers aren't as bright as they used to be. Oh, go on, smoke, you needn't ask my permission, that courtesy went out when the speakeasy era came in, though judging by the shakiness of your hand, Stewart, I'd suggest that you cut out tobacco for a while."

Mark looked at Jed Stewart. Jed shaky. It was incredible. He watched as his friend flung down the cigarette, perched on the arm of a chair, and clasped his hands hard about one knee.

"You're right, madam, I am smoking too much, but I was lighting that one to steady my nerves. I was fond of my client Mrs. Dane, and your reference to her last will brought back a picture of the delicate woman in her wheel chair with —"

"With that disreputable parrot swearing in the cage behind her. The bird was there when I witnessed the will; I didn't know but that she would insist upon Micawber's being the other witness, but she called in Clotilde and Henri Jacques, it was her nurse-companion's day off. If I had to choose between the parrot and that French butler as my co-resident on a desert island, I'd take Mr. Micawber. After they went out, Mary Amanda and I were alone for a few moments in the firelight. It was the last time I saw her —" Mrs. Gregory dabbed her reddening eyes with a lace-edged handkerchief.

"I'm traveling fast, Mark. You are too young to know that tightening of the heart as one by one friends vanish into the haze ahead; I'm getting used, though not re-signed, to picking up the paper and seeing that someone with whom I had played cards, perhaps the day before, had been paged, had been touched on the shoulder with that mysterious summons:

" 'Wanted on long distance, madam.'

"Perhaps the increasing number of empty chairs in one's friendship circle make it easier to leave one's own."

She straightened, demanded angrily:

"Why am I slobbering like that? I love life! I wouldn't give up my place in this problem-logged world for all the starry halos and golden harps you could offer. Thinking of your aunt set me off. The last few times I saw her I had noticed that she seemed distrait, as if something were worrying her. I've wondered since if she would have told me what she had done if I had not had to hurry away. I called Henri before I left. As I looked back, she seemed white and exhausted. As I drove away I saw that girl driving in."

"That girl! You mean —"

"The Reyburn girl, of course, Stewart. You ought to get a position somewhere as an echo. I'd met her several times and I liked her too before I knew what she had done to Mark. She made me forget that I was old enough to be her grandmother. Charming manners. Well, I must run along. I'm looking in at three debutante teas — mothers have waked up to the fact that it's advisable to invite older guests as well as younger. I had to come, Mark, and tell you that I was sorry for my share in that unjust will. I always liked you."

"Thank you for your interest in me, Mrs. Gregory. I'm going down to your car with you. Wait for me, Jed."

The woman turned on the threshold. "I hope, if ever you draw another will cutting out a rightful heir, young man, you'll be swished in boiling oil."

Stewart grinned. "Not boiling oil, madam, not boiling; couldn't you reduce the temperature a degree?"

She smiled. "We'll see, we'll see. You're an engaging boy, if you are a poor lawyer. I'm to spend the winter in my country house — not far from the Dane-Trent property — everybody's doing it this year. Motor down some Sunday for lunch. I like men. I grew up with three brothers, had two husbands and a son. They're all gone. I'm sick of seeing nothing but women. When I get too old to live alone I'll apply for admittance to a home for nice old gentlemen — and not too old at that. Don't forget to come to lunch, Stewart."

"Sure, I'll come. Meanwhile, would you mind not telling anyone that you witnessed Mrs. Dane's will?"

"You don't think I'm proud of my part in that robbery, do you? I wouldn't have mentioned it now, but I wanted to square myself with Mark."

Mark Trent's mind was in a tumult as he chatted with her in the corridor, inquired for her health on the way down in the elevator, told her that he thought of her rich fruit cake whenever he attended a wedding. She looked up at him sharply as they waited at the curb.

"Then you still attend weddings?"

"Why not? I rather like them."

"After your experience, I should think you would shun them. Ever see Lola?"

"No."

"Here's my car. That's Dominique at the wheel. Remember him, don't you? He drove my horses before I had an automobile, and the only thing I have against him is that he recommended his friends the Jacques to your aunt. She made so much of Henri that he got dictator-minded and tried to run the whole place. When God wants to destroy a fool He gives him power. It will be interesting to watch the man. He'll crack up some way. I hear Miss Reyburn has kept him and his wife as servants. Bring that Stewart man with you some Sunday. I like him. Good-bye. Don't hold my signature against me."

Mark Trent stood looking after the limousine as it shot into the line of traffic. Why did she question him about the woman who had been his wife? Had been. Why couldn't he think in the past tense always and not feel bound by that, "Whom God hath joined together let no man put asunder"?

Why spend a moment on the past, with Mrs. Gregory's startling revelation to be confronted that his aunt had made a later will than the one which had been probated?

Jed Stewart was walking the floor when he entered his office. He stopped abruptly.

"Well," he demanded, "did she talk any more?"

"Not about the will. Why the dickens didn't you ask questions?"

"Didn't dare. Don't you see, Mark? Boy, don't you understand? Someone has snitched that second will she witnessed."

"Did you draw it?"

"Never heard of it. Perhaps your aunt had an acute attack of remorse. I argued with her, as much as a lawyer can argue, against cutting you out; she wouldn't come to me about a new will. Didn't Mrs. Gregory say that she had been distrait the last few times they had been together? She thinks it was because Mrs. Dane was making up her mind to disinherit you; you and I know that the will to that effect already had been drawn."

"You passed up a grand chance to cross-examine her, Jed."

"Didn't dare. She thinks the will she witnessed is the one probated; doesn't know that if it had been she would have been summoned to prove her signature. We mustn't let a suspicion of this second will get out. Where is it?"

"She said the Reyburn girl drove in as she left the place. Do you suppose Aunt Mary Amanda told her what was in it and that she —"

Jed Stewart stopped his restless pacing. His eyes and voice were troubled.

"Destroyed it? But how could Brooke Reyburn have known what was in the first will? Perhaps your aunt had told her that she was to be residuary legatee — it doesn't seem probable, but women do fool things." He grinned. "Of course men never do. We've got to get busy. If it isn't destroyed, that will may be at Lookout House; you've never liked the Jacques and you say that they hate you. I have an idea. Open your house. Live there. Get friendly with the girl."

"I would feel like a sneak to go there to spy on her."

"You suspect that she may have influenced your aunt to make a will in her

68

favor, don't you?"

"I do."

"Then give her a chance to prove that she didn't. Take a couple of Japs and go down and live next door."

"I won't commit myself to that proposition in a hurry. If I decide to do it, will you come with me?"

"Sure, I've been hoping you'd ask me. Philo Vance is my middle name." Stewart picked up the note lying on the desk. "You'd better open the investigation by accepting this."

"The Reyburn girl's invitation to dine on Thanksgiving Day? I would feel like a spy, a traitor. The turkey would choke me."

"Do you want the truth about this will?"

"You bet I do."

"Then go. Don't write. 'We never send a letter when we can send a man.' Phone the night before that you are coming. She'll have less time in which to think why you are accepting."

IV

Brooke Reyburn stood in the doorway of the living-room at Lookout House. Behind her in the hall a graceful circular stairway wound up and up. She nodded approval. The room was the perfect setting she had visualized for the Duchess of Argyle since the day she had known that her father had willed her the portrait. The green of the walls and trim repeated the color of the satin gown of the woman in the dull gold frame which hung above the mantel of carved black Italian marble, repeated also the shade of the feathers of the dozing parrot in a gilded cage, threw into relief dark polished surfaces of mahogany. On each side of the fireplace in which birch logs blazed and crackled, choicely bound books lined the walls from baseboard to ceiling. Softly shaded lamps shed light on deep, inviting chairs and intensified the rich coloring of the hollyhock-printed chintz which covered them. A sun porch was filled from floor to ceiling with chrysanthemums in pots, shading from feathery white at the top through pale pink and rose to crimson.

Brooke's throat contracted as her glance rested on the large flat-topped mahogany desk. That, as well as the books, had been her father's. There had been no room for them in the apartment. If only he could have lived to share her good fortune. He had been such a wonderful father.

What would Mark Trent think of the changes — if he came? She needn't worry about that. It was evident that he wasn't coming, would not accept her last-minute invitation, he probably had dozens for the holiday. What was he thinking of her for having invited a man who had persistently snubbed all attempts at friendliness, to dine with her on Thanksgiving day? She needn't wonder about that either. She knew. She had sent the note two days ago, because she couldn't rid herself of the feeling that unwittingly she had robbed him, and she so wanted to tell him that she had known nothing of his aunt's will, and to thank him for saving her, if not from death, from being terribly messed up the day he had pulled her from in front of that speeding roadster. He had not replied to her invitation. It was her last flourish of the olive branch. She didn't like him anyway. Whenever she thought of his lordly declaration that he "wouldn't marry that schemer," she felt a furious urge to hurt him, hurt him terribly. So that was that.

She had had everything that she thought belonged to his family stored in the apartment over the garage. Curious that she had found so little silver. But she had found other things, heaps of useless things. Dozens of old corks, empty bottles galore, boxes in all shapes and sizes, bags of string neatly coiled and tied that had been taken from packages. Before she finished clearing closets and drawers, she had begun to wonder if everything that ever had come into the house had been saved.

She looked at the door which Mary Amanda Dane had told her opened into the twin house. Something uncanny about it. Whenever she was in the room it drew her eyes like a magnet. Mark Trent's house was on the other side. It had not been lived in for years. What a waste. Had his wife refused to live there? His wife? She couldn't think of him as having had a wife. Why think of him at all?

She resolutely switched her thoughts to her surroundings. This was the same room in which she had first seen Mrs. Dane in her wheel chair, but how different. Then it had been drab and heavy; now it glowed with soft color. She would never forget the pathos in the woman's eyes as they had met hers, nor the eagerness of her greeting. She had registered a passionate vow to make her lovely and attractive in appropriate clothes. That had been her job — then — and a thrilling job, too, to help women make the most of their good points.

Brooke smiled as she remembered the "Stop! Look! Listen!" with which the parrot had greeted her appearance; her face sobered as she remembered also the ill concealed animosity of Henri, the butler, as he had lingered in the doorway. In his beady black eyes there had been something menacing, something greedy which had stopped her heart for an instant.

How Mary Amanda Dane had fooled her about money. The crippled woman had kept her feet firmly on the ground when it came to spending. Planning inexpensive, attractive clothes for her had been an exciting challenge. She had succeeded. The frocks had been charming, and with her drab wardrobe the invalid had shed much of her crabbedness. Lovely clothes did that for a woman. Pity that more husbands didn't realize the fact. Now she was gone and had left a small fortune behind her. Why had she denied herself so many of the luxuries of life? Brooke blinked long wet lashes and said aloud, as she had said many times since she had come to live at Lookout House:

"Thank you for everything, Mrs. Mary Amanda. Thanks billions."

She swallowed the lump which rose in her throat whenever she thought of the woman's incredible kindness. Hardly the time to go sentimental when at any moment the family might burst in on her. They were on their way to spend Thanksgiving. For the first time they would see the changes in the house; she had postponed their coming until it should be in perfect order.

What sort of an evening was the weather clerk handing them after two days of storm? She had been too busy to think of it before. She pushed back the long chintz hangings at the French window. She leaned her forehead against the cool glass. Heavenly night. The sea was fairly quiet. There was a faint reverberation only as it drove against the rocks below the terrace, curled back on itself and drove again. Rows of lights, looking from a distance like a procession of cloudy jewels, outlined the causeway. A faint wind stirred the blinds as if ghostly fingers were running up and down the slats, moaned eerily at the corners of the house. Lights blazed and twinkled on the shore across the bay, but so far as she could see to the east, except for one jutting rock, the ocean stretched in unbroken immensity on and on to a distant continent. Where sea and sky met, a big red moon was rising. It cast a coppery mist on the shimmering water. That gorgeous gleaming bubble gave one a no-account feeling, a sense of being alone in a big indifferent world. Curious, it never had had that effect on her when she had seen it peering above the roofs of the city.

The city. The adorable city. Resolutely she shut out the mental flash of brilliantly lighted streets; of crowds of people, laughing, frowning, pushing; of processions of automobiles, all of them going somewhere.

She drew the hangings and crossed to the desk. The parrot opened one eye, muttered something deep in his throat, and shivered until every green and yellow feather stood on end as if electrified.

Brooke watched him from under her lashes as she rearranged the rich foliage of two perfect Templar roses in a bubble vase on the desk. He was dozing again, the old reprobate. Queer that she disliked him so. She distrusted Mr. Micawber almost as much as she distrusted Clotilde and Henri

Jacques whom she had kept on as servants. The man was so — so obsequious — oily was a better word. A cadaverous, gray-haired hypocrite. Particularly she hated his slack mouth, his false teeth which clicked when he talked. Uriah Heep with French manners. His wife was fat and sullen, but — an excellent cook. They had not been part of her legacy. She had kept them on only until the house was in order.

Now that it was in order, what next, she wondered with a touch of panic. Her life had been so full that she would grow mentally flabby without an absorbing interest. The business world had sharpened all her senses, it didn't seem as if home-making for herself would keep them keen. Since she had come to Lookout House, she had missed the stimulating impact of rival firms on her mind, the sting of ambition to make good, the glamour and color of fashionable clothes. Had the family come with her, it would have been different.

She crossed her arms on the mantel and studied the face of the portrait. How did the Duchess like being transplanted? The painted eyes looked down at her steadily. Brooke nodded and confided:

"Something tells me that your spirit never shirked responsibility which would broaden character, nor evaded experience which would give stamina and courage to carry on. I'll wager you went forward like an army with banners. What you could do, your descendant many generations removed can do. Watch her, that's all, just watch her go on!"

She wafted a kiss to the painted face. "With banners, Duchess! With banners!" Her smile vanished. She thought:

"That's all right so far as it goes, but I feel a pricking in my thumbs. I wonder what experience, what test of courage is lying in wait to pounce on me as I turn the next corner?"

The honk-honk of an automobile horn outside was followed by voices singing lustily:

" 'Over the river and through the wood,
   Trot fast, my dapple-gray!
   Spring over the ground
   Like a hunting hound
   For this is Thanksgiving day.' "

The gay chorus was followed by laughter and vociferous cries:

"Whoa there! Stand still, Lightning! Whoa!"

Laughing, Brooke dashed for the front

door. It was so like the Reyburn family to dramatize its arrival.

In a rush of cold air and excited greetings she piloted her mother and sister to the library. The startled parrot shrieked, "Stop! Look! Listen!"

"Boy, you don't need a burglar alarm with that announcer. You ought to loan him to a bank."

Lucette made a gamin face at the parrot as she slipped out of her ocelot coat. She dragged off her hat and patted the swirl of her dark hair.

Brooke hugged her mother. "It's wonderful to have you here, Celia Reyburn, and aren't you devastating in that eel-gray ensemble!"

"Not as devastating as you are in that shimmery white, daughter. It brings out the copper lights in your hair."

Brooke laughed. "We are like two diplomats exchanging compliments, the difference is that ours come from the heart. Where's Sam? Don't tell me Sam isn't coming!"

Lucette held a lighter to a cigarette with a faint hint of bravado.

"Don't cry, darling. Sam came. Didn't you recognize his voice singing as if his little heart would burst from joy as we approached this baronial hall? Doubtless he is kissing his peachy convertible goodnight in your garage. He's crazy about that coupe you gave him, Brooke. He has named it Lightning. And can it go! Who's the tall gent with the undertaker expression who pulled our bags from the car as if he were extracting upper and lower molars?"

"Henri. He and his wife, Clotilde, worked for years for Mrs. Dane. I kept them on to help me settle. They take a lot of handling, believe it or not."

"I believe it. This room looks like part of a House Beautiful exhibit. It's corking."

"Wait till you see the rest of the house, Lucette. Here's Sam. I would recognize his bang of a door if I heard it in Timbuctoo. Welcome to Lookout House, Sammy! It's wonderful that the theatre closed just at this time."

"Yeah! It's all in the point of view. There are them who think otherwise. However, I'm not kicking."

He caught Brooke in a bearlike hug. He kept his arm about her as he looked around the room.

"Swell joint you've got here. I like the greenhousey smell from those plants. Say listen, we've missed you like the dickens, haven't we, Mother?"

"We have, Sam." Celia Reyburn steadied her voice. "We'd better stop emotionalizing and get ready for dinner. I have kept house years enough to know that promptness at meals helps to keep the home-maker's life's walk easy."

"You would think of that, Mother. It isn't dinner tonight. I planned a buffet supper, not being sure at what time my relatives from the big town would arrive. Come upstairs and I'll show you your rooms."

A family might get on each other's nerves, as of course it did at times, but there was nothing like it, Brooke concluded fervently, as after supper on a floor cushion in front of the library fire she leaned against her mother's knees. And every family needed a house in which to spread out, and blazing logs around which to gather and exchange confidences, her thoughts ran on. People slipped aside their masks in a room lighted only by the flames on the hearth. Sam's face, usually gay and debonair, had settled into grave lines as he thoughtfully cracked nuts. Was he worrying about a job? Lucette's black brows were contracted in a slight frown as, on the floor, legs out straight before her, she leaned back against the broad couch.

Brooke couldn't see her mother's face. Was she remembering the evenings they had sat about the fire like this when her husband had been the sun about which all their lives revolved?

Perhaps it was because she had been too absorbed in her own concerns before to notice, but Sam and Lucette seemed to have grown older, to have changed, seemed also to have something weighty on their minds. What was it? What had happened?

As if she knew what she was thinking, Lucette burst out nervously:

"If Sam can stop that nut-munching Marathon, perhaps he'll announce the latest Reyburn news flash."

Brooke sat erect. "What news?"

Sam took careful aim at the parrot's perch. The nutshell struck its bullseye and roused the dozing bird.

"Hell's bells!" he croaked, and ruffled his feathers.

"Looks as if he were caught in a ty-phoon, doesn't he?" The laughter in Sam's voice vanished. "Mother has been invited to spend the winter in England with her friend Lady Jaffrey."

"Sam!" With the exclamation Brooke was on her feet. "Do you mean it? How perfectly grand! She lives in an old castle, doesn't she?"

"Hey, pipe down, Brooke. There's a nigger in the wood pile. Wait till you hear the condition."

"A condition in Lady Jaffrey's invitation, Sam? I can't believe it."

"Be quiet, children. Let me talk." Arms crossed on the back of the wing chair in which she had been sitting, Celia Reyburn faced her family. Her cheeks were pink; her eyes, as blue as her son's, were brilliant with excitement. She clasped her hands tightly as if to steady them.

"The chair recognizes the lady from the big city," Sam encouraged with a grin.

"What's the condition, Mother? Don't you want to go?"

"Very, very much, Brooke, but I shouldn't enjoy a moment of the visit if I left your brother and sister in that apartment alone. Quote. I'm old-fashioned, and my feelings date me. Unquote. Let me finish, Lucette." Celia Reyburn spoke in the tone her children never failed to respect. "I know by heart your argument that you are old enough to live by yourself, that most girls are doing it; that Sam, a man of twenty-seven, should live in bachelor quarters —"

"I've never even thought of that, Mother."

"I know, Sam, I know. You've been a tower of strength to me. When I am with you I feel warmed through, as if I had been sitting in the sun. When I hear your key in the apartment door at night, I close my eyes secure in your protection. I feel as if nothing could hurt me or your sisters." She steadied her voice and brushed her hand across her eyes. She laughed.

"I didn't mean to turn on what Lucette calls the waterworks. I would love to spend the winter with Elaine Jaffrey, Brooke; she was my room-mate for four years in college. I realize that I have been in a deep rut, that I have been stagnating. It's the water which keeps moving, if only a little, which gets to the sea. Perhaps I'm a selfish woman, but I would like to go and will go, if my mind is perfectly at ease about Lucette and Sam. If they will come here to you, and if you will have them —"

"Have them! Mother, don't be foolish! I have been rattling round in this big house like a dried coconut in a shell. Of course I want them — but will they come?"

"Who's being foolish now?" Lucette flung her cigarette into the fire. Her cheeks were almost as red as her painted lips. "Of course we'll come, Brooke Reyburn. Of course we'll play ball Mother's way. Sam

83

and I aren't cold-blooded fish. If taking to the sticks to be chaperoned by big sister will make Mother's visit happier, we'll settle down here with bells on. She's earned all the fun she can get. She'll have one grand time and mow those stiff Britishers down in swaths and come home Countess Whoosit, or I miss my guess."

"Lucette!" Celia Reyburn protested indignantly.

"Don't mind her, Mother," Brooke reassured. "By the time you return your younger daughter will have acquired all the social graces —"

"Just a minute! Now I make a condition. I come only if I keep on with my job."

"It would mean early and late commuting, Lucette."

"I've thought that out. In Sam's convertible we can make it."

"But you and Sam won't be coming down at the same time, and —"

"Don't be so sure, Brooke." Sam aimed a nutshell at the parrot. "The theatre has closed permanently and I'm up against one of those simple economic problems, where's the next job coming from? I'll go to New York to see off Mother and take my play. Now that producers have begun to sniff around for bargains, I may get my chance."

"Sam — dear —" Brooke attempted to lighten her dismayed voice. Bad enough for him to be out of work without having her turn sob-sister. "You'll find something. I read the other day that the theatre is on the up-grade. If you don't — oh, Sammy, what a chance for you to write! Why not give your play a try-out here? We'll do it for the town's welfare fund, in the Club House theatre. What a chance to try 'Islands Arise' on the dog!"

"News flash! The Reyburns stage a play!" Lucette cut in.

"Why not?" Brooke persisted eagerly. "Most of the summer homes are to be kept open during the winter and — Answer the phone, will you, Sam? Take the message for me. I've been pestered to death by tradespeople and insurance agents wanting to sell me something. Tell them I'm out of town for the evening — anything."

The silence of the room was broken only by the snap and hiss of the fire as Sam Reyburn put the receiver of the handset to his ear.

"Hulloa. — Yes. — Miss Reyburn is out of town for the evening. — Sure, she'll be back tomorrow. — Oh, it is! — Yes, I'll give her your message. She'll be pleased purple. — I get you. I'll tell her. 'Bye!" He

85

laid the phone on the stand.

"Who was it, Sam? What will please me purple?" Brooke demanded uneasily.

Sam backed up to the mantel. With hands deep in his pockets, he grinned at his sister.

"Holding out on us, weren't you, gal?"

"What do you mean? Sam, who called?"

Her brother cracked a nut with maddening deliberation and crunched the meat between his strong white teeth before he answered:

"A party by the name of Trent."

"Trent! Not Mark the Magnificent? Why didn't you let me answer?"

Sam struck an attitude. "Ungrateful female! Didn't I imperil my immortal soul by lying for you? Saying you were out of town?"

"Cut the dramatics, Sam. What did Mark Trent want?"

"Wanted me to tell you that he had been away."

"What of it? For goodness' sake, stop stalling! What did he want?"

"Not much. Only to say that he accepted your invitation for Thanksgiving dinner with pleasure."

$\mathcal{V}$

Brooke noticed Mark Trent's quick glance about as he entered the dining-room at Lookout House. Did he approve of the change from the dark figured paper and oak trim of his aunt's regime to creamy white walls and woodwork, white damask hangings, and the gorgeous Sirapi rug, with its ivory ground patterned in soft Persian colors, rose, cream, a touch of blue and a touch of green? If he had a flair for the beautiful, he must like the tile of Rembrandt's Man with the Pearls over the mantel. Her father had brought that home from abroad in his days of affluence.

She felt an instant of self-consciousness as she took the seat against the variegated yellow background of tall mimosas and acacias which filled a broad bay-window, which her mother refused with a quick shake of her head and a smile. She immediately forgot herself in pride of her sporting family. Each one was so gay, so determined to do his or her share to make the party a real festivity. Holidays were hard days since her father's death, but always someone who was alone had been invited to keep the feast with them. Thinking of others helped immeasurably to bridge the sense of loss, Celia Reyburn argued.

The oysters were big and cold and luscious; the turkey was cooked to a turn. When Sam's knife touched the joints they fell apart. The squash was a golden mound of lusciousness; the potatoes a fluffy mass of perfection; the broccoli Hollandaise of melting green tenderness; and the cranberry jelly a triumph. There was avocado salad, and plum pudding, and mince and squash pies. She had tried to have the dinner as much like those they had had in their own home as possible, even to the mass of yellow and bronze chrysanthemums in the centre of the table. When the cheese board was passed, her mother looked at her and smiled. Did she realize that her daughter felt that her home-making ways couldn't be improved upon?

Brooke breathed a little sigh of relief as she rose from the table. This Thanksgiving dinner had been the first entertaining in her own home. Of course the guests had been her family and Mark Trent only, but she had felt pride in having it a success.

As she served coffee from the massive

silver tray in the living-room, she glanced at Mark Trent standing before the fire. With his elbow on the mantel, he was talking to Celia Reyburn seated in a corner of the couch. The orchids he had brought her added the perfect touch to her amethyst frock. Orchids for her mother, gardenias for Lucette, and deep fragrant purple violets for his hostess. He had said it with flowers. A lavish gentleman. Had Henri turned chalky as he had announced dinner, or had she imagined it? He had stared at Mark Trent as if seeing an unwelcome apparition.

With a groan of repletion Sam pulled himself out of a deep chair.

"Boy, let's get out and walk! I feel like a stuffed, trussed turkey. Why do we eat so much more on Thanksgiving? Because we haven't any sense. Notice that I'm acquiring the analytic method, question and answer. Anybody here got the energy to take the shore walk?"

Lucette curled deeper into her chair.

"Can't go. I've got to finish this." She waved a mass of knitted wool.

"Don't apologize."

"I'm not apologizing. I'm explaining, Sam Reyburn. You never can seem to sense the difference."

"Won't go, you mean, lazy! If you don't exercise more, Lucette, you'll look like a butter ball stumping round on toothpicks."

"The Great Adviser on the air again! Butter ball or not, I stay right here. Knitted skirts have gone longer, and I'll never finish this if I don't keep everlastingly at it. Drag Brooke along."

"I'll go with you, Sammy." Celia Reyburn smiled at her tall son. "Elaine Jaffrey is a great hiker; she will probably walk me all over the British Isles. I must get in practice. Just wait until I change my shoes."

"Boy, I'm glad we have one sport in the family. I'll bet Lucette has a heavy date, and is expecting someone. Coming, Brooke? Don't tell me that you've gone knitting-minded. Coming, Mr. Trent?"

"Mark to you, I hope, Sam. Do come, Miss Reyburn," Mark Trent urged. "It's a grand day. After hours of storm, there is enough wind to make the surf worth looking at."

"Worth looking at" were colorless words to express the grandeur of the shore, Brooke thought, as, standing on a jutting crag, holding on her beret with one hand, skirts blowing, she looked down at the driving current, cold and stealthy in places, in others foaming and tossing white-edged green waves against ledges transformed by the magic of the slanting sun into ruddy copper, dark brown in the crevices. Spray, diaphanous as a mist from a giant atomizer, iridescent as jeweled malines, shimmered in the light. Beyond the surf a dozen lavender winged gulls floated on the water. Overhead, clouds, which had the pink depths and crinkled edges of a conch-shell, were encroaching stealthily on the limpid blue sky. Toward the east, the ocean, deeply malachite, stretched on illimitably till it merged into the purple horizon. Above the din, the suck and thud of the sea, floated the haunting wail of a distant siren, the screech of gulls, came a drift of music from a great ship outward bound. An amber green wave outlashed its predecessors, hissed, roared, broke against a ledge, and showered Brooke with crystal spray.

"Oh!" Instinctively she clutched Mark Trent's arm. "It — it took my breath!"

He drew her back to the path, pulled out his handkerchief, and wiped her wet face.

"I should have known better than to let you stand there."

"It wasn't your fault. I adored it. It made me feel as if every inch of me had been electrified. Why is it that when we are together I need to be rescued from difficulties? I want to thank you for —"

"Please, don't."

She wondered at the embarrassed fierceness of his voice.

"I won't, except to add that I know I owe my life to you. There, that's over. I promise never to mention it again." Spurred by the stimulating air, she took her courage in both hands and plunged.

"Won't you please be friends? I didn't know Mrs. Mary Amanda Dane had any money, really I didn't, Mr. Trent."

In the instant that she waited for his answer, sun, sea, the roar of the surf were blotted out. Only his straight-gazing eyes meeting hers were real. They touched her heart, quickly, passionately. Then Mark Trent thrust his handkerchief into his pocket.

"Forget that Mr. Trent stuff. Being legatees in the same estate — my aunt left me a bank account, you know — ought to make us friends, oughtn't it?" His voice was light, but she sensed a tinge of irony. "We'd better keep going if we are to walk around the Point before dark. Your mother and Sam went on some time ago. What did she mean when she spoke of hiking over the British Isles?"

"She is going to England to visit her college classmate. Of course, I'm crazy to have her go, but — but I didn't realize how precious she was until I thought of her being so far away."

Brooke hoped fervently that Mark Trent had not noticed the break in her voice. Apparently he hadn't, for he asked casually:

"Are your brother and sister going?"

"No. They are to be with me while Mother is away. I am so glad. It will give me heaps to do. I'm not used to this poison-ivy leisure that looked so alluring before I had tried it. My life was so full before —"

"Before you had Lookout House stuffed down your throat, you mean? I don't see why the dickens Aunt Mary Amanda tied that string to her legacy, forced you to live in this house."

"It wasn't a string, and she didn't force me. I like old towns, and I love Lookout House."

"My mistake." Trent's laugh turned to a frown. "What are the town fathers thinking of to allow a gas station stuck out on this road? Has that house been sold?"

Brooke promptly defended the brilliant equipment in front of a small white cottage.

"I don't know who owns the place, but doubtless the town fathers were thinking of giving the poor man who has started the filling-station another chance. I heard that he had money, lost it, began to drink too much, and that a friend set him up in business here hoping to steady him."

"Who told you the story of his life?"

"Henri."

"Henri! Does he know the man?"

"He will have to answer that question. He asked me to buy gas at the new filling-station, and I do to encourage the poor fellow to keep on trying to make good."

"How about encouraging honest Mike Cassidy who started the garage at the end of the causeway years ago and has served the public faithfully and unselfishly? He has a wife and five children to support."

Why did his voice rouse opposition in her, Brooke wondered. She had had doubts herself lately as to the permanency of the filling-station owner's reform. Twice when she had stopped for gas, a young Irish girl had reported the boss as "sick" and she had wondered if he were backsliding. Mark the Magnificent need not know that, however.

"Don't you believe in helping a man to come back?" she asked crisply.

"I do, most decidedly, but I believe also in helping an honest hard-working man like Cassidy, who has had the strength of character to leave drink alone, to keep his kids in shoes. Come on. We are almost quarreling. Why should you and I fight over a filling-station owner?"

"You're right, when we have so many other things about which to disagree."

Brooke's brown eyes met his, intent and darkly gray; wistfulness tinged her voice as she urged:

"Speaking of disagreeing — will you please behave like a sensible person and take the family treasures which belong to you?"

"Aunt Mary Amanda left them to you."

"I know, but it isn't right for me to have them, and what's more, I don't need or want them. I'd rather go without rings all my life than wear one of those gorgeous things she left, which are rightfully yours. Mr. Stewart has put all the jewelry in a bank vault for you. I have Mother's lovely china and glass and furniture which have been in storage since our home was broken up. I've had everything which belonged to your family moved to the chauffeur's apartment over the garage. There seems to be very little silver. Perhaps your aunt gave it to you?"

"Silver! Very little silver! She had the Trent service which came originally from England and any number of beautiful pieces. That silver is a family tradition. Where is it? She didn't give it to me. What does Stewart say about it?"

"He thought that because of the epidemic of crime reported in the newspapers, Mrs. Dane might have become timid about keeping valuables in the house and had it stored in a bank. But he found no receipt for it among her papers. Do you think she sold it?"

"Sold it! No. I'll bet —" he broke off abruptly. "See that great rock sticking up off shore? I used to imagine it the peak of a submerged island rising from the sea."

"Perhaps it is. 'Islands arise, grow old and disappear.' That isn't original. Sam has taken the title for his comedy from it. The first night I spent at Lookout House I was kept awake by the wailing of that distant siren. Now I don't notice it."

"You'll notice it if you stay here during the winter as Jed told me you were planning to do. There goes the sun behind the city! Couldn't you hear the kerplunk as it dropped below the skyline?"

Across the harbor, buildings, towers, and chunky blocks made a vast irregular pattern of unreal beauty against the crimson horizon, a pattern punctured by myriad blinking yellow lights which were windows.

"I could. See the lights springing up in the houses, see how the shapes of things are beginning to lose their sharpness of outline? I love twilight, love lighted windows. They are like the welcoming eyes of a home. I love this town. I'd like to help here, there is a lot to be done besides voting and paying taxes, even in this small place. Of course there is heartache, and suffering, and even wickedness, I suppose, but one doesn't run into it at every turn as one does in the city; there one sees constantly the neglected child, the small merchant with tragic eyes hanging on by his teeth, the hard-boiled women — out for all they can get — and all the time, one feels so powerless to help."

She felt rather than saw Mark Trent's sharp look at her before, straight and immobile as a soldier on parade, he walked on beside her. The light from the afterglow accentuated the lines of repression in his face. Was this his habitual self, and the man who had rescued her the self who emerged only under stress? What was he thinking, she wondered, and wished that she had not made that reference to hard-boiled women. From what she had heard, his wife must have been of that type. She said quickly:

"Don't mind my thinking aloud. I acquired the habit when working out problems in my office. I promise never to bore you again. Isn't that shimmery light on the water beautiful? See how it colors the sea-stained rocks. It has turned the roof of Lookout House a lovely pink. Here we are, home again."

She stopped to look at the massive stone houses set in cedar hedges, framed by sombre hemlocks, side by side on a ledge. They had a sort of splendid detachment from the world about them, a rugged picturesque beauty. They were a beautiful gray, not unlike that of weathered boards, toned by dashes of red and yellow iron rust, with hospitable doorways and long French windows on two floors opening on balconies railed and trellised in wrought-iron of lace-like delicacy, with great chimneys smothered in skeletons of vines. Brooke drew a little breath of sheer happiness.

"I adore Lookout House! To me home is not merely a convenience, a sentiment; it is a ruling passion." Embarrassed by her

98

burst of emotion, she asked quickly:

"Whose sleek roadster is that, I wonder?"

On the threshold of the living-room she stopped in startled unbelief. Jerry Field stood by the fire talking to her mother. Who was the brown-haired girl in blue beside Lucette?

"Couldn't wait for you to send out At Home cards, Brooke," Jerry Field greeted jauntily. "You remember that you said I could come to Lookout House when you were settled, don't you? I wanted to meet your family, wanted them to know that I'm in your stag line for sure."

His eyes flashed beyond her to Mark Trent on the threshold. There was laughter in his voice and a hint of challenge. Before she could answer, he commanded:

"Come hither, Daphne, and meet our neighbor. This is my sister."

"Neighbor!" Brooke smiled at the brown-haired girl as she welcomed her with a cordial handshake. "I would know that you were Jerry's sister, you look so like him; but is the neighbor stuff a joke?"

"No, Miss Reyburn, we really are staying on the Point."

Daphne Field's smile disclosed small teeth as perfect in color and size as a row of matched pearls. She turned to Sam.

"I've heard that you are the coming play-wright, Mr. Reyburn, that you have a touch of O'Neil's tragic outlook, a seasoning of Kaufman's humor, and a hint of Coward's sophistication."

Sam grinned. "Is that original, or did you get it from *The Times*?"

The girl pouted:

"Of course it's original. Why, Mark!"

Daphne Field's breathless exclamation, the radiance of her face revealed so much that Brooke had the embarrassed sense of having looked for an instant at a naked heart. Trent came forward. Was the fire-light playing pranks, or had his face gone dark with color?

"Where did you drop from, Daphne? How are you, Field?"

Why didn't someone say something and smash the strained silence, Brooke wondered impatiently. It was as if the firelight had cast a spell and tied all their tongues. Her mother's eyes were on Daphne Field as she thoughtfully pulled her gloves through her hands. Sam, back to the room, was poking at the parrot. He hated emotional scenes — off the stage. The atmosphere fairly quivered with things unsaid. Lucette came to life.

"Turn on the lights, Sam, this gloom may be artistic, but it gives me the merry-pranks. This has turned out to be meet-your-neighbor day, hasn't it? Who's the dame in the floppy hat, Brooke, who looks like a super-animated Bo-peep, and carries a cane which easily could be mistaken for a shepherd's crook? There's the chance of a lifetime for you to get in a little missionary work as clothes adviser; you'd better begin with a streamline diet. She thinks everything here, including Mother, 'charming.' "

"It must have been Mrs. Dane's friend Mrs. Gregory; they call her The Empress here. So she has called. That means, if she likes us, that we shall be admitted into the inner social circle. Jerry, I was so dazed by your appearance that I forgot to ask what you meant by that word 'neighbor.' "

The lamps in the room diffused a soft glow, set the chrysanthemums in the conservatory shimmering like mother-of-pearl, brought out the warm color in the chintz, and lighted the eyes of the Duchess over the mantel. Celia Reyburn was looking at Jerry Field. Brooke was familiar with that appraising scrutiny, it was the same look she had given Daphne who was perched on the arm of the chair in which Lucette sat knitting. Side by side, Sam and Mark Trent stood back to the mantel, almost as if they had joined forces against something. She felt Jerry Field's eyes on her and looked at him questioningly.

"I was waiting for your kind attention before answering your question, Brooke. Sure, we're neighbors. Daphne and I have taken a house here for the season."

"Season! What season?"

"This winter, of course. Didn't you say that many of the houses were to be kept open?"

"Ye-s. But why —" Surprise crisped Brooke's voice.

"I've been wanting for years to paint snow. Found I could hire a house with a studio here. You don't mind, I hope?"

"Don't be foolish, Jerry. Of course I don't, only —"

"No matter what Brooke thinks, I'm all for it, Mr. Field," Lucette encouraged. "It will be grand to have someone kind of young in the neighborhood — and — Oh, Sam, two more recruits for the cast of your play! Line of applicants for parts will please form on the left."

"Play! What play? I adore dramatics." Daphne Field's voice and eyes were eager.

"We've been talking about producing Sam's comedy, 'Islands Arise,' for charity. Of course it's a terrific job. We always paint our own scenery —"

"Hold! Jerry the boy artist will paint the scenery;" — Field's enthusiasm cooled — "afraid my box of a studio wouldn't be big enough though."

"There is a large empty room on the second floor next to Lucette's. Couldn't decide just how to furnish it, so I've waited. We can use that. Won't it be grand, Sam?" Brooke explained and demanded in the same breath.

"Yeah, but what does that prove? How do I know whether the Field team can act, or whether they'll gum up the show?"

"Don't be a grouch, Master Reyburn," Lucette jibed. "You'd better page the family Lost and Found Department for your manners. I adore neighbors. I'm pleased purple that we are to have two such snappy ones."

Mark Trent straightened and flung the cigarette he had but a moment before lighted into the fire. He kept his eyes on Lucette as he announced:

"News flash! Not two new neighbors, but four, lady. I'm opening my house next week. Jed Stewart and I will keep bachelor hall there. My announcement doubtless lacks the romantic overtones of Field's, but we'll do our best to make you Reyburns neighbor-conscious."

VI

In the firelit library of his house, Mark Trent was perched on the corner of the large flat desk. As he filled his pipe he compared the old-fashioned air of dignified restfulness of the room with its deep chairs in the smoking-room manner and its two-story book-lined walls, divided half way up by a gallery, with the charm of its twin on the other side of the brocade hanging which screened the door connecting the two houses. He might have the piano moved to the drawing room, the huge mirror taken out, and some figured stuff in place of those red curtains, he thought. Perhaps Brooke Reyburn would make a suggestion to pep up the place a little.

Jed Stewart, lounging in a crimson leather chair, hands in his trousers pockets, legs outstretched, was staring at the blazing logs, watching the blue and yellow, copper and green tongues of flame lick at the chimney. The faint thunder of waves dashing against ledges, the ceaseless crying of sea gulls stole through the heavy hangings drawn across the long windows.

Impatiently he sat up.

"Don't those mournful sounds ever stop?"

The question brought Mark Trent's thoughts right-about-face on the trail they were following.

"What sounds?"

"That infernal pound of the surf and those darned birds."

"What can you expect when the day blustered in with dark ragged clouds flying before a near gale? And gulls must live. You'll get used to it in time, Jed."

"So what! Remember the cow that was being taught to eat sawdust? When she learned she up and died?"

"Died! You're not planning to die on my hands, are you? You don't hate the place that much, do you? Because if you do, you don't have to stay."

"Who said I hated it? Who said I didn't want to stay? I think this house, stuck up on a ledge, is the berries. Because at times I'd like to soft pedal that surf doesn't mean that I'm quitting, does it? Couldn't if I wanted to, could I?" He lowered his voice. "We've been here a week, Mark, and we are not the fraction of a degree nearer finding that last will and testament of Mary Amanda Dane's — if there is such a thing."

"And the silver; don't forget the silver, Jed. I can account for the will being lost — if there was one — but what has become of the silver? I've had it so much on my mind that I consulted Bill Harrison."

"Who's he?"

"The Inspector in charge of Police Headquarters across the causeway. He's been on the force here since I was a small boy. He was my hero and when he sang at the A. E. F. celebrations — well, no grand opera celebrity ever has made my heart turn over as it turned when Bill sang 'Sweet Adeline.' He's keen. Never drinks. His voice is his only vanity. He loves to be asked to sing. He has had plenty of chances to go to bigger cities, but he stayed here because his children were in school and he wouldn't take them away from their friends."

"What did he say about the silver?"

"He didn't say, he doesn't talk much. He asked a few questions about the Jacques and said he would drop in here this afternoon to take a look around. Mrs. Gregory is coming later — hope they don't meet — I asked her to have tea with us. Met her yesterday on the street, and she let it be known that her feelings were hurt that I had not invited her before. I — I asked her to bring Miss Reyburn."

Mark Trent slid from the desk and absentmindedly twirled a globe which showed the countries of the world as they had been before the Treaty of Versailles had remade the map of Europe.

"Do you think Brooke Reyburn suspects that we are here as amateur detectives, Jed?"

Elbow on his knee, chin in his hand, Jed Stewart scowled at the fire. The licking flames cast curious shadows, for all the world like thoughts flitting across the ruddy brightness of his face.

"Amateurs! We may be, but you've called in a professional on the job, haven't you? You can't tell what that girl thinks, but why should she suspect our reason for being here more than Field's, and one couldn't suspect that lad of ulterior motives. He always looks to me as if he were on the verge of kissing a lady's hand. Why didn't you accept the lead in Sam's comedy? It was offered to you, wasn't it?"

"It was, but long ago I outgrew dramatics. What do you think of 'Islands Arise' — that's the name of the play, isn't it?"

"That it will get a fair hearing, at least. The theatre-going world isn't so cocky and hard-boiled as it was some years ago and it may appreciate Sam's ideas and ideals. You'd be a knock-out in the lead, fella."

"I wouldn't take part in the play if I were aching to act. I see the Reyburns as seldom as possible. Thanksgiving day when Brooke started to thank me for pulling her from under that car, I burned with shame when I remembered why I had accepted her invitation. I don't care for this spy stuff, even if I do believe that the girl by some hocus pocus hypnotized Aunt Mary Amanda. I'd let this missing will — if there is such a thing — slide if it weren't for the justice of the thing. The Missing Will; or Silver, Silver, Who Snitched the Silver? It sounds like a melodrama of the gay nineties."

"Mebbe so, mebbe so, but if you followed the court calendar as I do, you'd refuse to believe the fool things to which people sign their names. Only yesterday the number of wills in a contested estate we are handling was increased to five when a will dated before the death of the testator's husband was presented. The state ought to provide a university extension course devoted exclusively to wills. I'd donate my services as instructor. Gay nineties, sez you. There's nothing the matter with the experimental thirties for producing cockeyed wills, sez I."

"I'll take your word for it, but I hate the whole miserable business. Whenever I see one of the family from Lookout House I have a feeling of sick distaste."

"You show it. Getting to be the strong, silent type, aren't you, Mark? If you feel that way about her, why did you ask Mrs. Gregory to bring Brooke here this afternoon? You never have been fair to that girl. You started with the idea that she's crooked, and you're sticking to it like honey to a glass dish."

"Like her a lot, don't you?"

"I'm not the only one. I haven't dropped in at Lookout House yet without finding a lad or two from the big city — late business associates, I gathered — drinking tea or after-dinner coffee. I'll bet her stag line, if laid end to end, would reach from here across the causeway. She's got soul and —"

Trent blew a shrill whistle through his fingers. Stewart laughed.

"I get you, the stop signal. I'll toss her one more posy, then I'll quit. I'm supposed to be stage manager of Sam's play, but I'd sure make a mess of it without Brooke as my property woman. She's executive and then some. She never forgets."

"When does the play come off?"

"First Thursday in January. Sam thought of New Year's Eve but gave that up for fear he couldn't lure a producer away from New York festivities."

"That isn't far off. We'll have a grand celebration here for the cast and friends who come from town. We'll invite the neighbors to supper and dance after the show. Have you a speaking part?"

"If you can call one line a speaking part. I'm qualifying for what is called in the profession 'a short part and type actor.' You can't have an after-the-show party without inviting the Reyburns."

"Of course they'll be invited. Where did you get the crazy idea I would leave them out?"

"You're so suspicious of Brooke, and —"

"How can I help being suspicious? Didn't Mrs. Gregory say that the girl drove in as she went out that last day? That she —"

Mark Trent stopped speaking to stare at the ceiling. Had a door banged overhead, or had he imagined the sound? The servants, Taku and Kowa, were in the kitchen at this time of day; they wouldn't be on the third floor anyway, he had not had that opened up, plenty of room below for Jed and himself. It seemed as if he kept fasci-

111

nated eyes upraised for an hour, but it was a mere second by the tall clock in the corner before he crossed to the window and drew aside the curtains.

"What a drab December afternoon! The clouds are retreating and the setting sun is edging them with gold, but the temperature is dropping, must be near freezing point. The boom and beat and bang of the tide against the ledge rattles the shutters. I'll bet we're in for an old-fashioned New England winter." On his way back to the fire he stopped to listen.

"What pearls of wisdom were you about to scatter, Mark, when you stopped as if, like a Mohammedan, you heard the muezzin call, *'Allah, il Allah, Allah akbar!'*? Who's here?"

A man entered the room with a purposeful stride. He was ample of jowl, slightly opulent as to waistline; he had the flinty eyes of an eagle who can stare straight at the sun. A sense of force was his outstanding characteristic.

"Here I am, Mark. That Jap outside wanted to bow me in, but I shooed him off." Inspector Bill Harrison's voice was surprisingly soft with a persuasive inflection.

"Glad you've come, Inspector. This is

112

my friend Jed Stewart."

Inspector Harrison nodded. "How are you, Mr. Stewart. Does he know about the silver, Mark?" He lowered himself into a deep chair and accepted a cigar.

"Yes, he's staying here to help me — us solve the mystery."

"What else have you lost?"

"Why do you think we've lost anything else?"

"Would you two city guys come to this burg to stay just to find a lot of silverware?"

"It's more than mere silverware; the pieces are antiques of great value."

Inspector Harrison pulled himself from the enticing crimson depths to his feet.

"All right, Mark, have it your own way, but I ain't mixin' up in a case where folks are holding out on me. I work best when the interested party works with me. Get that?"

Mark's laugh was quick and disarming.

"Hold everything, Bill Harrison; you can't walk out on us like that. Sit down again. Jed, tell him what Mrs. Gregory told us about the will she witnessed. You understand, Inspector, that there may be nothing to it — so it's off the record."

"Say, Mark, do you suppose I climbed

up on the force by talking my head off? I play the rules. Spill it, Mr. Stewart."

Stewart repeated Mrs. Gregory's astonishing announcement that she had witnessed a will of Mary Amanda Dane's of a date later than the will allowed; told of the decision of Mark and himself to turn detectives and of their absolute unsuccess to date.

Inspector Bill Harrison blew a perfect smoke ring.

"Did Mrs. Gregory say there was anyone else present but Mrs. Dane and the other witnesses when she signed?"

"No."

Mark Trent's answer was nothing short of explosive. The Inspector's soft grudging laugh, in such marked contrast to his bird-of-prey eyes, brought guilty color to his face. It wasn't keeping back information not to tell that Brooke Reyburn had driven in that afternoon just as Mrs. Gregory had driven out from Lookout House, was it?

Inspector Bill Harrison rose. With a cigar tucked in one corner of his mouth, he nodded.

"I'll be going. Guess I've got all the dope. Don't give that Henri Jacques and his wife the idea that you've missed the silver. Let it drop out of their minds. When you have any news, come to head-quarters, don't phone. That reminds me. Know anything about the people who've started the filling-station here on the Point?"

"No. But I understand that Henri Jacques is recommending them."

"Oh, he is? That Henri's just naturally helpful, ain't he? Well, I must get back." He added in his soft persuasive voice:

"Whenever you're ready to come across with the name of the other party who was in the neighborhood of Lookout House the day that last will of Mrs. Dane's was signed, Mark, I'm just across the causeway. I'll be seeing you."

"Don't go yet, Bill!"

He mustn't leave thinking that he and Jed were holding out on him, Mark realized. He dropped to the piano bench and struck a few chords.

"Sing for us. Give us 'Sweet Adeline,' Bill. Not five minutes ago I was telling Stewart about the thrill I got as a boy from hearing you sing it."

Inspector Bill Harrison's generous mouth widened in a pleased smile, even his flinty eyes softened. He straightened and jerked down his waistcoat.

"Well, if I can remember it."

"Of course you can remember it. Atta-boy!"

Mark played a few opening chords.

" 'In the evening when I sit alone
   a-dreaming
Of days gone by, love, to me so dear.' "

sang Inspector Harrison in a powerful, un-trained, yet singularly sweet, tenor.

At the end of the verse he motioned to the two men to join in the chorus. Mark Trent contributed a rich baritone and swayed on the piano bench as he pounded out the accompaniment with gusto. Jed Stewart marked time with his pipe to a rumbling bass:

" 'Sweet Adeline,
   My Adeline.
   At night, dear heart,
   For you I pine.
   In all my dreams
   Your fair face beams;
   You're the flower of my heart
   Sweet Adeline.' "

Laughing as he had not laughed for years, Mark Trent spurred on the two

116

somewhat breathless men, who grinned back at him.

"That's showing 'em. Don't stop, Bill. Give us all the trills and trimmings. We've just got going. Come on!" He ran his fingers over the keys. Jed Stewart grabbed his shoulder.

"Hold on, Mark. See who's here!"

Mark Trent turned. Surprise brought him to his feet, wiped the smile from his lips. That couldn't be Lola on the threshold! It was. Hunt, her name was now, Lola Hunt, he must remember.

"Say, Mark, I'll be making my get-away."

He nodded response to Bill Harrison's mumble. Knew when he opened the door which led to the print room and vanished. Evidently the Inspector didn't care to meet Lola. Who did? With the question Mark thrust his hands hard into his coat pockets and took a step forward.

"Well?"

The sound was more a growl than a word, he realized, as he looked steadily at the woman who had been his wife. Had been. At last he had come to think of her in the past tense. It had taken three years to accomplish that. The shame, the humiliation, the unbearable heartache he had suffered in the years they had lived together swept over him in a sickening tide. What did she want now? She was the type of woman who constantly and everlastingly wanted something. Wasn't he giving her enough? There had been no justice in his giving her anything, but when she had written him that her current husband was out of a job and that she was hungry, what could he do but make her an allowance till the man found work? Her clothing had a cheap smartness; the dark brilliance of her eyes was intensified by artificial shadows; her skin was thick and flushed; her short black hair needed trimming; her mouth drooped at the corners. She pouted lips which resembled nothing so much as a bloody smear.

"Don't stare at me as if I were a ghost from out a purple past, Mark. I told your Jap that I was an old friend, that I wanted to surprise you. You were all bearing down so heavily on 'Sweet Adeline,' I began to think I never would make myself heard. Bill Harrison's voice was shaking the roof. If you don't close your mouth soon, Jed Stewart, your jaws will never snap back into place. I hate to keep the gentlemen standing. Won't you ask me to sit down?"

Without waiting for an answer, she sank into the large chair before the fire and flung back her cape of silver fox. It was the last extravagant gift he had bought her, Mark Trent remembered, and the only thing she was wearing that was not cheap. She drew off fabric gloves with the care she might have given the finest kid. She still wore her rings, he noticed, rare and brilliant stones; she need never go hungry while she had those to sell. Her dark eyes sparkled with malice as she looked up at the two men who stood side by side before the fire.

"Still pals you two, aren't you? Funny how much longer friendship lasts between men than love between a man and woman. Mark, I came here to talk to you. Jed, you may go."

Mark Trent's hand closed on Stewart's arm with a grip which turned his nails white.

"Jed will stay and hear what you have to say. Surely we can have no secrets from the man who saw us through the divorce court."

She shrugged. "All right with me. I've nothing to lose. Thought you might object to having what I say get on the air."

"Methinks the lady is implying that I'm a gossip."

"I don't like the twist you gave that

'lady,' Jed Stewart. Don't shake your head at the Jap, Mark. Why shouldn't I have a cup of tea with you? I'm famished. Place it here."

The servant looked at Mark Trent before he pressed the springs which released the legs of the tray he was carrying and set it before the woman. He brought in a muffin stand with sandwiches and cakes.

"You needn't wait," she dismissed the man as if she were the mistress of the house. Mark nodded confirmation as the Jap's eyes sought his. Did he know that the woman so dictatorially giving orders had been his wife?

"Pity this gorgeous silver service wasn't one of our wedding presents, instead of your mother's, Mark; then I could have claimed it. Still take two lumps, Jed?"

"No tea, thanks."

She shrugged. "Shall I ring for cocktails?"

"I'll order what Jed wants." Mark Trent spoke sharply. "Drink your tea, Lola, and —"

" 'Get out,' I suppose you're thinking, though being a perfect gentleman you wouldn't say it. You always were scrupulously polite, even when we were fighting, Mark."

With a moderation which fired Mark Trent with a mad urge to kick over the tea table, she filled her cup and selected a sandwich. It would be unbearable to have Brooke Reyburn see her here.

Side by side the two men watched her, watched her restless hands. Once she had been told by a stag that her hands were like pale butterflies, Mark remembered, and they had fluttered ever since. In the silence the tick of the clock set the air vibrating; the fire snapped and blazed cheerily; the tide against the ledges boomed a dull undertone.

Lola Hunt flung a crumpled doily to the table.

"Now a cigarette, Mark, and I shall be ready to proceed with my story."

"Sorry, haven't any."

She raised brows which had been plucked to a thin arch.

"You do want to get rid of me, don't you. Well, I strive to please." She rose and crossed to the desk. With a glance over her shoulder, she opened a box of Chinese lacquer.

"You see I still know my way around. Oh, by the way, your aunt's legatee is living at Lookout House, I hear. Henri wrote me —"

"Henri!"

"Yes. I always got on with Henri, perhaps because he knew that I detested your aunt as much as he did. He wrote that Miss Reyburn evidently didn't like his wife and himself, asked if I would give him a reference in case they lost the position."

Was that all Henri Jacques had written, Mark wondered. There was a hint of mockery in Lola's voice and eyes. What was behind that letter? He watched her thoughtfully as she perched on the corner of the desk, crossed her knees and lighted a cigarette. She blew a ring of smoke toward the two men standing back to the fire.

"Forgot these were in the box, didn't you, Mark? You really should do something about your memory; it's slipping." Her eyes and voice sharpened. "Well, here's my news. Bert Hunt — he's my present husband, in case you've forgotten — is planning to go into business in the residential part of this town, has gone, in fact. I shall help when he's rushed or — indisposed. When I heard that you had opened this house, I thought perhaps you wouldn't care to have your former wife working — I've been warned that I've been taking chances with my heart — that perhaps you'd like to buy us off. With twenty thousand dollars we could go abroad and

122

stay for a time. Don't stand there like a bronze Nemesis ready to swoop. Nothing shameful about any kind of a job these days, is there?"

Mark Trent laughed. It was not an especially merry burst of sound, but it would serve.

"Do you call extortion a job? Nothing doing, Lola. Your heart! You've used your weak heart as an excuse to get what you wanted for years. Why should I deprive the town of Hunt's business ability and so charming an assistant?"

She slid to her feet. Her face, which had been blank with amazement at his laugh, went white with anger.

"You mean that you don't mind my working — here?"

"If it's what you like, why should I? But," his face was as colorless as hers, "if you do stay in this town, the allowance I am making you — which, you may remember, is purely voluntary — will stop."

"Are you threatening me?"

"Not for a minute. I'm merely reminding you —"

"Then I'll remind you that it may cost you more —"

"Mrs. Gregory, Miss Reyburn," murmured Kowa at the door.

In the instant of silence which followed the servant's announcement, Mark Trent frowned at the figures reflected in the great mirror which covered one wall. The looking-glass was old and played queer pranks with faces. It turned normal shadows into smudges, drew a mouth down, tilted a nose unduly. It reflected Anne Gregory, the broad brim of her hat, her ebony cane, her sable cape and long black taffeta dress, her white gloved hand extended as she advanced like a trim yacht under full sail, the shocked amazement in her deep-set tired eyes as they stared at Lola Hunt.

The mirror faithfully reproduced the flippant tilt of the chin of his former wife, showed up pitilessly her shallow, vain face in contrast to the vivid, beautiful face of Brooke Reyburn in her smart green knit frock, her swagger coat of beaver; mirrored Jed Stewart in his checked suit, red carnation in his buttonhole, with a cigarette half way to his lips. He met his own eyes in the mirror, eyes blazing with anger at the awkward situation in which Lola had placed him. Had he ever loved the woman? He knew now that his feeling for her had been nine parts chivalry and one part physical attraction. He had been conscious that he was wilfully shutting his eyes to grave faults. Hadn't he plenty himself, he had argued.

Mrs. Gregory moved and the spell of the mirror was broken. Her skin mottled, her eyes flashed as she thumped her cane on the rug and went into action.

"What are you doing in this house, Lola?"

"I might ask you that." Lola Hunt's eyes moved insolently from her to the girl beside her. "Matchmaking mayhap? As I remember it was one of your passions." Her glance brought color to Brooke Reyburn's face.

"Just as cheap in your answers as ever, aren't you, Lola? Wisecracking, I believe they call it now. Don't tell me you have taken her back, Mark."

"Taken me back! That's the joke of the week. He couldn't get me back."

Lola Hunt pulled the silver fox cape about her shoulders and drew on her fabric gloves.

"So glad to have met you here, Mrs. Gregory. It will save sending you a card."

Anne Gregory's face took on a purple tint. She thumped her cane on the rug.

"A card! A card to what, you brazen hussy?"

Lola Hunt shrugged. "Don't try to stop

125

her, Mark. She would call a woman who chose to live her life according to modern ideas of marriage, a hussy. You'd know that from her clothes, they're so deliciously Victorian. I really must go."

She stopped on the threshold. "Dear Mrs. Gregory, I didn't answer your question, did I? The card to which I referred is an invitation to patronize the business which we have started in my old home on the Point. You remember that house, I am sure, remember how you and your friends tried to freeze out the girl who came there to live. She didn't freeze, did she? She burned up a few of the husbands and all the lads. Is it any more shocking for me to go into business than for some of your pet socialites to sponsor cigarettes, soap, or bedding in every magazine in the country?"

She turned to Brooke.

"You are Miss Reyburn, aren't you? I'll give you a tip. Had I been left the late, not too lamented, Mary Amanda Dane's money, I would be wondering why her rightful heir and his lawyer had camped down in the house next to mine, why they were hob-nobbing with Inspector Bill Harrison. In a movie it would be because they intended to prove 'undue influence' or, perhaps, because the dispossessed heir planned to marry the heiress to keep the money in the family. That's a thought!"

She looked back over her shoulder.

"Think over my proposition, Mark, darling. It maybe cheaper for you — in the end."

VII

Lola Hunt's malicious laugh lingered eerily in the silence which followed her theatrical exit from the room. Somewhere a door closed with a bang which clanged through the house.

Her spiteful warning stuck like an irritating burr in Brooke Reyburn's mind. She glanced at the two men standing back to the fire: Stewart's eyes, still on the doorway, smoldered with anger; the tortured look in Mark Trent's hurt her unbearably; even with his pride knifed, his courtesy had been invincible. The woman had warned him also. Why think of him, she asked herself angrily. Better have her mind on what Mrs. Hunt had insinuated. Had those two men come to live in this house because they suspected her, Brooke Reyburn, of dishonestly influencing Mary Amanda Dane? If so, what could they do about it? Drag her into court? Was that why Inspector Harrison had been with them? It was fantastic, incredible, yet hadn't she wondered times without number why they, city men so obviously, should have come to this village for the winter? Why was she so amazed? The day she had met Mark Trent in Jed Stewart's office, he had intimated that he thought her a schemer. As for that marriage-to-keep-the-money-in-the-family stuff, it was too absurd to think of.

Had the woman's first suggestion been merely a haphazard thrust because she was angry? Whichever it was, she was a hateful creature. She was Trent's former wife! No wonder his face had been colorless if a woman like that was trying to re-enter his life. As if her thoughts had drawn his eyes to her, Mark Trent regretted:

"Sorry, Miss Reyburn, that you should have been bored with a scene."

He pressed a bell beside the fireplace. With a little snort of anger, Anne Gregory settled heavily into a chair and flung back her sable cape. The color of her face suggested a red-hot balloon. Temper and voice blew up.

"How about me, Mark? Do you think I liked meeting that shameless woman here? Shameless! Perhaps I'm too hard on Lola. She was right. We old residents did our best to snub her when she came here to live, and she did have every man in the place parking on her doorstep sooner or later. From the time she was a little girl she was shuttled from her Spanish mother living with her fourth husband to her father living with his third wife. What can you expect of children who have light-o'-love parents?"

"That's the modern technic of marriage, I understand."

"Modern fiddlesticks, Jed Stewart! You don't believe in this modern technic, as you call it, do you?"

"No, Mrs. Gregory, I believe passionately in what are at present called the old-fashioned virtues, honor, chastity, friendship, fidelity to ideals." There was a tone in Jed Stewart's voice Brooke never before had heard.

Mrs. Gregory sniffed audibly. "I might have known you were like that when you are Mark's friend. You're nice boys. Come to dinner on Wednesday, Stewart. I want to change my will. In spite of the trust fund, I have something to leave. You're sitting there like a mouse, Brooke Reyburn. What do you think of this modern code?"

"I? Oh, I'm old-fashioned too, even if I am a modern little electromagnetic field made up of nicely assembled atoms complete with protons, electrons, and all the other 'ons.' If a woman came after my man, first I'd pull her hair out by the roots, figuratively speaking, then I'd go on such a spree of extravagance that friend husband would wear himself to a shadow trying to earn money enough to pay my bills."

Jed Stewart chuckled.

"Judging from the fervor with which you remodeled Lookout House, you could do it — and how!"

Brooke hoped that Mrs. Gregory's thoughts had been switched from Mrs. Hunt, but the older woman went back to the subject like a deer to the salt-lick.

"What did Lola mean, she hoped I'd patronize the business she and her husband were about to start?"

"She didn't say what sort of business, did she? Let's forget her. Let me take your coat, Miss Reyburn." Trent stood behind Brooke as the servant appeared in the doorway.

"Kowa, take out the tray and bring fresh tea."

"All things out, sir?"

"Yes. Be quick."

Brooke noticed the crumpled doily as the servant passed. Had Mark Trent's former wife had tea? Did he want to clear the room of everything she had touched? If only she herself could as easily rid her mind of the suspicion the woman had planted. Its barbs still pricked. Had those two men settled down in this house to watch the girl to whom Mary Amanda Dane had left her fortune? That Mark Trent had any thought of marrying her was too absurd. Why couldn't she forget that silly suggestion? Yet, how red their faces had been after the Hunt woman had flung her warning.

Mrs. Gregory removed her gloves and resumed cross-examination.

"Did Lola really mean that she and her present husband are going into business in this village?"

"What's strange in that? It's being done every day." Mark Trent crossed his arms on the mantel and stared at the fire.

In spite of her suspicion of his motive in coming to live next door to Lookout House, Brooke's sympathy surged out to him. Why didn't Mrs. Gregory drop the subject of the Hunts? Couldn't she see that he was sick at heart over the whole sordid situation? With more kindness than finesse, Jed Stewart plunged into the breach.

"Has that pair of Japanese goldfish I ordered for you arrived yet, Mrs. Gregory?"

Anne Gregory looked up at him with

eyes made shrewd by years of living, by joys, by uprooted affections, by hopes unrealized. She shook her head.

"You can't sidetrack me, young man, even with goldfish. I mean to get at what Lola is after — not merely customers, I am sure of that, she was here to hound Mark, I know her. I'll see that she doesn't get a license to carry on business on this Point. I still have influence. Miss Reyburn will pour the tea," she directed, as Kowa approached her with the replenished tray.

Involuntarily Brooke looked at Mark Trent. He smiled.

"Please. Stewart and I have given up cocktails, they're too effeminate. We have become tea-minded since we came here. The cup that cheers offsets to a degree the pound of the surf outside. Have a sandwich, Empress?"

"You haven't forgotten that nickname, have you, Mark? I like it from you. You use your mother's silver, don't you? By the way, what became of that gorgeous antique service of your aunt's? I haven't seen any of it at Lookout House, Brooke."

The girl felt as if the eyes of both men were regarding her with suspicious attention. She finished filling a cup, added a slice of lemon and two lumps of sugar.

133

"For Mrs. Gregory, Mr. Stewart. Will you have yours the same strength? Oh, about Mrs. Dane's silver. There isn't any."

"Isn't any! You say there isn't any silver? Where is it, then? Did your aunt relent and give it to you, Mark?"

"No. Miss Reyburn and I were wondering about it on Thanksgiving day. Glad you brought up the subject. Aunt Mary Amanda didn't speak of having disposed of it, the day you wit— the last day you saw her, did she?"

Why had Mark Trent floundered in his question? What had he meant by "The day you wit—"? Why change the end of the sentence? Witness was the word he had started to use. What had Mrs. Gregory witnessed?

The questions jostled each other in Brooke's mind as she carefully prepared a cup of tea. Witnesses of signatures were required on all sorts of papers, she knew that. Deeds and wills especially. Mrs. Gregory's name had not been on the will of Mary Amanda Dane which had been probated and allowed. Hadn't she a copy of it? Hadn't she read the amazing document through an hundred times? She felt the tug of an undercurrent. Suppose there was a foundation for the Hunt woman's warning? Suppose those two men had Lookout House and its occupants under a microscope? What would she better do about it? Nothing yet, she answered her own question promptly. They must not suspect that she even remembered the ex-wife's suggestion. She would take a hand in their game of watchful waiting.

Even while she was driving Mrs. Gregory home, under a sky already freckled with stars, making what she hoped were intelligent responses to her monologue of question and answer, Brooke was weighing and disposing of conjectures as to the meaning of the Hunt woman's warning. It was with a sense of strain lifted that she helped the older woman out of the car. Mrs. Gregory laid her hand on her arm.

"You're a darling, Brooke. I appreciate now the color, and the sense of 'God's in His Heaven, all's right with the world' you brought into Mary Amanda Dane's life. I had intended to start a boycott against you and your family here because you had cut Mark out of his inheritance, but he asked me to be nice to you. I adore that boy. I would do anything for him. He lived in a nightmare of humiliation with a wife who came home night after night barely able to keep her feet. Why, why can't women realize that it's their privilege to keep up the standards of decency? He stood by her, though, and held his head high, and wouldn't allow his soul to be warped by the experience."

She turned on the threshold as an elderly parlor-maid opened the door.

"Don't remember a word that shameless woman said, about being suspicious of Mark and Jed — she hasn't a tongue, she has fangs and poisonous ones at that — and don't think she'll be allowed to start any kind of business in this community. I'll stop that. Good-night! It was a nice party."

How could she help remembering what Mrs. Hunt had said, Brooke asked herself, as she started her car. She went over in her mind the conversation in which Mrs. Gregory had vigorously denied having received confidences from Mary Amanda Dane as to the disposal of her property.

It had not been imagination that Mark Trent and Jed Stewart had firmly led her away from the subject. Stewart had plunged into a recital of the difficulties Sam had encountered in casting his play. He had been amusing and Mrs. Gregory, who knew most of the subscribers for the charity benefit, had added blistering comments to his. There had been some truth in Mrs. Hunt's hint — not about Mark planning to marry the residuary legatee of his aunt's property; that was too silly to remember — or the two men would not have shifted conversational gears so quickly. So Mark Trent had asked "the Empress" to be "nice" to her. Was that part of the espionage plan?

She reached the question and Lookout House at the same time. She left her town car in the garage. She was thoughtfully drawing off her gloves as she approached the garden door of her house. A stream of light laid a golden path on leafless shrubs and graveled walk. A woman was at the door! A woman in a fox cape. Mrs. Hunt! Talking with Henri.

Brooke stepped into the purple shadow of a spruce. She could see and she could hear:

"If you keep a level head we can't lose, Henri."

The man's murmur was indistinct. He closed the door softly as the woman went down the steps. She flung a furtive look at the windows of the house before she vanished in the dusk.

"That seems to be that," Brooke said to herself, before she started around Mark Trent's house that she might enter her own front door unobserved by a possible watcher in the garden.

As she entered the living-room at Lookout House, she rang for Henri. The green parrot squawked, "Stop!", ruffled his feathers, and hopped up and down in his cage. She was standing near the fire, letter opener in hand, looking over the mail she had found on the desk when the butler entered.

"Did anyone call, Henri?"

"On the phone, Miss?"

"At the house."

Henri opened the door of the parrot's cage. Mr. Micawber hopped to his shoulder and began tweaking his ear.

"Never mind about the parrot, Henri. Answer my question."

"But I take him out like this for a walk around three times a day, Miss; the old madame wanted him to have a change of scene. Not a person called at this house. Were you expecting someone?"

"Yes, the lady who is to have charge of selling tickets for the play phoned that she might come this afternoon. Probably she couldn't make it. That's all."

Her eyes followed him as he left the room with the green bird muttering on his shoulder. Always she had distrusted the man of whom Mary Amanda Dane had been so fond. Why should he have lied to her about Mrs. Hunt's presence at the garden door of Lookout House? Because the woman was there to see him of course. With her thoughts still on Henri and his evasions, she slit one of the envelopes in her hand and drew out the letter it contained. All thought of the butler fled as she saw that the letterhead was that of the firm for which she had been fashion adviser.

Dear Miss Reyburn, — she read —

Any chance of your wanting a job? We are opening a dress shop at Palm Beach under the name of Carston's Inc. Very swank, very expensive. Céleste will be business manager. We'd like you to be top mannequin — with a salary, of course, and percentage on the sales of the frocks you model. We'll put on a fashion show later in the season. Society girls as mannequins. We'll open this year January first. Don't say 'No' until you think it over. Come in and we'll give you more details.

Céleste and the directors are all for you on the job.

Yours truly —

Brooke's face flushed as she reread the letter. Of course she couldn't accept — some girl who needed the money should have the chance — but it was thrilling to know that she was wanted. Palm Beach. All sunshine and fragrance and flowers. What a contrast to this stern and rockbound coast with the pound of surf, the wail of the siren, and the cries of gulls, to which she was anchored for the present.

The contents of the letter glowed in her mind as she dressed for the evening. It was heart-warming to know that her hard work had been appreciated. Better not speak of it. Sam's mind was on his play and Lucette might go temperamental because she had not been given the chance, and lose her job. Women in business couldn't afford to admit that their feelings had been hurt; there was no place for the person with a grievance; she had learned that while working.

Not until later, as, snuggled in a big chair before the fire in the living-room, she waited for Lucette and Sam to change for dinner, did the memory of Mrs. Hunt's presence at the garden door recur to her. Now it surged to the top of her mind. With unseeing eyes on the green parrot back in his cage, she thought of the woman's warning to her, of her threat to Mark Trent — it had been a threat, in spite of that sugary "darling." What had she meant? What object could Henri have had in denying her presence? Why should the remembrance of the low voice declaring: "If you keep a level head we can't lose, Henri," send icy prickles crawling up her spine and coasting down; why had it flashed upon the screen of her mind the glaring headlines of an editorial in last night's newspaper:

WOMEN! YOU HAVE SHOWN YOUR POWER. WHAT ARE YOU, SITTING BEFORE YOUR FIRES, DOING ABOUT THE CRIMES BEING COMMITTED? TOMORROW IT MAY BE YOU, YOU WHO WILL BE THE VICTIM!

Cheery thought! Brooke surreptitiously glanced over her shoulder. The charming room was still and cozy in the flickering firelight, fragrant with the breath of the Templar roses in the bubble vase, and the smell of moist earth from the chrysanthemums in the conservatory. She drew a long breath. Silly, as if criminals would attempt to operate on this point of land where they would be caught before they could leave it.

Mrs. Gregory's question about Mary Amanda Dane's silver had started the train of thought. Just the same, where was it? A silver service couldn't walk off by itself. Was it possible that Mrs. Hunt knew of its whereabouts? Evidently she was terribly hard up for money, and the need of money sometimes killed a person's soul. What could she and Henri "lose"?

Brooke thoughtfully smoothed the lace of her dinner frock, lace the very shade of the high lights in her hair. If this were a movie, there might be a trick cupboard in the green paneling in which the silver had been hidden, but there was nothing so exciting here. She had been at Lookout House when the walls and trim were painted.

"Calling car 5! Car 5! Car 5!"

The frenzied call brought Brooke to her feet, set her heart thumping madly. Then she laughed as the parrot with a squawk preened his green and yellow feathers. She made a disdainful face at the chuckling bird.

"Mr. Micawber, sometime when you yell like that I'll forget that I'm a perfect lady and wring your neck. Sam, did you teach the parrot that police radio call?" she demanded, as her brother entered the room.

His eyes twinkled behind the lenses of his horn-rimmed spectacles. He pulled a piece of cracker from the pocket of his blue coat.

"Sure, I taught him. I've been at work on that bird ever since I came. Here, stout fella!"

The parrot twisted his head completely round, blinked lidless eyes, before he nipped at the reward which Sam had thrust through the bars of his square cage.

"That bird's a peach, Brooke. You can teach him anything if you try hard enough. Boy, I wish I had him in the play. He'd show some of the stiffs how to speak their lines."

"Who's the biggest problem?"

"Daphne Field. She's pretty enough but dumb. She'll stop the show, all right, but not because she's an actress. Hers is a feed-part for the leading woman. She's one of those darnfool girls who go off their heads in a crisis — in real life, I mean, not in the play. Glad she's not in the lead. Laura Crane, who is, is good; she's got plenty on the ball."

"How is Jerry in his part?"

"Okay, but I don't like the man who is playing the male lead. He's a spotlight hog. I wish Mark Trent would take it. He's just

the type and a natural. I think he's great —
and — he's darn friendly, but —" Sam
leaned against the mantel and faced his
sister. "Have you ever thought that he is
not particularly keen about the Reyburn
family?"

Brooke, perched on the arm of the wing
chair, put her hand to her face to screen it
from the heat of the fire and incidentally
from Sam's observation. His question set
the Hunt woman's warning echoing in her
mind. Should she tell him? No. Better not
until she was sure that it had been more
than a random shot she had aimed at her
former husband; better not tell him that
she had been talking to Henri, either. She
said thoughtfully:

"Would he be likely to be keen, as you
express it, about a family which was spending money that he felt should be his? I
think he has behaved decently."

"Who said he hadn't? I have a kind of
feeling, that's all. He told Jed Stewart that
we might take anything we liked from his
house for stage setting." Sam's grin was
broad. "If Mother were here, she could tell
him what scavengers we are."

"Poor mother. She was a heroine; she
would see her treasures trucked off to set a
stage without one protest. Now that I have

144

a house of my own, I know how it must have hurt. The drop for the forest scene is great, Sam. Jerry Field's tree trunks are so real that I have to touch them to make sure they haven't sprung up through the house; Mark Trent gave him a hand on them. I stopped in the studio before I went out this afternoon and added a splash of red to the cabin roof and a few leaves."

"Leaves! Those daubs of paint look like an explosion of green worms, and it's lucky Field put a red roof on that brown cabin or it might have been shot for a deer. However, it will all go great when the foots are on. I'll be glad when the show is over; sometimes I think I've written a smash hit and sometimes that the play is just a lot of tripe. I daren't hope for one or two first-string critics to give me the low-down on it. Anyway, a manager who liked those two sketches I wrote for the Workshop is coming for the opening to give it the once-over, and he'll bring a New York producer."

"Really, Sam! How perfectly grand! We —"

"Hi! Soft pedal! Here comes Lucette. I don't want her to know that they'll be in front, it might rattle her."

There was the sound of running feet on

the stairs, a gay voice singing. Lucette dashed into the room. Her black hair was silky; her thin frock was only a shade redder than her lips and cheeks and finger-nails. She dropped to the rug in front of the fire, hugged her knees, and looked up at her sister.

"How soon do we eat, Brooke? I'm starving."

"Henri waits till he hears you tumble downstairs before he announces dinner. What kind of a day did you have?"

"Hectic. Every woman in the city appar-ently has gone sports-clothes minded. They've stopped boasting of the extreme age of their frocks and hats and have begun to spend real money. They are buying for themselves and for Christmas gifts in spite of the fact that prices are being stepped up. I should worry. I get a sliver of commission on my sales. The girl who has taken your place had just one of those days, today. Madame Céleste was on the warpath. Her heart, like the Mother Goose man's little gun, is made of lead, lead, lead. I brought Jerry Field down in the car. He was a gob of gloom when he came in and you were not here. He had no interest in this T. B. W. though I tried to be a little ray of sunshine. I told him that probably you had taken your knitting to Mrs. Gregory's. You certainly are a hit, Brooke, with what in the store we call the older woman."

Brooke laughed. Lucette was being subtle. Since the children had grown up, there was a live-and-let-live law in the Reyburn family that no member of it should be asked why or where she was going or where she had been. Celia Reyburn argued that living close together was sufficient strain on dispositions without having every move commented on.

"Cagey, aren't you, Lucette, trying to find out without asking what Brooke did with her afternoon, and say, instead of looking like the fingers of a Tired Business Woman, your nails look as if you'd been digging out the entrails of some animal, old Greek and Roman sacrifice stuff, or what have you."

Sam's tolerant man-of-the-world voice was especially pitched to aggravate his younger sister. Brooke recognized storm signals and spoke before Lucette could think up a sufficiently caustic reply.

"If you'd like to know, Mrs. Gregory and I had tea with neighbors. Home-town boys."

"Not in there?" Lucette's eyes were round with incredulity. She nodded toward the connecting door. "Did you go in that way?"

"Good heavens, no! You don't think I would be the one to unseal that, do you? We were ceremoniously admitted at the front door by the Jap with the black eyes which always make me think of those little nuggets of obsidian we picked up near the cliff at the Yellowstone."

"What's the Looking-Glass house like? Gloomy?"

"Not gloomy, but, except for the lovely circular stairway, like ours, completely gay-ninetyish. Entering it is like stepping back into another century. I like it though; like the great domed library shelved with books which look as if they had been read, put back, taken down and read again; I liked the woodfire on the deep hearth, the tick of the old clock in the corner, the portrait of a man in a periwig above the mantel."

"My word, it sounds pre-historic to me. I'll bet after a few weeks of exposure to this peachy room Mark Trent will be doing his over. Other guests?"

"It wasn't a party, Lucette."

Better not mention Mrs. Hunt, Brooke decided, it would start a fusillade of questions; besides, the woman had not been a guest, it had been quite apparent that she had been neither invited nor welcome.

"Then someone else was there. Going secretive on us, aren't you, darling? I get you. I'm not! News flash! Who do you think runs that new filling-station in the white cottage?

"Mark Trent's ex-wife and her husband!"

VIII

Brooke stood before the fire in the softly lighted living-room at Lookout House. Three days had passed since she had received the letter offering her the Palm Beach position, since she had heard that the Hunts were the proprietors of the filling-station she had been patronizing. She had refused promptly the business offer and had dropped it from her mind, but she couldn't forget the other. Sometimes she wondered if she would ever think of anything else. Questions were everlastingly popping up. Could Mrs. Gregory wipe the filling-station off the map? Had Lola Hunt gone to Mark Trent's house to tell him about it, or had he known already? Why later had the woman been talking so confidentially to Henri at the garden door of Lookout House? What had she meant by: "If you keep a level head we can't lose, Henri"? What was behind that snapped off "wit" of Mark Trent's?

She had built a high, strong, impregnable wall of dislike between herself and him; hadn't he called her a schemer? But for some inexplicable reason it hurt to think that he was being heckled by an unprincipled woman. Mrs. Gregory had said he had not only been fair in his treatment of his former wife, but that he'd been maddeningly quixotic. What would he do about that filling-station? It must be unendurable for him to know that his ex-wife was selling gas.

Why was she spending a moment's thought on Mark Trent's problems? Hadn't she plenty of her own? She frowned at the empty gilt cage. Where was Mr. Micawber? When she had come in this afternoon, Henri had been wringing his hands. He had gone completely French as he chattered, but she had gathered from the jargon that when he had stepped out on the lawn with the parrot on his shoulder, the door had banged behind him and the frightened bird had flown away. It wasn't that she cared for the parrot, she detested him, but Mrs. Dane had loved him and she felt as if she had broken faith with her benefactress.

"Wake up, sister!" Lucette prodded from the doorway. "Sam and I have been staring at you for three minutes, trying thought transference. Nothing doing. We couldn't penetrate your skull. You've been scowling as if addressing a hall full of women who refused to rally to your one-time battle-cry:

"Old age isn't necessary, it is nothing but a germ! Watch out that you don't pick it up!"

Brooke laughed. "I had no idea that the precepts of her elders made such an impression on our little sister, had you, Sam?"

"No. I — Where is Mr. Micawber?"

Brooke told him.

"No kidding, what do you know about that! I'll bet Henri let him go."

"He wouldn't do that, Sam, though he should have known better than to go to the open door with him. Mrs. Dane wouldn't have the bird's wings clipped; of course he would fly when he got the chance. Henri takes all the care of him, thank heaven. I think he adores him, if he can adore anything. Curious, Mr. Micawber likes Henri and you; he doesn't try to conceal the fact that he dislikes Lucette and me. I'm really troubled about the parrot. He may be flying outside, and Mrs. Dane was so careful never to expose him to draughts. Who is calling, I wonder?" Brooke asked, as the butler passed in the hall on his way to the front door.

"Cricky! I forgot! Jerry Field is coming

152

to dinner. Thought we could all go to rehearsal together. Do you mind, Brooke?"

"Of course not, Lucette. Did you tell Henri to set a place for him?"

Lucette nodded before she greeted Jerry Field.

"How are you, stranger?"

"Little girls shouldn't be sarcastic, Lucette." He unfolded a green waxed paper. "For you, Brooke."

"Gardenias! I've never seen more perfect ones. What wax-like petals! What lovely leaves! Thanks billions, Jerry."

Brooke turned to the mirror and pinned on the flowers. She saw Jerry Field watching her as he said:

"I strive to please. Sam, you slave-driver, why did you call a rehearsal again tonight? We've been working every evening this week."

"What does that prove? Call what you've been doing working? I calls it playing. We'll run through the three acts tonight, and, m'lad, for the love of Mike, put some punch into your part, even if we are rehearsing with no props. Last night when the woman lead gave the cue for your quote:

" 'Islands arise, grow old, and disappear,'

153

you mumbled your lines as if you were going to sleep on us. If you talk like that the night of the show, you'll have the audience in an hypnotic slumber."

He ran his fingers through his hair.

"Boy, 'Islands Arise' is the name of the play! Don't you get what that play stands for, Jerry? The birth of a man's soul; the waking of love; the breaking up; the forging to steel by sorrow and disillusionment, and the renewing to full and abundant life. Can't you convey some shades of meaning of it in your voice? It isn't the lead but yours is a fat part."

Sam's outburst died down as quickly as it had flared. Only Brooke realized the sense of frustration which had smoldered in her brother's heart as he had watched scenes, listened to lines over which he had spent days of passionate enthusiasm being butchered because the cast wouldn't settle down to real work, to be line-perfect.

Jerry Field's eyes and voice were ludicrously awed as he demanded:

"My eye, is all that in the play? I thought it was a comedy."

"It is a comedy, but even a comedy has to be built on life, hasn't it, and aren't there tragic undertones in life? That play is my declaration of faith that there is a big

154

theatre public for things that matter, for something besides sordid infidelities and bawdy lines. Oh, what's the use trying to make a lot of dumbbells understand!"

There was a break in the last word as Sam crossed his arms on the mantel and dropped his head on them.

"Ain't the life of a playwright grand!" Lucette mocked, but there was a suspicious moisture on her lashes. "Come on, Sammy, let's eat. Life won't seem so dark after dinner.

" 'Just around the corner there's a rainbow in the sky,' " she sang, as she linked her arm in her brother's.

The dining-room was cheery with firelight and the flames of tall yellow candles, which matched to a tint the acacias in the bay window. The blue of bachelor buttons, the soft pink of carnations, the yellow of Souvenir roses in the golden bowl on the table repeated the colors in the rare Persian rug. The flickering lights threw fantastic patterns on the walls and smudged the butler's face with shadows as he drew out Brooke's chair. She smiled at her brother who sat opposite.

"Cheerio, Samuel. Something tells me that 'Islands Arise' will be the hit of next season. Picture your adoring family in a box at the opening, fairly swooning with pride when the audience yells:

" 'Author! Auth—' "

The telephone interrupted. Henri answered it and returned to the dining-room.

"Call for you, Miss Reyburn."

"Probably someone panicky for fear she can't get tickets to the great and only show of the season, Sam," Brooke said on her way to the door.

In the living-room she answered the call:

"Brooke Reyburn speaking."

"This is Mark Trent. I want to show you something. Make an excuse to stay at home from rehearsal, will you?"

"Yes."

"Get Henri and Clotilde out of the house. Can you?"

"It's movie night in the village. They'll go."

"Phone me as soon as they start."

"I will."

"Good-bye."

What could Mark Trent have to show her? His voice had been drenched with mystery. Brooke was projecting and rejecting answers to the question as she went back to the dining-room.

"How many did they want?"

She wrinkled puzzled brows as she looked across the table at her brother.

"How many of what, Sam?"

"Has the little old memory gone blotto? Didn't you say the call was about tickets?"

"Don't beat me, Sammy. I thought it was. It was only a — an insurance agent who has been on my trail. How did the market behave today, Jerry?"

Field reported jauntily and in detail on the rise of certain of his pet stocks, and the shuttlecock of conversation was in the air again.

As Brooke poured coffee in the living-room after dinner, she planned to plead a letter to her mother as an excuse for staying away from the rehearsal; as property woman she wasn't important yet. She was positively tingling with curiosity. What had Mark Trent to show her? Why had his voice been hushed as if he feared he might be overheard?

"Boy, you wouldn't think old Micawber making his getaway would leave such a hole, would you? It's almost as if someone in the house had died." Sam's voice interrupted her thoughts. "When we get back from rehearsal we'd better make this find-the-parrot-night. Suppose he's hiding up in a tree on the grounds, Brooke?"

"If he is, Henri will get him. He was white when he told me he had lost the parrot. I'll slip into a coat, go out and whistle for him myself when you've all gone to rehearsal."

"What's the big idea walking out on us, Brooke?" Jerry Field demanded in his most spoiled-boy tone as he held Lucette's coat in the hall.

"I told you, a letter to Mother, and sandwiches to make. Bring the cast back here after rehearsal, Sam, for a bite to eat."

"What's the use having two servants and doing a lot of work yourself?"

"Don't mind Jerry, Brooke. It's evident he's never seen our sunshiny Clotilde on location when asked to do something extra. I'll help you when I get home. Come on, boys, the stage waits!"

Lucette dashed out with the two men at her heels. As she watched from the porch, Brooke saw Jed Stewart join them from the Other House. Their voices and laughter drifted back. Did Jed know that Mark Trent had phoned? She waited, drawing in long breaths of the cold salty air, until the rear light of the car was but a red spark in the distance.

When she returned to the living-room, Henri was collecting cups and saucers. She watched him in the mirror while she pretended to be absorbed in fastening the two gardenias more securely to the shoulder of her lace frock. He stopped on the threshold, holding the silver tray.

"Anything more this evening, Miss?"

"Nothing, Henri, except that I wish you would impress it upon Clotilde — I can't seem to — that when I order Rocquefort cheese dressing for a salad, I mean that, and not mayonnaise. This is the third time she has made the mistake."

"She thinks mayonnaise more suitable. You don't like Clotilde and me much, do you, Miss Reyburn?" His smile was an ugly thing, having under it the suggestion that it would be to her advantage to like them.

"I don't!" was on the tip of Brooke's tongue, but she caught the words back. With the production of the play so near, this was not the time to change servants. After that she would get rid of the couple if it meant doing the work herself. She temporized:

"Because I insist upon having my orders carried out, doesn't mean necessarily that I don't like you, Henri. Can anything more be done about finding the parrot?"

"I'll look round before I go to bed, Miss, but I think in the morning we'll find him huddled in a corner near the house."

"This is movie night in the village, isn't it?"

"Yes, Miss, though if you are to be alone and mind —"

"Of course you are to go, Henri." Brooke had an instant of panic. Suppose he insisted upon staying at home? "I shan't be alone long. Mr. Trent and Mr. Stewart will be here with the cast after rehearsal for a little supper."

"Will the supper keep up till late?"

"Probably, but we will take care of the dishes."

"Thank you, Miss."

"Have you put plenty of gingerale and White Rock on the ice?"

"Yes, Miss. The mint is chopped and the fruit juices are ready for the drink just as you told me." Henri's eyes seemed but sparks in cavernous depths.

"Excuse me, Miss, you'd better like Clotilde and me. We could put you out of this house if we wanted to. Anything more?"

Brooke was too indignant to answer. What did the man mean by the threat he had inserted so casually between two sentences? What did he know? Had Jed Stewart and Mark Trent confided to him their suspicions as to "undue influence"? Were they grooming him to testify for them? Had they set him spying upon her? Should she repeat his threat and demand to know the truth when Mark Trent came? No. Better cool down. She was too furious now. She would wait until after Sam's play. That must go smoothly; it might be his big chance — after that — well, after that she would investigate a few things, she would find out why Mrs. Hunt and Henri were so friendly, to begin with.

She attempted to read the evening newspaper as she waited for the servants to finish their work and depart for the movies, but her thoughts kept reverting to Henri's insinuation:

"We could put you out of this house if we wanted to."

Had that threat any connection with Mrs. Hunt's:

"If you keep a level head we can't lose, Henri"?

She flung down the paper after she had read a paragraph three times. She hurled defiance at an imaginary Henri:

"Of course you can't put me out! Suppose you could? It isn't too late to get the Palm Beach job."

Curious how heart-warming was the

161

knowledge that she was wanted in the business world. Not half so heart-warming as this house, she corrected herself, as she glanced about the room she had planned with such thrilled pleasure. It seemed empty without the parrot. Was it possible that she had begun to like Mr. Micawber?

With eyes wandering to the tall clock, ears strained to hear the chug of the servants' flivver on the drive, inhaling the scent of gardenias with every breath, her thoughts returned to Mark Trent's message. Why had he phoned? Perhaps she was dramatizing his voice, perhaps it hadn't been mysterious except in her imagination.

"There they go! I'd know the wheeze of their car if I heard it among a million. I'll wait five minutes before I phone Mark the Magnificent. Must be something in the air. First I have a hot chill and then a cold chill, I'm so excited."

She watched the clock. Dialed. Waited. Probably Kowa had gone to the movies. He — She put her mouth close to the transmitter.

"Mr. Trent? Brooke Reyburn. They've gone."

"Okay. I'll be there like a shot."

Brooke replaced the telephone. His voice

was excited. It had set her nerves tingling. She would be at the front door to open it before he had a chance to ring.

In the hall she listened for his step on the terrace. Why did he take so long? His "like a shot" was more like an hour.

"I'm here," a low voice announced behind her.

In her surprise, Brooke leaned back against the door and looked up at Mark Trent. She never before had realized how tall he was, nor how black his gray eyes could be.

"How did you get in?"

"The connecting door upstairs. Took the quickest way. Lock that door. Give me the key. I'll put it in my pocket. Queer things are in the air. We won't take a chance at being locked in or — out."

That didn't sound as if Henri were his tool, Brooke thought, as she entered the living-room.

"Where is Mr. Micawber?" Mark Trent demanded, his eyes on the empty cage.

Brooke told him what Henri had told her.

"Um, lost him, did he? The plot thickens."

His voice was uncompromising, his eyes unflinching and direct as, hands in the pockets of his dinner jacket, his brows knitted, he looked at her.

"Ooch, I'd hate to battle with you," Brooke thought. "It would be like trying to dent a steel wall." Aloud she said:

"What is the mystery? It is a mystery, isn't it? I've been jittery ever since you phoned."

His smile was a flash of white teeth below his small dark mustache.

"Glad I got my Big Moment over. Can't have Sam monopolizing all the drama in the neighborhood. Sure the Jacques have gone?"

"I heard their car go out. One couldn't mistake its wheeze. I told Henri that we would have supper here for the cast after rehearsal and that he would not be needed."

"Fair enough." He caught her hand. "Step on it!"

Why was Mark Trent afraid to have Henri, his tool, — if he were his tool — know what he was doing, Brooke wondered, as, side by side, they hastily mounted the winding stairs. She felt as if she were in a dream, as if at any moment she might waken to find herself snuggled in the wing chair before the fire. But the squeak of a tread was real; Mark the Magnificent's muttered execration at the sound was real; so was his grip of her hand. Why was he so careful about being heard? He appeared friendly with her; was that part of his plan, his and Jed Stewart's?

On the second floor before the door which opened into his house, he stopped.

"Look," he whispered. "I tried this, had a hunch I might get through quickly this way. When it opened, that key was in your side." He turned the knob. "Better leave it where it is. We don't want anyone to know that we have seen it. Come."

He followed her into the hall of his house and closed the door gently behind him.

"Now we can speak aloud. Kowa and Taku have gone to the movies. You're not afraid?"

"Afraid! Of what?"

"Of being alone in the house of the enemy?"

"Are you my enemy? Was your — was Mrs. Hunt right that afternoon when she warned me that you and Jed Stewart had come here to — to watch me?"

How maddening! She had let him know that she attached significance to Lola Hunt's warning, and she had intended to keep the two men guessing as to what she thought. She watched his color darken, his brows knit in a frown.

"Why take that silly question of mine seriously? I don't know why I asked it. Must have picked up one of the theatrical germs with which the air has been filled since Sam started the play. Jed rants by the hour."

"Most interesting, but did you bring me here only to explain your reaction to the Reyburn dramatics?"

The wave of Brooke's hand included the hall hung with massively framed paintings, the circular stairways descending and ascending, the doors opening into dark rooms in some of which furniture was dimly outlined.

"I brought you here to show you something. Come on."

"You're so like the Red Queen in Alice. She was forever saying, 'Come on!' and never getting anywhere. I hope ordering me about is not getting to be a habit with you," Brooke protested.

He pressed a button which switched on a light in the floor above and ran up the stairs.

She followed slowly. Where was he taking her? It seemed hours since they had left her living-room. Suppose Henri slipped back and found her gone? Would he suspect where she was? Of course he had left the key in that connecting door. Who else would have done it? What business had he in Mark Trent's house? Did he come for instructions?

She reached the question and a door at the same time. As Mark Trent opened it, a slightly musty smell, a blend of camphor and old books and ancient furniture, stole out. He motioned with the flash in his hand. Brooke's eyes followed the light. She set her teeth hard in her lips to keep back an exclamation of astonishment. On a large table, illumined by the spotlight, surrounded by boxes and trunks and storeroom litter, was a massive tea-service and perhaps a dozen dishes and pitchers of silver, tarnished to a light copper color. A scrap of paper drifted to the floor.

"It's a great hide-out, isn't it?"

She nodded in answer to the low, amused question.

"When did you discover it?"

"Thought I heard strange sounds upstairs when Jed and I were waiting for you in the living-room the other afternoon. The Japs' rooms are in the L on the first floor, and when I had this house opened I told the caretaker not to touch the third.

After you and Mrs. Gregory left, I investigated and found this silver. I've been on the watch ever since to discover who put it here. This afternoon someone slipped a cog, and left both keys; must have been frightened off, or else they were left purposely so that a second party might have access to the loot."

"Who put the loot, as you call it, in that room?"

"That's what you and I will find out."

That "you and I" was fuse to dynamite. Brooke leaned back against the balustrade.

"You will, you mean, you and your sleuth Jed Stewart. You and he are spies, aren't you? Amateur detectives. 'Mark, to you,' you say to Sam, and all the time you are spying on his sister and accusing her of 'undue influence,' of hypnotizing an old woman into leaving her a fortune. I ought to have known what you thought of me when you said that. I do now. Find out who stole the silver. You've put Inspector Harrison on the case, haven't you? I wish you luck."

She jerked her wrist free and ran down the stairs. She stopped at the foot of them. A tirade like that she had just delivered took one's breath for a minute. Why, why had she let Mark the Magnificent know

168

that she suspected his reason for occupying his house? She, who had prided herself on her self-control in business? Why couldn't she be diplomatic? Her outrageous temper was the answer. Thank Heaven she had had sense enough not to tell him of Henri's threat that he could put her out of Lookout House.

A sound! Someone had touched the knob on the other side of the door! Had the person remembered that both keys had been left? Now — now Mark and she would find out who had taken the silver.

Stealthily she touched the button and plunged the top floor into darkness. She raced up the stairs. Caromed into Mark Trent coming out of the storeroom. She clutched his sleeve; whispered:

"Shut the door! Quick! Someone is fumbling at the hall key. Perhaps he'll come for this one."

He held her by one arm as he noiselessly closed the door. In the dark he drew her into another room. Side by side they waited. Brooke's heart shook her body. How could the man so near her help hearing it thump in the tomblike silence?

A spot of light. Creeping up! Creeping up! Her breath caught in a gasp. An arm slipped round her shoulders and held her so close that the scent of the crushed gardenias was sickish.

"Ssch! Mustn't let him know we are here!" Mark Trent whispered.

The spot of light illumined the key in the door, illumined the black-gloved hand which gently turned it and as gently drew it out.

IX

Mark Trent felt the hard beating of the girl's heart as his arm tightened about her shoulders, the softness of her skin against his hand. He didn't dare release her for fear she might make a sound and reveal their presence to the unknown person in the hall. What a good little sport she was. She had followed him into his house with no embarrassment, but with a modern girl's interpretation of propriety, her ignoring of outworn conventions. Just the same, he wished fervently that she was back in her own living-room in that chair before the fire, for there was no dodging the fact that black-gloved fingers had withdrawn the key from the lock. To whom had they belonged? The words on the scrap of paper he had picked up from the floor of the storeroom and replaced on the table teased at his mind.

"Make X on cover when —"

That was all. What cover? Much as he wanted to know, he couldn't let Brooke Reyburn get mixed up in the mess. When he had discovered the silver, his first

171

thought had been of her and the thrill she would get from seeing it. If he hadn't brought her, he would be on the man's neck by this time.

It seemed hours that he stood rigid, listening, with the only sound the roweling of the tide against jutting ledges, like the underground roar of a great city, the faint wail of the distant siren, and the girl's unsteady breathing. He strained his ears. Was a door being closed cautiously, or was his imagination playing tricks? He must find out. He couldn't stay here forever. He put his mouth close to Brooke's ear. He felt the softness of her hair against his face.

"Don't move. Don't speak. I'll come back."

Whenever in after life he smelled the fragrance of a gardenia, he would remember this night, he told himself.

He took a cautious step into the hall. Listened. The house was so quiet that he could hear the tick of the old clock on the stairs below. He tiptoed to the door of the room in which he had found the silver and ran his fingers lightly over the knob. The key was gone.

He felt his way down; he didn't dare use the flash. The lamp in the lower hall provided a faint light. Gently he turned the knob of the connecting door. It was locked. Someone had followed him down the stairs! He felt a presence. Fool, not to have suspected that an accomplice might be hidden in the dark. He shouldn't have left Brooke. He must get back to her no matter who was between them.

He wheeled with pantherlike agility. Raised his flashlight to bring it crashing down on a head.

"Mark! Mark!"

It was Brooke Reyburn's voice, her hand on his arm. The stiffening went out of his knees. Relief was submerged in a mighty rush of anger as he gripped her shoulders.

"What do you mean by coming down when I told you not to move? What do you mean? I might have struck you!"

"But you didn't, Mark. I felt like a quitter hiding in the dark while you came down alone, so I crept after you. What did you see?"

"Nothing here — but the door is locked."

"A black-gloved hand did pull the key from the store-room door, didn't it? I didn't dream it, did I?"

"If you did, I was in the same dream, Brooke. Wonder when they intend to remove the stuff."

"You think someone is planning to take it away?"

"Why else should it be there? It probably was moved from Lookout House to this one, which has been unoccupied for years, before I came back here to live. After Aunt Mary Amanda went, I was the only person who would know about the silver, and I was far away in South America. That's why Henri's face turned chalky when he saw me enter your living-room on Thanksgiving day."

"Then you noticed it too? I thought it might be my imagination."

"He was white, all right. Come on, we can't get back to Lookout House through this door. We'd better beat it downstairs and out that way. Lucky I pocketed your key."

"Hurry! Hurry! Suppose it was Henri who left those keys in the doors? Suppose he remembered that he had left them and stole back from the movies? I told him that you and Jed Stewart would be with us for supper after rehearsal. He may be looking for me now to see if I was telling the truth."

In the lower hall, which was slightly scented by the smoky aroma of open fires, Mark laid a detaining hand on her shoulder.

174

"Wait! Listen!"

The stillness of the high-ceilinged rooms was accentuated by the low moan of the wind at a corner of the house, by the muted thunder of the sea, by the sharp crackle of a burning log; was haunted by the weird wail of the distant siren, but no human sound intruded.

"Coast's clear. Let's go. Hold on!" Mark Trent frowned at her bare arms and throat, ivory tinted above the lace of her frock. "You need a wrap."

"To go from one door to another! Don't be foolish. If we don't hurry, Henri may get there before us and then —"

Why had she stopped? Was she afraid of Henri? Had he a hold on her? He and she had been the only persons with Mary Amanda Dane after she had signed the will Anne Gregory had witnessed. Even while remembering all that, he couldn't distrust her, Mark told himself.

They stepped from the warmth of the house into a cold world of starlit beauty. Frosted shrubs, brown tree trunks glittered. The long vistas of lights on the causeway were like opaque opal helmets on the heads of prim rows of soldiers. Bare branches tinkled like the iridescent pendants of a crystal chandelier; the high note of a startled bird was a thin thread of sound above the steady boom of the sea as it foamed against the ledges throwing up a silver-gray screen of spray. A star fell, clear and green as a huge emerald; followed a shower of meteors thick as the golden rain of a rocket against the black velvet of the sky.

"That was so beautiful it made me shiver," Brooke confided breathlessly.

"It was beautiful, but it's standing out here in the cold with no wrap that makes you shiver. Give me your hand. The steps are frosty."

In the green-walled living-room at Lookout House, Mark Trent threw a log on the smoldering fire and poked it into flame.

"Come here and get warm, Brooke. You are still shivering."

"If I am, it is from excitement, not cold." She toasted her fingers at the blaze. She closed her eyes and opened them. "I have been trying to convince myself that the happenings of the last half hour — it seems more than that — were not a dream. I've been checking up. There is the newspaper I flung to the floor when I started to phone you, and that flashlight bulging from your pocket is real, isn't it?" She touched it. "It is. I haven't been in a nightmare. I'm awake. That fact being settled to my satisfaction, what do we do next?"

"Watchful waiting seems our best bet."

"You would say that."

"I don't like the implication, but we'll let that ride — for the present. What move would you suggest?"

"I don't know, but let's do something. I hate sitting on the sidelines. I hate waiting. First we must find out who took the key from the storeroom door. If you hadn't held me, I would have dashed at him and found out."

"I had a hunch you would; that's why I grabbed you. Afraid I crushed your gardenia."

Brooke put her hand to her shoulder. "They're gone! Where could I have lost them?"

"Don't make a tragedy of it. I'll get you another."

Mark Trent had never seen brown eyes so flamingly gold, cheeks so red as Brooke's.

"I'm not making a tragedy of it, and I don't want another gardenia. For an amateur detective — amateur is the word with a capital A — you are dense, Mark Trent. Suppose the person in the attic went back for something and picked them up?

Wouldn't he know at once that he was being watched?"

"I thought of that so — I brought this along." He held a flower in the palm of his hand. The once waxen petals were brown at the edges, but they had the feel of velvet in his fingers. "You don't want it now, do you?" He slipped it back into his pocket. "I'll keep it as a souvenir of our late dive into the underworld."

"I do want it and the other too."

"Because Field gave them to you? I don't know where the other is; didn't realize that there were two. You dropped this as you came into this house. Better let me keep it. Would you want him to know that it had been crushed out of shape against my shoulder?"

From the depths of the wing chair before the fire Brooke disdainfully looked back at him. Her eyes were so clear, so forthright; her mouth when not smiling was so wistful, so tender, how could he have thought that she would deliberately influence a sick old woman to leave her a fortune? That line of R. L. S.'s expressed her:

"Honor, courage, valor, fire."

"Just why should Jerry assume that it was your shoulder against which the gardenia was crushed? You are not the only man

178

in my life, you know," Brooke reminded disdainfully.

"I intend — to keep the flower."

Mark Trent felt the color surge to his hair and recede. He had caught back "to be" in time. What had become of his conviction that he was still the husband of a woman who had been untrue to him, who had married another man; of his certainty that this girl had cajoled his aunt into making an unjust will, of his faint suspicion that she might know the whereabouts of a later one? Swept away, all of it, by the light in her eyes, by the magic in her smile.

It was evident that she didn't like him. On Thanksgiving day she had been warmly friendly. Was that infernal insinuation of Lola's that he would try to keep his aunt's money in the family by marriage, making trouble? He said quickly:

"I haven't had a chance, Brooke, to tell you how ridiculous Mrs. Hunt's suggestion was that — that I had any thought of trying to keep Aunt Mary Amanda's money in the family by —"

"Why stumble over it? Why tell me again that you wouldn't marry me? This is the second time. First in Jed Stewart's office and now here. To save a third attempt to impress the fact on me, I'll tell you that I wouldn't marry you if you were the only man in the world. Divorced men leave me cold. Sometime perhaps I'll have the privilege of refusing to marry you."

He knew now the sensation of a knife being plunged into his heart. He drew the gardenia from his pocket and dropped it into her lap.

"Here it is. Water may revive it."

She twirled the stem in her fingers.

"It is past recovery." She flung it into the wastebasket. "I don't care for rejuvenated gardenias any more than I care for warmed-over love. That sounds like a car. Can they have come so soon?"

"Better not speak of what we discovered," Mark suggested hastily, as she started for the hall.

She left the room without answering. He salvaged the flower and thrust it into his pocket. He was not keeping it for sentimental reasons, he assured himself, but as a reminder of how near he had come to forgetting that all he had to offer a girl was "warmed-over" love.

Sam Reyburn entered the living-room and flung his blue covered script to the table. He dropped into the wing chair with a groan. Voices in the hall thinned in the distance. Mark Trent could distinguish

Jerry Field's laugh, Lucette's rather high-pitched tone, Brooke's questioning murmur, and Daphne's drawl. He looked at the dejected figure in the chair, at the long legs outstretched.

"What's wrong, Sam? Aren't you home early?"

"What's wrong with you, you're white as a sheet?"

"I'm okay, it's these artistic lights that play the dickens with one's color. Didn't Stewart and the rest of the cast come with you?"

"Jed stopped at your house for a minute, he'll be here pronto; the other actors — so-called — have gone home. I'll say I'm here early. After they'd walked through the first act, it was a choice between dismissing the cast or shooting them. I had a sane interval and decided not to shoot. I'm giving them tomorrow night off."

"Then I'll throw a party for the Reyburns and Fields at that new Supper Club just opened in town. Give them a let-up from the play. What say, maestro?"

"Okay with me. It's darned good of you. Perhaps I have overworked them, but there is so little time before the performance." Sam sat up and ran his fingers through his hair. "With that so near, wouldn't you think those dumbbells would know their parts? I ask you! Besides that, the leading man has walked out on us."

Mark Trent's throat tightened in response to the despair in the boy's voice. It must be devastating to care so much, to have one's heart shredded to shoestrings because the work one loved was being murdered. It made him wonder if he had cared deeply for anyone or anything since he had lost his mother. In spite of the humiliation, Lola's going had been a relief, she had grown so impossible to live with. He flung off the past.

"It's tough. Can I help, Sam?"

"Can you help! I'll say you can. 'Now is the time for all good men to come to the aid of their party.' Take the lead." He caught Trent's arm. "Be a good scout. Help a poor, distracted playwright-producer, will you? With you and the Crane woman in the leads, we'll make a two-star offering of it. That girl's good."

Sam's despair had changed to exultation. Mark Trent temporized:

"How do you know I'm good?"

"How do those bozos out in Hollywood know an actor will be a wow on the screen sometimes before they give him a try-out? Something here, m'lad, something here,"

Sam tapped his broad brow, "tells me you'll be stopping the show."

"That same something couldn't tell you where I'm to get the time for a theatrical career, could it? All right, all right," Mark conceded in response to Sam's groan, "I'll take the part. Give me the sides and I'll try to know the lines at the next rehearsal."

"A break at last! I didn't like the way that male lead was looking at Lucette. I feel the responsibility of her while Mother is away. I kept one eye on him while I rehearsed the gang. It kind of cramped my style at directing."

With a whoop he caught Brooke as she entered the room. He hugged her as he exulted:

"What d'you think, gal? Trent has signed up for 'Islands Arise'! Will he pack 'em in as the lead? I ask you!"

"What's happened to the man who had the part?"

"Walked out on us. When he comes round tomorrow ready to eat out of my hand, he'll find he's not wanted. Get that?"

"Not quite, but I suppose a playwright-producer is a law unto himself." Brooke looked at Mark. "I can't imagine you acting — behind the footlights."

There was a hint in her light tone that

she could imagine him acting off the stage. He smiled.

"It has been suggested that I am getting stale, old, with a capacity for warmed-over affection only. Here's where I step out for romance and adventure."

Had the emphasis he had given the last words brought that sudden color to Brooke's face? Jerry Field appeared at the door beating a huge spoon against a tin pan.

"First call for the dining car! First call —"

Sam held up his hand.

"Just a minute! We're all invited to dine and dance tomorrow by the new male lead in 'Islands Arise,' Mark Trent! Sam Reyburn announcing."

"You in the play, Mark?"

"How exciting!"

"Dinner and dance in the big city! What a break!"

Jerry Field interrupted the excited comments.

"Where are your gardenias, Brooke?"

His tone set Mark Trent's lips twitching. Under cover of lighting a cigarette, he caught the girl's furtive glance at the wastebasket. She put her hand to her shoulder.

"Why — why I must have dropped them."

"Where've you been?"

"Hi there, m'lad!" Sam's tone and manner were those of a stern parent guarding his offspring. "That isn't a topic for group discussion. We don't make people punch the time-clock in this family."

Jerry Field's face turned a bright and lively crimson; his voice and eyes were furious.

"I wasn't asking Brooke to punch the time-clock. I thought I might find the gardenias for her. I —"

He stopped as Jed Stewart appeared on the threshold. He was tapping a gardenia against his lips.

"Run to earth, Mark. Who's the charmer who leaves a flower outside your door?"

X

An hour later Jed Stewart slumped deeper into a crimson-cushioned chair in Mark Trent's library and demanded:

"How was I to know that Field had brought Brooke the gardenias? Didn't he look like a meat-axe though, when I barged into Lookout House waving that flower and giving the whole show away by telling where I picked it up? I'm the original village cut-up, I am." He lighted his pipe.

"It wasn't all my fault. I didn't know, did I, Mark, that you and she had been cruising round this house?"

"You didn't. I hadn't told you then that I had discovered Aunt Mary Amanda's silver parked in a storeroom. Decided to wait till I had the goods on someone, but I couldn't resist the temptation to show it to Brooke. You should have seen her eyes when she saw it piled on that table."

He poked the fire till orange and scarlet flames, shot with pale green, roared up the chimney and sent a tangy puff of wood smoke into the room.

"Going to tip off Inspector Harrison that

the stuff has been located, Mark?"

"Not tonight. Every person who knows where it is increases the possibility of its whereabouts getting on the air. I would like to catch the thief myself. Dollars to doughnuts he's hooked up with the paper Mrs. Gregory witnessed."

"Apparently you've eliminated Brooke Reyburn from the list of suspects."

"I have. Haven't you? I thought you liked her, believed in her, that I was the doubting Thomas."

Jed Stewart scowled at the fire. "I did believe in her. I was sold on the whole family. They're such straight-shooting youngsters — doubtless they know plenty about the evil in the world — they're omnivorous readers, and they go to plays and movies — but it doesn't smirch them. Their home-training has made them world-proof. Decent instincts, that's the answer. But Brooke might be all that and yet be tempted beyond her strength. Who doesn't stumble occasionally? I thought her the eighth wonder of the world till Mrs. Gregory prattled about the will she had witnessed and let out that the girl drove into the yard just as she drove out."

"We've been on the wrong track, Jed. I set out on the will hunt with the conviction that the girl was guilty. I would be chucked off a jury if I tried to serve with my mind made up against the defendant in a trial, wouldn't I? At the time Mrs. Gregory witnessed that paper, Brooke Reyburn didn't know that Aunt Mary Amanda had left her a fortune, did she?"

"Not unless your aunt had told her, and it would have been out of character for her to do that. The only way she could have known was by some reference to the former will in this last one Mrs. Gregory witnessed. Suppose she had read it? Suppose your aunt at the last moment had relented, had made you residuary legatee? Could one really condemn a girl who had had to work her head off the last few years, if she were tempted to hold back a document — perhaps for a few months only — which would deprive her of a fortune? Now we are back where we started. Where is that paper? It couldn't have been casually mislaid; neither could it have walked out and lost itself. Why doesn't your wonder-sleuth, Bill Harrison, find out something? Mrs. Gregory wouldn't spin that witness yarn out of whole cloth, would she?"

"No, she is a racy raconteuse but she's not a liar. Suppose we lay our cards on the table and tell Brooke what we have heard? It wouldn't surprise her. She accused me tonight of having settled down in this house for the sole purpose of espionage. She referred to the way I switched the subject when we were questioning Mrs. Gregory about the silver the other afternoon."

"She did! Well, that's nothing to get steamed up about; it may have been merely a shot in the dark; Lola's confounded insinuation may have started her on that line. She may suspect, but she doesn't know why we came. We'll keep her guessing. Do you think Brooke took in that catty suggestion of Lola's that you came to this house with the idea of marrying her to keep the Dane money in the family?"

"Do I think! I know that she took it in. I had her reaction to it tonight. Forget it."

"Okay, you're the doctor. Have you ever wondered why the Fields dropped down in this particular spot for the winter? Nuts as Daphne is about you —"

"Tune in on another wave length, Jed."

"Gosh, you're touchy tonight, aren't you? I was merely about to remark that she couldn't have known when she came that you were to open this house, because she and her brother had hired theirs before you thought of coming."

189

"It's evident enough to anyone who sees Field at Lookout House that he followed the gleam."

"The gleam being Brooke Reyburn? Sure, she's his heart-beat at present, and was he sore about the flower and your invitation to dine and dance in town tomorrow night? I'll say he was."

"I thought a bit of whoopee would pep up some of the actors and actorines. They are stale from too much work."

"It's a grand idea. Field will be all for it when he thinks it over. 'Twill be easy for him to monopolize Brooke in a crowd. I felt as if I were deserting the ship to come away and leave him there this evening though. Having proclaimed the fact that her gardenia had been found on your doorstep, I should have stood by. I wonder if he would be so keen for her if she had no money?"

"What difference would money make to a man who loved her?"

"Nicely put. You've answered two questions in one, Mark."

"Two! I didn't hear but one."

"All right. Call it one. The little tongue must be slipping. I — Who's phoning at this time of night?" Seated on a corner of the broad desk, Mark answered the ring:

"Trent speaking. — Lola! What do you want? — Not interested. If you like selling gas, sell it, only remember that the allowance stops. — Is she? Mrs. Gregory's word goes, here. You should have made sure of that before you set up shop. — What? What sort of paper?" Mark Trent looked at Jed Stewart who had come close and was moving his lips without making a sound. He nodded understanding. "I haven't rung off. — Yes, I heard what you said. I can't imagine how any paper you may have will interest me, but bring it here tomorrow at five. — Sure, I'll be alone. — Yes. Good-bye."

Mark Trent cradled the telephone. He looked up at his friend.

"Lola has a 'paper' to sell me. She suggested that I have my cheque-book in hand tomorrow. What do you make of it?"

"If it is the 'paper' Mrs. Gregory witnessed, how could she get hold of it?"

"Henri?"

"She said he had written to her, didn't she? She's bringing it tomorrow afternoon! There's a catch in it somewhere. It sounds too easy. You don't think she'll back out at the last minute, do you, Mark?"

"Not if there is money in it. She said also that Mrs. Gregory was putting the filling-

191

station out of business. It was started without a license. Started for the sole purpose
of chiseling money off me, I suspect."

"Right as usual. What say we call this an
evening? I'm due in court in the morning
in my best Gentlemen of the Jury style;
furthermore, we'll need our brains running
wide open when Lola comes at five. She
has a 'paper' to sell! Won't we feel cheap
about our suspicions of Brooke if it proves
to be the 'paper' we're after?"

"I stopped suspecting her some time
ago. Shall we go up? We are getting provin-
cial. If we were in town we'd be just beginning to go places. Toddle along. I'll put out
the lights."

Mark banked the fire before he ran up
the stairs. Jed Stewart yawned as he stood
at his door.

"In spite of the late excitement, I'm
sleepy. Nightie-night, Mark. I'll drop our
problem into what the psychologists call
the deep mind. Perhaps it will float to the
top in the morning all nicely solved." He
was whistling softly as he closed his bedroom door.

Mark crossed his dark room to the
window. What a night! The sky was powdered with stars. The sparks of gold were
like the lights in Brooke Reyburn's eyes

when she was happy or thrilled, and she had been thrilled when she had heard of his plan to dine and dance in town. A white ruffled tide curled around the ledges. The ocean, dark and mysterious, stretched on and on illimitably. The distant siren wailed monotonously. It got on his nerves at the end of this hectic evening. He jerked the long hangings across the windows to dull the haunting sound and snapped on the lights.

What would Lola try to sell him tomorrow? He and Jed had jumped to the conclusion that it was the will that Mrs. Gregory had witnessed, but how could she get hold of it? Perhaps it was merely a paper she had trumped up in regard to the divorce.

He drew the gardenia from his pocket. Nothing beautiful about it now but the leaves. He didn't need a paper which Lola Hunt might produce to clear his mind of suspicion that Brooke had influenced his aunt in any way. Had she really meant that she wouldn't marry a divorced man, or had she been furiously angry at his bungling attempt to assure her that he had not come to live in this house with the idea of marrying her to keep the Dane money in the family? He drew the flash light from his coat pocket. Lucky he had thought of it when he had taken Brooke to see the silver.

"Mark! Mark!"

Jed's voice? He laid the flower on the dresser before he opened the door. There was no sound in the hall save the creak of a stair, the tick of the old clock, the slight rattle of a shutter as if skeleton fingers were tapping for admittance. Must have been his imagination. He turned back into the room. Stopped. Queer things were happening. He'd better make sure that Jed hadn't called. With the electric torch still in his hand he crossed the hall and knocked at Jed Stewart's door. He knocked again. Why didn't he answer? He flung open the door. A coat had been hung over the back of a chair. A shoe lay on the floor. Cold air was stirring the chintz hangings. Where did it come from?

The bath-room! Mark sprinted to the door and stopped in amazement. The window was wide open, but the air was strongly scented with perfume. The shower was dripping. Shaving materials were flung about as if hastily dropped.

Jed hadn't had time since closing the door to do all that. Had he surprised a man in the room? A man who had come for the silver?

In spite of his anxiety, Mark chuckled. Would a big, bad burglar stop for a shower and shave? The idea was a riot. Not so funny if Jed were in danger. Where was he?

There was no laughter in his eyes as he thrust his head out of the window. There were two ways to escape from the little balcony under it. Drop to the terrace, or through Lookout House. Had the two men crashed in there? Brooke would be frightened. He'd follow them. He swung his leg over the sill.

"Stop!"

He went rigid in obedience to the hoarse warning, but only for an instant. Why was he perching like a dummy with the light from the room behind making him a perfect target for the person who had grunted? He moved his leg. No response to that from the balcony. Quickly he flashed his powerful light in the direction from which the sound had come. That would blind the person watching.

His eyes followed the light. In his amazement he lost his balance and pitched forward. At one corner of the railing, blinking and shivering in the glare, huddled the run-away green parrot.

Held up by a bird! He slid to the balcony. Reached for Mr. Micawber, grabbed him, flung him into the room behind him. He could hear the parrot squawking with fury as he closed the window.

"That seems to be that! Now, where's Jed?"

He peered over the railing. No uprights on this balcony to slide down. The next one had iron trellises which connected it with the stone terrace. Had Jed entered Lookout House by the window? Who occupied the room of the next house which opened on it? He would investigate.

He tiptoed to the window, reduced the light in his torch before he flashed it over the glass. The shade was closely drawn and the sash locked. No one could have gone in there. Cracks of light were visible in the two rooms beyond where French windows opened on another balcony. Had Jed entered that lighted room? How could he get there? He was too stout to swing across. Could he himself do it?

He appraised the distance, stepped over, and swung. As he gripped the frosty railing of the other balcony, his foot slipped. He hung by his hands, hands which seemed to freeze to the iron. He floundered for a foothold. His heart stopped. Was he going down? He was not! He had started out to find Jed. Was he a quitter?

For a second he hung relaxed. Then he lifted one foot to the edge of the balcony. Dragged up the other. Cautiously stepped over the rail and ripped his hands from the frosty iron.

With his heart drumming like an airplane motor he concentrated his attention on the window. A crack of light showed between the hangings. Whose room was it? Should he take a chance that it was Sam's or Brooke's and tap lightly?

A window was being opened cautiously. Where? He flattened himself against the house. Must be the end balcony outside the studio. He visualized the interior as he had seen it the day he had helped Jerry Field sketch in the tree trunks on the backdrop. Someone was crawling out! A man! He was sliding down an iron trellis like a monkey! Now he was running across the lawn bent double! He was entering the garage!

Mark Trent crammed the electric torch into his pocket and swung a leg over the railing. He hitched along till his feet found an upright, went down hand over hand, his palms sticking painfully to the iron as he moved them.

From purple tree shadow to purple tree

shadow he skulked. Near the garage he hid behind shrubs. The click of a lock! He held his breath as he listened. Who had been in the Lookout House garage at this time of night? Whoever it was, was leaving. He could hear cautious footsteps. An automobile starting! He strained his ears. It was speeding down the street toward the causeway. That didn't prove anything, it would be easy enough to turn into a side road and cut back. Was the man who had sneaked from the house driving? Had he stolen the car? Even so, he couldn't follow it, he must find out why he had entered the garage.

He crept to a window and peered in. Dark as pitch except for a white blur. That must be the cover of Aunt Mary Amanda's old limousine. Why was the unused car directly opposite the door? He remembered now. Jed had told him that he had o. k.'d an offer Henri Jacques had reported for the out-of-date machine. Probably the butler had planned to drive it off in the morning.

The man who had just made his get-away had stopped here. Why? Had he hidden loot? The silver? But the silver had been in the storeroom only a few hours ago. A few hours! Much could happen in a few hours while the occupants of the Other House had been at supper at the Rey-burns'. He'd better investigate. Lucky he still carried the key to his aunt's garage on his ring. In the days when they had been friendly, she had insisted upon his having a key to the house as well. Soundlessly he slid back the door, squeezed in, closed and locked it.

With the light in his torch dimmed, he tiptoed carefully between the automobiles. Brooke's long, sleek town car. Sam's convertible coupe. The white cloth cover of the old limousine was awry as if it had been hastily adjusted. Part of it lay on the floor. What was that mark? A footprint! A footprint faint but bloody!

XI

With a childish impulse to clutch their coats and keep the men with her, Brooke Reyburn had listened to the closing of the door behind Mark Trent and Jed Stewart. They had pleaded an early morning start for the city, but she was sure that they had gone because they resented Jerry Field's sulky silence. She would have been glad to get away from his gloomy presence herself. She glanced at him as he stood before the fire. From the back of the house came the crash of dishes, a shout of laughter.

Brooke sprang to her feet. "I wonder what went then. I suspect that Lucette and Sam started rough-housing and that Daphne was drawn into the scuffle. I should have known better than to let them wash the dishes. Come on, Jerry. Let's investigate. I'd rather know the worst at once."

Field straightened and thrust his hands hard into his pockets.

"Same here, Brooke. I want to know what you were doing in Mark Trent's house while we were at rehearsal."

"Why should you think I had been in his house?"

"Didn't Stewart find a gardenia outside his front door?"

"So what? I suppose there couldn't be another woman in the world who might call on Mr. Trent wearing a flower, or did you corner the gardenia market today, Jerry?"

Field's expression changed from gloom to cheer.

"There's something in that. Trent certainly is a wow with the ladies. I hear that he could dine out three times an evening if he'd accept the invitations heaped on him. It gets me why he settled down in this burg. Don't be sore at me, sweet thing. Wasn't it natural for me to think the flower yours when Stewart produced the gardenia that he found at Trent's front door when you weren't wearing any? Where are they?"

Brooke fought an impulse to glance at the wastebasket.

"Took them off. I had a letter to write to Mother, had a lot to tell her, the room was hot, and the heavy fragrance of those flowers got on my nerves."

"Sorry my gift annoyed you."

"Don't be silly. I adore gardenias."

She drew a breath of relief as Sam and

the two girls entered. She didn't like Jerry Field in the role of inquisitor, neither did she like the way in which she had evaded his questions. She hadn't been quite honest, but Mark Trent had asked her not to speak of what had happened in the Other House. Did he think her a chatterer? Why had she thrust at him about his divorce? It had been cruel, no matter if he had again assured her that he didn't want to marry her. It wasn't like her to be cruel, she hated to hurt anyone. Aloud she inquired:

"What smashed in the kitchen, Sam? I thought the chimney had fallen in."

"Nothing but a stack of those warranted unbreakable plates Clotilde keeps things on in the ice-box. And did they crack up? The floor looked as if there'd been a snowstorm."

"The sound brought Henri down the backstairs in a hurry. Ever seen him in his *robe de nuit*, Brooke?"

"What a giggler you are, Lucette! Of course I haven't."

"You've missed the laugh of your life. He was something straight out of a Cruikshank edition of Dickens. Night cap with tassel; night shirt, I believe it was called back in the dark ages; thin bow legs, and flapping slippers."

"Was he embarrassed?"

"He was not. He behaved more as if he were afraid we'd miss the appeal of his costume. He ran around like this." She trotted across the floor.

Lucette frowned at Field. "Can't you smile for the lady, Jerry. I'll tell you one thing. I'd rather be a giggler than a gob of gloom. Good-night!" She dashed from the room and sang defiantly as she bolted up the stairs:

" 'Take me where the daisies cover the
    country lane.
We'll make hay while the sun shines,
We'll make love when it rains.' "

Daphne ran into the hall.

"Lucette, don't forget that Mark Trent is giving us a party tomorrow night at that swell new Supper Club."

Lucette hung over the mahogany rail. "Forget! Not a chance. Think I'll forget a night off from rehearsing? Nothing short of an act of God will keep me away. Sam, the old tyrant, is giving us a break. I'll be seeing you."

Jerry Field picked up his sister's coat.

"Come on, Daph, let's go. If I'd known

that we were to have a night off, I would have taken you dining and dancing, Brooke."

"Nice of you, but I think that a party will be heaps more fun."

"You would think that. I don't know why but this whole evening has gone haywire. Come on, Daph."

Daphne Field snuggled her hand into Sam Reyburn's.

"Good-night, Sammy. Don't love me much, do you, darling?"

Sam shook off her hand. "I'll love you when you learn your lines, and what's more, if you don't learn 'em, you'll be tossed off the lot."

"You mean that I'll be fired?" Daphne opened her eyes at their widest. "I, fired, after I've had gowns made to wear that will simply stop the show? Come on, Jerry. Nobody likes us here."

From the threshold she threw a kiss to Sam.

He grinned.

"Why direct your talent for fascination at so unimportant a target, gal? I'm a poor struggling playwright, and you belong to the internationalized upperclass, so-called. Good-night."

As the front door closed, Brooke turned

to her brother as he stood back to the fire.

"What's wrong with Lucette, Sam? She seems always on the verge of tears. Is the rehearsing too much for her on top of her day's work?"

"Rehearsing! She's fallen for Field and fallen hard, that's what's the matter, and he doesn't know she's in the world when you are around."

"But, Sam, I don't care for him that way."

"Sure you don't, you don't have to tell me. He isn't big enough for you. In a month you'd be fed up with his conversation, if you call it that, which is geared to run on stock quotations and art with a capital A. Don't get me wrong about that last, I believe in trying to make an art of whatever profession one's in, it's just that I can't take Field's enthusiasms seriously. He'll be all right some day, but you don't want a boy to bring up, you want a full-grown man, Brooke."

"Sam, sometimes I think you're psychic. Do — do you like Daphne?"

"She's good fun. Swell looker, isn't she? She's got those big you'll-look-after-me,-won't-you? eyes and all the time she knows her way around. You're a kid beside her."

"A kid! This aged business-woman a kid!

Why, I'm fairly bent with years and care."

Sam grinned. "Oh yeah! Brooke, you're the star actress of the family. Why wouldn't you play the woman lead in 'Islands Arise'?"

"Too much Reyburn. The townspeople would think we were putting on a benefit for the family instead of for the town's pet charity, at which, I understand, the gilt-edged subscribers will appear in their crown jewels. I'm going up to finish a letter to Mother. She has had you and Daphne on her mind."

"Tell her to take us off, pronto; tell her that there is no girl living who means as much to me as this play — excepting herself and you and Lucette."

"Thanks billions for including me in the preferred class, Sammy. Mother will be relieved when she knows the exact state of the light-of-her-life's affections."

"Doesn't she like Daphne?"

"Well enough, but apparently she thinks that her soul must do a powerful lot of growing before she covets her for a daughter-in-law. Good-night. I'm thrilled when I think of Mark Trent's party. I haven't dined and danced in the bright lights since I came here to live. You're coming, of course?"

"Yep. It's an awful waste of time, but it will pep me up to get the play off my mind for a few hours. You do think it's good, don't you, Brooke?"

"I don't think; I know." She laid her cheek against his for an instant. "Don't take it so hard, Sam; even if the critics do pan it —"

Sam straightened. "They won't! They can't!" He grinned sheepishly, "That gives me away, doesn't it? Well, if I don't like what I write, who will? Good-night."

In the room she had made her boudoir, Brooke slipped out of the lace frock. If only she could shed with it the haunting sense of having said the wrong thing. She had been bitterly unkind when she had reminded Mark Trent of his divorce. If she could apologize to him and get it off her mind, it would help. Well, she couldn't. Perhaps if she wore the hair shirt of remorse for a while, it would teach her to guard her tongue.

In a heavily embroidered Chinese housecoat of vivid green, she pulled forward the chair at her desk. She paused long enough to enjoy the effect of the room, with its ivory panels painted with huge bunches of leaves and flowers, blue, pink, pale yellow, and amethyst, with a touch of crimson;

pale, smooth ivory chairs cushioned in green; green chintz at the windows; green rug edged with a lighter tint; of the glint of her tawny hair against the ivory and silver of the bit of the bedroom hanging reflected in the mirror above her. She thought:

"I'm mad about this gorgeous coat, this room, and for the first time in my life I have all the flowers I want. I don't wonder people struggle for money; it will buy such heavenly things for themselves and others. It must be harder to get along without much after one has had it than never to have had plenty. Suppose I were to lose the legacy? What would I do? Take the Palm Beach job pronto, of course. How can I lose it? Would Jed Stewart have allowed me to spend money on this house unless he had been sure that it was mine to spend? Of course he wouldn't. The Hunt woman's hint is responsible for this attack of imagination. Even if those two men are here to prove 'undue influence,' they can't do it. Why worry?"

She picked up the letter from her mother she had been answering before dinner and skimmed the first few pages which described the charm of English country life, the superannuated sporting Earl at the head of the family who grunted complaints from morning till night, the youthful exuberance — in spite of her father-in-law — of Lady Jaffrey, the stiff courtesy of her husband, the superfluity of servants and the meagre supply of bath towels. Brooke settled deeper into her chair to reread the paragraphs which had set her questioning Sam in the living room. Her mother had written:

Your first long letter came yesterday and confirmed my judgment that it is better for my young people that their mother is away for a time. If I were there I would be watching Sam's every move, for — between you and me — I don't like Daphne Field. You wrote that she is in the play. You know what dramatics do to people. What sudden friendships, what swift intimacies develop between men and girls, which, under ordinary circumstances, wouldn't form at all. She is pretty, she has that you're-so-big-and-strong manner which is deadly to the male. My Sam is vulnerable to flattery about his work, and the girl's, 'I've heard that you are the coming playwright, Mr. Reyburn,' sent little creepy chills over me.

Sam thinks now that he does not

want a wife and children. He will, and when he does he'll want a girl who hasn't cheapened herself by a series of engagements. I hear that Daphne has experimented five times. Of course, it is better to break five engagements than to make one mistake in marriage, but at about the third break, wouldn't a girl with any ideals at all begin to look inside her mind and wonder what was wrong with her judgment? You know that I have a sympathetic understanding of the modern girl. She's gallant, and beneath the shellac of indifference I believe she is tender, but she's wrong in her belief that it hurts a woman no more to experiment in amorous adventure than a man. This is a decade of political experimentation, of radical ideas and impossible plans, but marriage won't bear much tinkering. In spite of the broad and shining target it offers to the cynics, it has brought out more nobility of character and selfless devotion than any other human institution. No amount of scrapping of old standards, of setting up new freedom, of half-baked arguments can alter the fact that woman is the mother of the race and will be to the end of time, that as she climbs, so will her children climb. Give me the girl who proclaims herself as something better than one of a herd by holding some of these dangerous trends in check; whose roots of integrity and honor and faithfulness to her man go too deep to be stirred by passing fancies after marriage.

Brooke dropped the letter and frowned at her reflection in the mirror above her desk. Her mother had seen Daphne Field but once and she had put into words an instinctive distrust she herself had felt without being able to express it. She drew her own unfinished letter forward on the desk. At least she could set her anxiety about Sam at rest. She faithfully reported his reaction to the probing of his sentiments in regard to Daphne Field. That finished, she nibbled the end of her pen. Should she tell her mother of the business offer? No, it might get back to Lucette, and Lucette would be aggrieved. She was touchy enough now without adding another irritant. She wrote:

And so, Mother, you may close your eyes at night secure in the thought that the light-of-your-life is immune to the wiles of the fascinating Daphne — even if he were not, but I'm sure he is — she is after bigger fish. She has her net spread for Mark the Magnificent.

Don't worry about us. You and Father taught us to hate cheapness. You put the best of your fine lives into your children. That must count. What a waste your love and care would be if it didn't. Have a grand time. If that sporting Earl grunts at you, flap the wings of the American Eagle in his face. Use those Express cheques I gave you for clothes for yourself when you get to Paris, every cent of them. As I said before, have a gorgeous time — but don't forget to come home, Celia Reyburn.

Devotedly,
BROOKE.

She reread the letter and nodded with satisfaction as she slipped it into an envelope. That ought to set her mother's mind at rest about Sam. Curious that even after her daughters and son had become financially independent, they were children to her. Perhaps all good mothers were like that. What had she seen in Daphne Field's face that made her distrust the girl? Faces were masks anyway. Who could tell what she was thinking if he saw her in the mirror as she was seeing herself now? She —

Her heart mounted to her throat and stuck there, beating, beating. Reflected in the looking-glass, the silver-shot hanging between bedroom and boudoir filled and swung like the sail of a boat. What had set it in motion? Had a window been opened? She was too far from the bell to ring. Suppose she rang? Who would answer? Henri and Clotilde were locked in their room probably. What should she do? She stared at the mirror. How could a person get in? From the balcony under the bath-room window? That meant that he had come through Mark Trent's house. Was it the black-gloved man who had been in the attic this evening?

She swallowed her heart. She couldn't sit here forever. She must move. How still the room was! The silence of fear enveloped her like a cold mist and turned her finger-tips to ice. Perhaps she was in a nightmare and could waken herself. Glorious thought. She'd scream.

Her mouth remained open as a hatless man in blue denim slipped past the swaying hanging. His head was wet and sleek as a seal's; his face below his eyes — bad eyes

— was so thickly plastered with white as to be unrecognizable. He gave one furtive glance over his shoulder before he flitted in ghostly silence from the room.

Brooke pulled out the drawer of her desk. It crashed to the floor spilling the contents. Maddening! It would do that when she was in a hurry. On her knees she scrambled after an electric torch which had rolled under a chair. She dashed to the hall. Who was the man? What was the stuff on his face? She'd never forget those wicked eyes above a smear of white. The house was dark and still. She ran toward Sam's room. Stopped. Better not start him on a man hunt. He was so impetuous. How did she know that the intruder hadn't a gun? She must go Scotland Yard herself.

The hall clock told the hour. The sound echoed through the house. Only twelve? It seemed hours since she had said good-night to Sam in the living-room, and years since Mark Trent and Jed Stewart had gone home. She tiptoed to the balustrade and listened. Had the man gone down the stairs? The scent of roses and burning logs drifted up. Above the dull beat and suck of the tide against the ledges she could hear the sizzle and crack of a smoldering fire, the wind fumbling at the windows, the faint, weird wail of the siren.

A squeak! She put her hand hard over her heart to stop its thumping. Was a window being opened cautiously? If only the wind would stop for a minute. The sound again! Lucette's room?

In a moment she was at her sister's door. She looked into the room and guardedly flashed her light. Lucette was asleep; she could see the glisten of cold cream with which she plastered her eyelids at night. The salty air blowing through two wide-open windows gently stirred a wave of her dark hair and the photographs of movie stars with which the mantel was crowded.

Brooke soundlessly closed the door and leaned against it. The squeak had not come from that room. Had it come from the next which had been used for scenery? It had a small iron balcony like the one which connected Lookout House and Mark Trent's. Why hadn't she thought of that before? A person might easily slide down the trellis.

She tiptoed into the room and closed the door softly behind her. This must be the window that had squeaked; it was wide open. It had been closed this afternoon when she had come in to scatter green paint on the flats and to give another splash of red to the peak of roof on the backdrop. In spite of her anxiety, she chuckled. Sam was right. The foliage of the trees on the canvas did look like an explosion of green worms.

She flashed her light around the room then on the floor over which a sheet had been spread. A can of red paint had been overturned! It was sluggishly spreading.

Tipped over recently! Slowly Brooke's light traveled. A red footprint! Uncannily like a bloody one. The man must have stepped into the thick paint. Another! One beyond that under the window. Cautiously she followed the trail. A smooch of red on the window sill. He had gone that way. Was he on the balcony? What would she see if she looked out? She must look out. She wouldn't close her eyes tonight unless she knew that the man had gone — where, she wouldn't care, if he were gone.

She leaned out cautiously. There was nothing human in sight, only a one-eyed moon was watching through a maze of branches. One of the four hundred million meteors, drawn by gravity into the earth's atmosphere daily, shot across the dark heavens leaving no trail. Stars twinkled. Distant street lights shone steadily. Cold winter moonlight turned a towering hemlock to purple, shadows to amethyst, and scattered a shimmering trail of golden topaz on the dark water of the harbor. Had one of the shadows moved down by the tree?

It had. That meant that the man was out of the house! She cautiously closed and locked the window. Pulled the hangings across it. That was that! She curtained the other window, turned to switch on the wall light. Stopped. The door was opening! A glare of light. Had the man come back? Had he a pal? Had her heart parked in her throat forever? She couldn't see, but she could still hear:

"Well, for the love of Mike!"

The wall light snapped on.

Brooke's blood, which she had thought frozen, surged through her veins. Sam was staring at her, Sam in pink and white pajamas which made him look for all the world like an animated stick of striped candy. His copper colored hair was on end; without his spectacles his eyes were big and dark and vague. He shook her arm.

"Hey! Snap out of it, Brooke! Have you got that darn scenery so on your mind that you're walking in your sleep to sling paint in here?"

Brooke swallowed the lump in her throat.

"I wasn't asleep, Sam, and I wasn't sling-ing paint. I heard something." Her voice sounded hoarse to herself.

"A window being opened? That's what I heard. But how could you get here so soon?"

Breathlessly she told him of the man who had slipped through her room, of fol-lowing him into the hall.

"You're kidding! No? Then why didn't you yell for me?"

"You're so reckless, Sam, I was afraid you might be hurt."

"That's the funniest thing I ever heard. How about yourself? Beat it back to bed. Sam the boy sleuth is hot on the trail."

"You mustn't go downstairs."

"Who says I mustn't. I'll snoop around outside to be sure the guy has gone. Beat it."

"If you go down, I go too."

"Oh all right, all right. I know better than to argue with you when you use that tone, Brooke. Got a flash? We'll creep down the backstairs. Follow me. We'll get into the front of the house that way."

He switched out the wall light, opened the door and stood motionless, listening.

"Let's go!"

Brooke nodded in response to his whisper. The hall seemed miles long as she tip-toed through the dark; the backstairs end-less in number as she stole down, stopping at every creak, holding her breath at every sound which echoed as if amplified in the walls.

Sam stopped at the kitchen door to listen. Crept on to the front hall. Brooke controlled an hysterical urge to laugh as she stole after him.

"The Reyburns go sleuthing," she thought, and chuckled.

She felt Sam's quick turn and glare, though she couldn't see it. The turn was catastrophic. He lurched into a chair. His muttered, "Thunder!" was submerged in a hoarse command:

"Don't move! I've got you covered!"

XII

The dusk about Mark in the garage went black. A bloody footprint! Had the crime horror spread to this small point of land? Brooke! Had anything happened to her? The possibility stopped his heart. He had been so intent upon finding Jed, upon identifying the prowler that he had not thought of danger to the occupants of Lookout House. Sam was there. Nothing could happen to his sister with that boy near. Why was he letting his imagination loose? Would a man who stopped for a shave and a bath in the midst of house-entering be guilty of a bloody crime? But — the footprint?

He dropped to his knees and touched it. Sticky! He flashed his light on it. Sniffed. Turpentine? He sank down on his heels and choked back a shout of laughter. He had been fooled by red paint.

How had it come here? What was that dark heap beyond it? Overalls! Blue denim overalls still warm from the wearer's body. The driver of the car he had heard a few moments ago must have shed them before he left the garage. Why had he worn them?

Mark projected and rejected explanations with lightning speed. The man who had shinnied from the balcony had come from the room where the scenery was being painted. Wasn't the roof of the cottage on the backdrop red? Why the shower? Why the shave? Was it he who had removed the key from the door of the storeroom tonight? But that man had disappeared via the connecting door, presumably into Lookout House.

He flashed a dim light over the white cover. More red! A clumsy X.

"Make X on cover when —"

The words on the scrap of paper in the storeroom were explained.

"X marks the spot where the body was found."

The sentence flashed into Mark's mind as if set in electric lights. Body! Jed was missing! Perhaps his body had been dumped inside the limousine!

He set his heel on the thought. He would imagine a horror like that. That infernal cross probably meant nothing, but he'd take a look-see so that he wouldn't ask himself later, "Why didn't I?"

Soundlessly he reached the other side of the limousine. The disarranged cover which left the door exposed revealed also a license plate. All set to go! He flashed his light inside. Something long, something rounded on the rear seat was covered with an automobile robe.

Dread paralyzed Mark's hand for what seemed to him hours; then with a muttered imprecation he thrust it under the robe. The silver! Nothing but the silver! That X on the white cover was a sign that it had been moved from his house. Who had moved it? That was easy. It had been removed while he and Jed had been at the Reyburns' by the man who had driven away. Sure of plenty of time he had stopped for a shower and shave. Moving the loot to the garage had been his share of the job. Would a pal appear to drive the stuff off?

"He will, and here he is!" Mark muttered, as the frosty gravel outside the garage crunched faintly.

What next? Find out who was prowling at this time of night, of course. Had someone come to check up on the loot, to make sure that it was inside when the limousine was driven off in the morning? Hadn't Jed given Henri authority to drive the car away to be sold?

A key in the lock! Not a minute to waste. Where should he go? Inside Brooke's town car! The breaks were with him. It wasn't locked.

The garage door was sliding back. Mark saw a patch of sky. He banged his forehead as he plunged headfirst into the sedan, and saw a million stars. His head spun as he crouched in the space left by the turned back seat and drew the door shut without latching it. He held it in place as barely breathing he listened.

"If only I had a piece of Alice's mushroom to nibble to make myself shrink," he thought, as he tried to dispose of his elbows and knees with a minimum of sound and maximum of effort. He put his hand to his aching forehead. The bang had raised an ugly welt. Lucky the skin wasn't broken.

Footsteps on the cement floor! Cautious footsteps. A light on the ceiling! Suppose it should flash into the town car? It had stopped. Whoever it was, was taking his time. Evidently giving the confederate a chance to make a clean get-away. A door clicked! Someone checking up on the loot in the limousine? What a title for a mystery story. "Loot In the Limousine." He would pass that on to Sam. He'd better keep his mind on the situation, he wasn't sitting any too pretty.

An engine turning over! Was some darn fool starting a car with the garage door closed? Mark raised his head turtle-fashion. No, the door was open. He might have known it. Was it likely that the bandit would allow himself to be bumped off by carbon monoxide? Not that bad boy. He had too much at stake.

He must follow. How? He couldn't trail in another car. He would be heard. Could he hang on to the empty trunk-rack? That was an idea. He would follow the limousine out of the garage, slip into the shadow of a shrub when the man went back to close the door, then grab the trunk-rack when the car started again. A stunt, but he'd make a stab at it. If he were to hold the man now he would learn nothing of his destination.

He cautiously tiptoed after the limousine. He was safe behind the shrubs when the driver returned and noiselessly closed the garage door. A soft hat was drawn low over his eyes, but Mark knew him. Henri.

He was behind the wheel again! The limousine was coasting down the incline! Mark crouched as he ran after it. As the engine started, he drew himself carefully to the trunk-rack. He barely breathed. Had the driver felt a jar? Evidently not. He was increasing speed. He was not headed for the causeway. He was going in the opposite direction. What did that mean?

Clinging to the rack with one hand, Mark turned up his coat collar. For the first time he realized that he was off on this joy ride in dinner clothes without hat or topcoat. The air had a crispness and cleanness born of sea and frost and the smell of salt. He crouched close to the body of the car, it kept the wind from his back and his head out of sight of the man in front. What move should he make when the driver stopped? Time enough to plan that when he knew what he was up against.

The landmarks he passed turned his thoughts back to his youth. There was the old house in the cupola of which he and a boy pal had first experimented with radio, then an intriguing puzzle of wires, coils and sparks. The red and green lights of boats swinging in the harbor conjured up the memory of the night he had met Lola at a dance on board a yacht; he could see the decorative pattern made by strings of colored lanterns, her face upturned to his. He thought of the tornado of protests from family, friends, and neighbors that his engagement to her had set in motion, and he thought of his stunned realization after their marriage that the Count, whom he had thought her friend, was more than that, much more; of his unbearable humiliation when he had literally carried her home from parties because she had had too much to drink. He remembered how he had icily given her the choice between her lover and himself. She had taken it promptly and had gone to Europe; he had secured the divorce; she had married the Frenchman, had been a countess for a short time. The next he heard of her she had married Hunt. From her appearance it was evident that she had started down the toboggan slide of promiscuity. Would anything stop her from plunging into the black pit at its base? Why had he never felt free since she had left him? The divorce had been as legal and complete as the law of the state could make it, no subterfuges, no placing himself in a compromising situation to save her good name. She had had none to save. She had left him for another man. And he was legally free. Free! For what? To ask a girl to marry him who wouldn't marry a divorced man if there was not another in the world? He was crazy to think of Brooke Reyburn.

He visualized her slim, vivid beauty, her brown eyes like deep pools reflecting gold stars when she was eager or moved, the ruddy satin of her hair; he could hear the lilt in her charming voice — a lilt when she was not speaking to him. There was an edge to it then which set him on the defensive.

He on the defensive with Brooke Reyburn! That was a joke. Sometime — not until after the play; nothing must interfere with Sam's play — he would tell her that Mrs. Gregory had witnessed a later will than the one probated, and ask her to tell what she knew about it, if she knew anything. Meanwhile the car was slowing down! It had stopped.

The white cottage. The filling-station. The Hunts had dared start it at Lola's house without a license, and the old residents were after it like a pack of hounds. No doubt but that it had been a plot to force twenty thousand dollars from him. Had he fallen for it, what would have been their next extortion scheme? He would know tomorrow — today, it must be after midnight now. Wasn't Lola coming with a mysterious "paper" to sell? He must not be seen here. Surely the driver would make contact with someone inside before he left the limousine.

Henri stepped out of the car. He stopped

as if to make sure he was not observed. How still the night! Far, far away a hound was baying. Sinister sound! Blood-chilling! It gave one the creeps.

Mark slipped off the trunk-rack. He was cramped and stiff. He hobbled rather than walked into a deep purple shadow cast by a pine. He could see the cottage. He held his breath as Henri gently turned the knob of the front door and entered. What would he do next? Come back to the limousine? What a chance to grab him.

What was he doing inside the house? He was taking his time. The door was opening again! Mark hardly breathed. A man slipped out. His hat was pulled down over his eyes. He slunk along in the shadows. Reached the shore road. Ran on the dried grass which bordered it as if pursued by furies.

Had that been Henri? Had he delivered his message? Had he been warned to beat it? Couldn't have been a fight inside. No loud voices. Had the limousine with the silver been left for someone else to drive away?

Someone else! What a break! What a break! He would drive it back and park it in his garage — no, that wouldn't do, he would leave it with Mike Cassidy. Mike was as dependable as the sun. It wouldn't be safe to take it across the causeway to-night. Someone might be lying in wait to relay the driver. In the morning he and Jed would transfer the silver to his car and take it to the bank, and then have the laugh on Inspector Bill Harrison.

He stole from the shadow of the pine. With every faint scrunch of his feet on the frosty ground his blood stopped running. Could he reach the limousine before some-one came? Only a few feet more. He was behind the wheel. With a hand stiff from cold he touched the self-starter. Hang it! Wouldn't you know the motor would back-fire! A light! In the front dormer! He had wakened someone! He hadn't a mo-ment to lose.

With his ears strained to detect pursuit, with his eyes roaming from side to side, Mark shot the car ahead. He went in an opposite direction from that taken by Henri, — if the man who had burned up the road making his getaway from the white cottage had been Henri — he wouldn't run the chance of overtaking him. It seemed years before he reached Mike Cassidy's garage at the entrance to the causeway, hours before he could rouse the man, before he partially opened the door.

"Let me in quick, Mike," he whispered to the blinking, cursing proprietor, who was gripping something that gleamed dark and blue and ugly in a hairy, ham-bone fist.

"It's only you, Mr. Mark! Thought it might be a hold-up."

Cassidy's lower jaw swung like a gate on loose hinges. He slipped the automatic into his pocket before he rolled back the garage door.

"Where can I hide this?"

Cassidy pointed.

Not until the limousine was stowed behind a motley collection of broken-down cars did Mark Trent explain.

"I've just rescued the family silver, Mike. The yarn I have to tell you will beat any of the thrillers you get over the radio. Not afraid to keep the car here, are you?"

Cassidy's red-rimmed eyes grew moist. He wiped his nose on a shabby coat sleeve.

"I ain't afraid to do nothing for you, Mr. Mark. You an' your family give me my start; sometimes you've kept me goin' when I didn't know where the next meal was comin' from. I felt mean when I let my Maggie go to work for Mrs. Hunt who treated you so bad, but we needed the money somethin' terrible, so she took the job, though it was at that new fillin' station that's tryin' to put me out of business."

A telephone rang. The two men stared at one another. Mark's blood turned to ice. Cassidy whispered:

"Holy mackerel! Who's callin' this time of night? Have they traced you and the silver this quick? Perhaps there's a gang after you!"

Mark nodded toward the telephone. "Answer!" His muscles tensed as he listened.

"Cassidy's garage. — You, Maggie! What I'll — Stop blubberin'. — What! Who? — I can't hear, you're cryin' so. — Something terrible? — Never mind, never mind. I'll call police headquarters. — You've got to stay there, girl, till I get Bill Harrison. If anyone comes, don't talk. Don't talk! — Sure, I'll come. Just as soon as I get the police."

"Mike! What's happened?"

Cassidy's face was ashen as he shook Mark's hand from his arm.

"Wait!"

He dialled. He spoke into the transmitter.

"Someone's hurt bad at the white cottage — that new filling station on the Point. — Mike Cassidy talkin' — I got to

231

go. You don't understand — my daughter's there. — All right. I'll wait here."

He hung up and wiped a grimy hand across his sweat-beaded forehead.

"That was my girl, Maggie, who called."

"Talk, man, talk! What's happened?"

"Someone hurt bad."

"Who?"

"I couldn't make out."

"Someone hurt at the white cottage! But I was there not more than ten minutes ago, Mike."

"If I was you I wouldn't say that, Mr. Mark. It wasn't just hurtin'. I was breakin' it easy. Someone's dead."

XIII

"Don't move! I've got you covered!"

In obedience to the hoarse warning, Sam and Brooke Reyburn stood as if turned to stone in the dark hall of Lookout House.

"What does a perfect lady do when she is 'covered'?" the girl asked herself. "Will he shoot if I move?" Her thoughts raced on. "Tonight can't be real, it's too much like a movie. Such things couldn't happen in this little village. I'm in a nightmare — I —"

Lights flared. She stared incredulously. Was that Jed Stewart with his hand on the switch glaring at them with wide dilated eyes, with his mouth open as if he had just swallowed a salt wave? That was a flashlight he was pointing at them, not a pistol. It was Jed Stewart without his coat, with his black bow tie under one ear, with only one shoe on. He was the funniest sight she ever had seen.

Her taut muscles relaxed. She flopped to her knees before Sam; her body shook with nervous laughter as she held out supplicating hands:

"Please — pl-ease, Mr. Ban-dit, sp-spare

my little brother in — in his cun-ning little p-pink pajamas. Cut! Lights! Camera!"

Sam grabbed her shoulder and pulled her to her feet.

"Quit your ranting, Brooke. Think this is a joke, don't you? For the love of Mike, Jed Stewart, perhaps you'll tell me why you're holding us up in our own house? Why this Public Enemy No. 1 touch?"

Stewart swallowed.

"There goes his Adam's apple," Brooke thought, and giggled hysterically.

Stewart blinked.

"What are you two doing wandering round this house half dressed at this time of night?"

Brooke tightened the cord of her green lounge coat.

"Stop shouting, Jed. You'll have Lucette down here. Don't you know a perfectly g-orgeous mandarin coat when you see one? As for Sam's pa-pajamas — he could walk across the causeway in them with per-fect propriety."

"Now you've got the giggles again. Stop laughing, Brooke."

"I can't — can't help it, Sammy. Jed's — Jed's — so fun-ny. All I can th-think of is, 'Diddle diddle dumpling, my son John, went to bed with one s-shoe on —' "

"You've got to stop, get me? Come into the living-room and tell us what you're doing in this house, Jed."

"Let's go to the kitchen instead, more likely to stabilize our emotions," Brooke suggested. "I'll make cocoa and we'll scramble eggs. Jed must need food after the late ex-excitement — he's fairly twitching with it — and I feel hollow to my toes. Come on, Sam."

"Sounds okay to me. I'm a growing boy, I need lots of nutriment. You'd better eat or you'll go hysterical, Brooke; you didn't touch a thing when we came back from rehearsal. I'll run up and get a couple of bath robes. Take these, Jed." He kicked off his slippers. "I'll put on shoes upstairs."

Jed Stewart gulped, nodded, and pulled off his shoe.

Brooke held laughter rigidly in check. It wouldn't take much to start it ringing in peals. Jed's hold-up was the funniest thing she ever had seen. Her brows contracted. Whom had he thought he was holding up? Why was he in this house at midnight?

The questions were still chasing each other in her mind and never getting anywhere, like the horses on a merry-goround, when she reached the kitchen, that white and green "step-saving" kitchen which she had had more fun in remodeling than any other room in the house.

"Much as I dislike her, I'll hand it to Clotilde for keeping this place spotless," she confided to Jed behind her. She thought of the man who had dashed through her room. "Draw all the shades, quick!"

"Sam can be speedy when he wants to be," she admitted, as her brother entered with a lurid bath robe over his pajamas and another all red and green stripes which he flung at Stewart.

"There you are, m'lad."

"Bring the milk, eggs, butter and bacon from the icebox, Sam. Toss me that apron, Jed, the big white one — that's right. Toast some bread, Sammy."

Brooke, enveloped in a capacious apron, measured and mixed at the white porcelain table, brought plates and cups from the pantry, while Sam sliced bread and cooked bacon, and Jed Stewart stirred the contents of a double-boiler on the electric range.

Sam sniffed. "Doesn't the bacon smell dandy! Here you are, folks." He arranged thin, crisp strips around a mound of fluffy scrambled eggs. "You and Jed sit down, Brooke, and I'll bring the cocoa after I find the marshmallows to drop into the cups. Where does Clotilde, our little ray of sunshine, keep them?"

"She doesn't keep them, she eats 'em. You'll find a box I hid for emergency under the buffet."

Brooke slipped off the apron and waited until Sam had served steaming hot cocoa with a little melting white island floating in each cup and helped himself lavishly to scrambled eggs and bacon, before, with elbows on the porcelain table, chin on her clasped hands, she suggested:

"Now that the shock of discovering us roaming round in our own house has somewhat worn off, perhaps you'll tell us how you got in and why, Jed?"

Stewart leaned back in his chair with the air of a man whose appetite has been abundantly satisfied.

"Little Tommy Tucker, sing for your supper, stuff, what? You're a grand cook, Brooke."

"What does that prove? I cooked that bacon," Sam reminded. "Get going, stout fella, it's your cue to break down and confess All. How did you get into the house?"

"Any chance that someone may be listening in?"

"Take a look-see into the back hall, Sam." Brooke's voice was a note lower than Stewart's.

"All quiet on the Western Front," her brother reported. He straddled a chair. "Shoot, Jed."

"Well, it was like this. I had said good-night to Mark and gone into my room. I had pulled off my coat, had yanked off one shoe when I began to sniff." He reddened. "Perhaps it's effeminate but I like a lot of 4711 in my tub, and I asked myself, 'Who's been using my bath crystals?'"

" 'The Three Bears' gone modern. 'Who's been using my bath crystals?' growled Father Bear."

"Stop interrupting with wisecracks, Brooke."

"I'm sorry, Sam, but when I think back over the last few hours, my funny-bone tickles. Go on, Jed, I'll be good. You'd just sniffed 4711 crystals. What next?"

"Heard sounds in the bath-room. It sort of took my breath for a minute and my brain whirled like a pin-wheel. Then I grabbed up my flash from the table beside the bed and tiptoed to the door."

"Don't stop to swallow; keep on!" prodded Sam.

"I banged it open. Water was gurgling out of the tub, dripping from the shower, my shaving things were scattered every-where, and — a shoe was going out of the window." Stewart pulled out a handkerchief and mopped his red, moist face.

"A shoe!" Brooke and Sam exclaimed in unison.

"I presume there was a foot in it. For an instant amazement paralyzed me. I made a strategic error. Instead of beating it after that shoe, I poked around. The razor was gone. That fact gave me a nervous chill. 'Why would a man take that? Who could it have been? Kowa?' I asked myself. 'But he has his own bath; why should he use mine?' Then I came to and realized I was wasting time."

"I'll say you were and you're fairly spilling it now. Keep going! You did go after him, didn't you?"

"I did, Sam, but first I shouted for Mark. I hadn't much hope that he would hear me but I didn't dare wait to make sure. I squeezed my boyish figure through that window and wriggled to the balcony. I listened. I could hear only the pound of the surf and the crack of frost in the trees. Cautiously I peered over. Nothing moving. A sound! After this I'll never doubt that hair can rise. Mine felt like that green stuff you see growing up straight on one of those terra cotta heads. I listened. Sounded like a curtain flapping. Then I noticed that the window next to mine was open. Had the man gone in instead of over?

"I knew that it was a Lookout House window, Brooke, but I didn't know whose room. I couldn't be fussy about that. All the horrors I'd ever heard rushed through my mind as I thought of the missing razor and of what might be happening to you and Lucette and Sam."

He ran his fingers under his collar.

"It chokes me even to think of it. Where was I? Oh, yes, I squeezed through and dropped softly to the floor. I stopped to lock the window and draw the shade — my late visitor might have a pal, I reasoned — before I tiptoed into the adjoining room. It was a bedroom unlighted. Behind a hanging I reconnoitered. A mirror over a desk in the next room reflected a boudoir with flower panels; then I knew that the room was Brooke's. All the lights were on. No one there. I crept in. A desk drawer was on the floor, its contents scattered in all directions. A chair was overturned. I lived years crossing that room. What would I see? What would I find on the other side of that door? The hall was dark. The man —"

"Call him the Bath-Crystal Bandit and be done with it, but get him out of this house, Brooke's eyes will pop out of her head in a minute."

"Don't interrupt, Sam. Go on, Jed. Did you see anyone?"

"Couldn't see anything. Didn't dare use my flash for fear I might be spotted. I figured that the man had heard me enter my room, had beat it to the balcony, had seen the open window of this house, had crawled in planning to make his get-away from the lower floor. I gum-shoed down holding my breath at every creak of a stair board, expecting every minute that I'd be sniped at.

"In the hall I stopped to listen. Sounds upstairs. Faint sounds. I hunted for the light switch. Found it. It seemed years that I waited in the dark with my finger itching to press that button. The house was so still I could hear my brain working. Stairs creaked! Back stairs! A door swung! He was coming! A chair crashed! I had him! I shouted:

" 'Don't move! I've got you covered!' Snapped on the hall light. When I saw you two blinking and staring like owls, you could have knocked me over with a toothpick. That's the end of my installment of the serial. Now, perhaps you'll explain why you were prowling round this house?"

With her arms in the big green mandarin sleeves crossed on the white porcelain table, her eyes deep shining pools of excitement, Brooke leaned forward and told him. Stewart's lips and cheeks puffed and deflated at second intervals as he listened. She concluded:

"I've brought my installment to a crashing finale with your line, 'Don't move! I've got you covered!' Where do we go from here, Jed? Put your master-mind at work on it, Sam."

"Are you sure that there was white on the Bath Crystal Bandit's face?"

"I'm sure that the face of the man who streaked through my rooms was covered with something. Was it soap lather? I'll never forget his wicked eyes, probably the whiteness below them intensified the effect. I can't swear that he was the person whose shoe Jed saw vanish." A suspicion gave her pause. Perhaps the man had moved the silver from Mark Trent's attic! Perhaps he had felt hot and grimy. Silly, would he dare move it a bright night like this? If he had, would he stop for a shower?

"It gives me the creeps to think what he might have done with that razor," she said aloud.

Sam administered an affectionate pat.

"Hey, cool off, gal. 'What the eye doth not see the heart doth not grieve over.' If I had your imagination I'd be the world's leading dramatist — and how! Jed, it looks to me as if the guy had been there to lift something, but why the shower, why the shave? Listen, folks! Footsteps! Stealthy! Outside! Who's coming?"

Jed Stewart sprang up. He caught his chair before it could crash, and swung it experimentally as Sam pressed the light switch and plunged the room into ghostly gloom.

The back door opened softly. Brooke held her throat tight in one hand to stifle an exclamation. A blast of cold air swept in. Someone came with it. She could see a dim shape, could hear labored breathing as if the person had been running. Had the Bath Crystal Bandit returned?

The light flashed on. She closed her eyes. Opened them. Was that Henri, Henri standing in the middle of the floor, with the blinking green parrot making queer noises under his arm, or was this more nightmare? She was awake. Sam was real, as he stood with his finger on the switch. Jed Stewart was real, as he puffed his lips in time to the swing of the chair he clutched. Henri's ghastly face, distended

eyes, and the savage invectives which grit-
ted through his chattering teeth, were real.

"Cut that line!" Sam took a step toward
the butler. "You should appreciate this
little surprise party instead of acting as if
you'd stepped into a nest of scorpions. It
wasn't but a couple of hours ago I saw you
in this very kitchen dressed — or un-
dressed — for bed. Why did you go out?
Go back to your entrance and take it over,
Henri. Come in as if you were pleased
purple to see us. Why are you skulking into
the house? That's your cue."

Henri made a desperate attempt to
steady his quivering mouth. He looked like
an innocent prisoner hailed before an accusing judge; his expression was incredibly
grieved as he huddled the parrot under his
arm and twisted his soft hat in one hand.
He appealed to Brooke.

"I don't know why your brother should
speak to me as if I was a criminal, Miss.
Haven't I the right to go out at night, even
if I had started for bed?" He attempted to
inject the virus of defiance into his uneven
voice.

"Of course you have, Henri, but the
papers are so full of burglaries and hold-
ups that when we heard you stealing in we
didn't know but what it was our turn.

Where did you find Mr. Micawber?"

"That's why I went out, Miss. Couldn't go to sleep, had him on my mind. Queer where I found him. Everything's queer to-night." Henri shuddered. "Nothing strange has been happening in this house, has it?"

"Nothing at all, Henri, nothing at all," Sam assured quickly. "We sat up talking and got hungry again."

"I'm glad of that, Mr. Sam, that nothing strange happened, I mean, because I — I found things terrible wrong outside."

"Wrong!" Not until she felt Sam's foot on hers was Brooke conscious of her explosive exclamation. She noticed that the butler's long cruel fingers shook as he passed them over his slack mouth.

"I don't wonder you're upset, Miss; you'll be more so when you hear that the old madame's limousine is gone."

"Gone where?" Sam demanded.

Henri shrugged thin sloping shoulders. "That's what I asked myself when I opened the garage door and the big car wasn't there."

"Why did you go to the garage at this time of night?"

"Well, you see, Mr. Stewart, I couldn't settle down. I'd had the parrot on my mind while I was at the movies. I kept thinking how worried the old madame would be if she knew he was out in the cold. 'Twas my fault he got away. And after I went upstairs I got more anxious, so I dressed and went out. I ran around under the trees calling him. When I got to our garage I had a hunch to look in. Then I saw that the limousine had been taken. Queer, ever since the old madame left us, I've had a feeling that something wasn't quite right, and when Mr. Mark came down and opened the Other House, I was sure he felt so too." The man's voice was steadier, his face was not so livid.

"Felt what? What are you insinuating?"

It was Brooke's turn, and she ground a heel into Sam's foot with a force which made him flinch. Henri must be encouraged to talk, no matter what he said. Had the man who had flitted through her rooms and gone out the studio window, driven off the limousine? Had he been Henri's tool, had he listened to the clink of the cadaverous-eyed butler's pieces of silver, and was this Henri's method of dragging a red herring across his own trail? Had the Bath Crystal Bandit double-crossed him? She prodded:

"Go on with your story, Henri. What did you do after you discovered that Mrs.

Dane's car was missing?"

"I ran to the Other House — you'll excuse me, Miss, for going to Mr. Mark first; I've always thought of him as being the heir, you see."

"Don't apologize, Henri."

"I wasn't apologizing, Mr. Sam. I was just explaining."

Brooke bit back a smile. Henri had caught Lucette's very inflection when she responded to her brother's teasing.

"Don't stop even to explain, Henri. Can't you see that we are frightfully excited? Perhaps something more than the car has been stolen. Did you find Mr. Trent?"

"No, Miss, and there's something queer there too. That Jap, Kowa, came rushing to the door when I kept my finger on the bell, and he shouts:

" 'Where's my boss? I been over house, one, two, t'ree time. Boss gone! He been kidnaped, I t'ink! Loud noise, Mr. Jed's room. I run there quick. Green parrot in bathtub, swearing fine.'

"I ran upstairs for the parrot, thinking the Jap had a bad scare on and I'd see Mr. Mark somewhere. But I didn't. The Jap and I looked everywhere but he was not there."

Tense silence in the white and green kitchen. Chilled and exhausted by his foray into the outside world, the parrot huddled within the curve of Henri's arm making sounds in his throat like a tribal dialect. The faint scent of bacon lingered in the stillness, a stillness haunted by tragic conjectures and possibilities which turned Brooke's blood to ice. Sam laughed from sheer nervous tension. Jed Stewart lashed at him furiously:

"You would do that! It's all theatre to you Reyburns, isn't it, and side-splitting theatre at that. Where's Mark? That's the only thing I want to know. Where's Mark?"

"Present."

Mark Trent answered from the doorway. Brooke's heart stopped, raced on. What had made that deep welt across his forehead? His face was colorless. Had a ghost appeared it couldn't have produced a more paralyzing effect. Jed Stewart's face was darkly red as he stared at his friend. Sam's brow was furrowed as if he were appraising the substance, the color, the theatrical value of the situation; the green parrot blinked lidless eyes; Henri's thin quavery voice broke the spell.

"Have you been hunting for the parrot too, Mr. Mark?"

Mark Trent's hand was unsteady as he held a lighter to his cigarette. His eyes reflected the flame as he looked at the butler.

"Not for the parrot, Henri. I'm hunting now for the man who killed Mrs. Hunt."

XIV

Mark Trent flinched as he approached the white cottage. It seemed days since he had driven away from this very house in the limousine filled with his aunt's silver; days since the message had come to Cassidy's garage from the police that Mrs. Hunt was dead and he had left there in a flivver with Mike at the wheel. They had stopped at Lookout House to make sure that the Reyburns were safe before they had burned up the road to get here. But it hadn't been days, not much more than an hour had passed. No use waiting, he must go in.

With his hand on the knob of the door, his mind came to a jangling halt as from somewhere near a blood-curdling howl rose to a piercing wail, broke, quavered away.

He stood transfixed, powerless, too numbed by horror to move. In the stillness which followed the frightful sound, he could hear the rustle of unseen things in the shrubs, hear the thump of his heart. He looked up at the stars. Silent, immutable, they shone steadily as they had shone for thousands of years. What was a hound's howl to them? What was the snuffing out of a woman's life?

He drew a long ragged breath, forced his motor nerves into action, and with icy fingers turned the knob.

As he entered a small living-room, Inspector Harrison was kneeling by the fireplace. His piercing eyes glittered as he looked up and nodded to Mark.

"They got her all right."

Mark Trent stepped forward, blindly for an instant. He sunk his teeth deep in his lips to steady them before he looked down.

Lola, the woman who had been his wife, lay on the floor. She was dressed for the street — had she been about to drive away the limousine full of silver? The question flashed through his mind only to be instantly submerged in a flood of pity. She looked so young, so shabby, so helpless. Her shabbiness hurt him most, she had been so exquisite. He was glad that he had made her that allowance. Her hat had fallen off. A current of air stirred a lock of her dark hair. Her hands were still now. One gripped an open bag, the fingers of the other were bruised. He dropped to his knee beside the Inspector.

"Can't something be done? Can't we

move her to a couch?"

"No! No, not until the coroner comes."

"What happened?"

"They got her rings. She had rings, hadn't she?"

"She had when I saw her — a few days ago. Valuable rings. Other jewels too."

"Then I guess we got the motive. She let you down, boy, but it's tough for you just the same."

Motive! Had robbery been the motive, or had Lola been mixed up with the crooked gang which had stolen the silver? Had he told Bill Harrison at once of the loot in the limousine, would Lola be alive? As he knelt beside her, Mark looked about the room in which she had been living. The furniture was cheap. The linoleum rug on which she lay was blocked with garish colors on a glaring shiny white ground. What a setting for a woman who had loved luxury!

"Better come away, boy, you can't do anything," Inspector Harrison suggested in his persuasive voice. He crossed the room. His solid, resourceful personality steadied Mark. He got to his feet and stood straight and tall and rigid. He frowned down at the still figure on the rug as he acknowledged:

"Life hasn't seemed as smooth as a trotting park to me to date, Bill, but tonight it seems a terrifying, horrible thing."

"I know, boy, I know. Bring her in, Tim." The Inspector spoke to the policeman with ears like clinging bats, who appeared at the door.

"It's the Cassidy girl," he explained to Mark. "Kinder tough to bring her into this room, but there don't seem to be any other place. We've waited till her father got here before questioning her. Mike's a grand fella and me friend since we were lads together. Here you are, Maggie!"

The hint of joviality in his soft voice missed its mark, for the sixteen year old girl, who entered the room as if dragged by unseen hands, regarded him with terrified Irish blue eyes. Her curly auburn hair made her egg-shaped face seem bloodless in contrast. She was shivering uncontrollably as she gripped her father's arm with one hand and crushed the front of her blue and white print dress with the other.

The Inspector placed a chair with its back to the still figure on the floor.

"Sit here, Maggie."

As she sat down, Mike Cassidy laid his heavy ham-bone hand on her shoulder. The Inspector cleared his throat.

"Now, don't be frightened, Maggie.

Ain't I just the same Bill Harrison who's been chumming round with your dad ever since you was a little girl, and ain't I got kids of my own? All you got to do is to tell me what happened in this house tonight."

"I don't know what happened," the girl answered in a strained whisper. She glanced furtively over her shoulder. The Inspector tapped her arm.

"Keep looking at me. Don't look behind you. Sure, I'm not handsome, but you keep your eyes on me, Maggie. Tell us what you heard that brought you downstairs tonight. You're not afraid of Bill Harrison, are you? Ain't you stuck out your tongue at me plenty of times when I've told you to quit hanging on trucks?"

The Inspector's soft persuasiveness warmed even Mark's cold heart as he stood with hands thrust into his coat pockets. It reassured the girl for her body stopped shaking and her lips parted in a trembly smile. Her voice was almost normal as she agreed:

"Course, I ain't afraid of you, Inspector. I'll tell what I know. I sleep in the attic, it's got a dormer back and front. I was dead beat when I went to bed, what with the housework an' havin' to run out to fill tanks. The boss was sick till afternoon an' —"

"Drunk, wasn't he? Tell it straight, Maggie."

"All right, Inspector, he was. I don't know what time it was when I was woke up by a car stopping at the garage; sounded like a classy car. We don't have much late trade — an' the boss told me today that the crowned heads here, that's what he said, 'crowned heads,' had put him out of business — so I got up and looked out to see what 'twas all about. I can see into the garage from my back window."

"Check up on that, Tim."

"Yes, Inspector." The policeman with the ears vanished into the hall.

"Go on, Maggie. You looked down and then what?"

"I see a swell dressed fella talking to the boss. I couldn't see his face 'cause his hat was pulled low; you know, the kind you see in the classy ads."

"Could you hear what they were saying?"

"No. That window was closed. I open the front one in cold weather, an', gee, has it been cold in that attic!"

"What did you do next?"

"Went back to bed, Inspector." The girl's voice had cleared. Rising excitement was driving out fear. "I must have gone to sleep

again for the next thing I knew I was sittin'
up straight in bed calling out:

" 'Who's shootin'?'

"I switched on the light and ran to the
front window, and I saw a big car going
lickety-split down the road."

The policeman appeared at the door.

"Okay 'bout the back window and
garage, Inspector."

"All right, Tim. Stay where you are.
What next, Maggie?"

"I stood looking out a minute, thinking
that the big car must have back-fired an'
what a hick I was to think the sound was
shootin' when I'd grown up in a garage, an'
then I had a kinder creepy feeling; you
know, the kind when they say a rabbit's
walkin' over your grave —"

"Don't shiver, Maggie, there won't be
nothing walking over your grave for years
yet; don't the papers say we're all going to
live to be a hundred — barring accidents?
Then what?"

"Then I began to wonder what that big
car was doing out here in the middle of the
night, and then I began to think of hi-jack-
ers an' kidnapers an' bandits till I thought
I'd scream, an' then I remembered Mrs.
Hunt's rings an' jewelry — she had classy
jewelry."

The girl's voice had risen till the last word was shrill with excitement.

Mike Cassidy patted his daughter's shoulder.

"Take it easy, Maggie. Tell the Inspector the rest that happened; then I'll take you home to your Ma. Won't I, Bill?"

"Sure, Mike, sure. What did you do after you thought of Mrs. Hunt's di'monds, Maggie?"

"I stuck my feet in slippers an' pulled on my blanket wrapper. I beat it downstairs an' come into this room. It was lighted an' she — she was lying there — just like she is now an' — an' — oh, gee!"

The girl drew a long shuddering breath and covered her face with shaking hands. Her father patted her shoulder; the policeman at the door shifted his feet; the Inspector frowned at his fingers. Mark Trent felt as if the hard throb of his heart must be audible, the room was so still. Bill Harrison was shattering all his preconceived ideas of the police force, he was showing infinite tact, infinite patience in getting the girl's story.

"We're almost through, Maggie," the Inspector encouraged. "You liked Mrs. Hunt, didn't you? You want us to find out who took her rings, don't you?"

"Sure, I liked her all right, but not as much as I liked the boss. Mister Hunt was one grand guy when he was sober, always kinder joshing her an' friendly like when she was whiny — an' she was whiny most of the time — an' saying awful sweet things to her an' what he'd do for her when his ship come in. Sober or not, he always treated me as if I was a lady."

"Glad to hear you liked your boss, Maggie. What did you do when you came into this room and saw —"

"I guess I let out a yell first; then I just flopped to my knees beside her. I didn't touch nothing though; I learned that in the movies. When I saw she wasn't breathin' I beat it to the garage, an' I know I yelled then for the boss was on the floor face down, his hands behind him, an' his feet tied. I grabbed his shoulder an' turned him over. There was a big bump on his forehead and his eyes were closed. I shook him. When he didn't say nothing, I rushed to the phone and called Pop. I guess you know the rest." Her lips quivered, and for the first time her eyes filled with tears. The Inspector patted her shoulder. "Good girl, Maggie, just one more question and you can go. Did you hear any rowing between the boss and herself lately?"

"He was awful nice to her."

"Sure, Maggie, but even folks who think a lot of each other — take your Pa and Ma now —" he winked at Cassidy — "have a cat and parrot fight sometimes, don't they? You know they do. So Mr. and Mrs. had had a quarrel, had they? What about?"

The girl twisted her print dress in unsteady fingers.

"It was last evening, late — it's tomorrow now, isn't it? An' she'd been phoning — I was in the kitchen, you can hear plain in this house — an' I heard him say loud:

" 'What's this about a paper?'

"I couldn't hear what she said, but he kinder shouted:

" 'I didn't mind starting this joint to gouge money out of Trent, but what you're planning now is different. It'll be jail for us if we —' The door closed hard an' I didn't hear any more."

"All right, Maggie. Make a cup of strong tea for her in the kitchen, Mike; then take her home." Mike Cassidy put his arm about his daughter as they left the room. Mark Trent watched them out of sight.

"My hat's off to you, Inspector. That girl told you everything she knew without being frightened into it."

The Inspector's eagle eyes retreated into bony caverns.

"My boy, 'bout two thousand years ago a Man laid down a rule for living that I ain't never heard improved on. I've got a girl of my own, and all the time I was questioning Maggie I was thinking how I would feel if my daughter'd been mixed up in this mess. Has Hunt come to?" he demanded of an officer who entered. The steel was back in his voice.

"Yes, Inspector, but he's groggy."

"I'll go to the garage. Will you come along, Mark? Cripes, I never can remember to call you Mr. Trent."

"Why should you? Didn't you hand me my first and only summons for speeding? I'll go with you, but you won't leave —" he glanced at the still figure on the floor.

"Tim will stay. The coroner ought to be here any minute now. Come on. I'd like to have you hear what Hunt has to say. According to my church, you are the woman's husband."

The garage was lighted by one glaring bulb, littered with tools and cans; the floor was patched with oil stains, and the air was strong of gas. On a pile of old tires, a man was braced upright against the rough cement wall. He was blond and must have been fine looking before life and dissipation had done cruel things to his face. He opened his eyes as the Inspector spoke to him. He tried to smile.

"Another dick? Maggie sure called out the whole police force. 'Twasn't necessary. I'll be all right in a minute."

Didn't the man know what had happened in the house, or was he acting, Mark asked himself. The Inspector rolled an empty gas can on its side and sat down.

"Course you'll be all right. As for Maggie calling out the force, she got an awful jolt coming out here an' finding you all tied up like a bundle of old clothes."

Hunt put an unsteady hand to his head.

"Why did the girl come out here at this time of night? She's never done it before." His eyes narrowed. He clenched his hand. "What are you doing here, Trent? You can't get Lola back!"

"Take it easy, Hunt, take it easy. Mr. Trent was with me in Cassidy's garage — I'm Inspector Harrison, in case you don't know — when his daughter phoned that you were hurt. He came along to help. What happened to you, Hunt?"

"Someone beat me up, you can see that, can't you? I was working late, I — I hadn't been feeling well all day and I was making up time, when a man drove up in a roadster and said he had a punctured tire and could I put on a spare. I said, 'Sure, I guess there's no law against my doing that if the old tabbies here won't let me sell gas.' I turned to get my tools, and that's the last I knew until I looked up to see an officer bending over me."

"Who was the man?"

"I don't know, Inspector."

"Ever see him before?"

"No."

"Sure?"

"Sure."

"Go on," prodded the Inspector.

"Nothing to go on about. I was blackjacked. I thought the man took a crack at my head, but my feet feel as if they were in iron casts."

"Probably those ropes stopped the circulation. Were you —"

Mark didn't hear the rest of the Inspector's question. His eyes were on Hunt's right foot. Between the upper and sole of the unlaced shoe was a faint line of red.

XV

From behind the tea-table in the living-room at Lookout House, Brooke Reyburn watched the sun fling the earth a spectacular good-night. The western sky was a field of crimson and gold glory. The water in the land-locked harbor was a sheet of flame. The snowy roofs of distant houses blushed rosily under the warm regard of the Orb of Day, and every pane of glass within its radius gleamed like polished brass. Dusk was spreading a silver-gray veil, fine as a bride's tulle, between her eyes and the sunset. She said impulsively:

"Look out of the window, Mrs. Gregory! I had forgotten that there was so much beauty in the world."

Mrs. Gregory, in a chair beside the crackling birch fire, set down her cup.

"It would take an Inness to paint that sunset. I can't believe that you would ever forget beauty. You've lost flesh in these last two weeks, Brooke."

"Is it only two weeks since the tragedy at the filling station? When, last October, I told Jerry Field that I was coming to Lookout House to live, he said:

" 'What will you do marooned on a rocky point of land in a place where the residents dig in and nothing ever happens?' "

"He can't say that nothing ever happens here now. The days have flown and have left behind them hours smeared with police questioning; men swarming over this house for finger-prints; newspaper front pages shrieking clues which were corrected in the next issue; skating and lots of it; poinsettias in place of chrysanthemums in the conservatory in honor of Christmas. It was such a strange Christmas without Mother, and with Sam absorbed in the production of the play. Now New Year's has slipped into the limbo of yesterdays, and in forty-eight hours the curtain will ring up on 'Islands Arise.' "

"I'll be glad when it's over. Your eyes seem tired, Brooke."

"Do you wonder? They have looked at the scum and dregs of the underworld, at pictures in rogue galleries, at line-ups, at patients in hospitals, trying to identify the man who ran through my room."

"I heard that the police were sure that Hunt was the man when red paint was found on his shoe."

"The trouble with that clue was that it

wasn't his shoe. When he first regained consciousness in the garage, he complained that his feet felt as if they were in iron casts. Then the police with their steam-shovel methods hurried him into the living room of the white cottage. When he saw what lay on the floor he collapsed. After he was taken to the hospital — he's still in a coma — his shoes had to be cut off. Then it was found that they were a size smaller than his at the cottage. The man whom the Cassidy girl saw in the garage must have changed and taken Hunt's shoes. He was a quick worker."

"Bill Harrison may be smart, but what has he done toward clearing up this tragedy? Nothing."

"He wants the case to drop out of the headlines. He says that the guilty parties will then think that the hunt for them is cooling off."

"I wish they'd put me on the force, I'd show them a thing or two." The brim of Mrs. Gregory's large hat flopped in unison with the thump of her cane. "I'm not afraid of bandits. I've ordered some of my jewels from the bank to wear to Sam's play."

"Oh, Mrs. Gregory! Is it safe?"

"Safe! Do you think I'll be frightened

out of wearing what I like? Besides, lightning never strikes in the same place twice. Lucky the performance is coming off soon; everybody is getting edgy."

"We'll relax tonight. Mark Trent is giving the Fields and Reyburns a party in town at that new Supper Club. It was planned for two weeks ago but it was postponed. It seems a century since I have been to a real party."

"Mark needs a change of thought too. It's an ill wind that blows nobody good. Lola is out of his life, thank heaven. The way she went is one of two logical conclusions to the rig she has run and perhaps this one is the less tragic. I've always felt a twinge of guilty responsibility about his marriage to her. If some of us older people hadn't banded together to run her out of town, Mark wouldn't have rushed in to champion her. He was young and chivalrous and hot-headed. I seem to be in a chronic state of regret about that boy. Much as I love you, Brooke, I'll never forgive myself for signing my name as witness to Mary Amanda Dane's will which cut him off."

Brooke's mind whirled and steadied. Mrs. Gregory's signature was not on the will which had been probated; she had made sure of that again recently. Perhaps the one to which she referred had been drawn earlier.

"How could you know what you were signing? Witnesses are not supposed to see the contents of a will, are they? When did you witness it?"

Brooke asked the question quickly. She must know and get the uncertainty off her mind.

"Just a week before Mary Amanda died. Perhaps you remember the day. You drove in just as I went out and — good heavens, I forgot! I promised Jed Stewart that I wouldn't mention it. Forget I told you, Brooke. It wasn't very tactful of me anyway, but when was I ever tactful? I like that rust-color gown on you. Now I suppose every would-be smart woman in town will appear with one like it. One Sunday at church you wore violets at the neck of your dress and that week every female in the place wore violets. You have a flair for clothes. It's a wonder you haven't tried to make me over."

Even as Brooke answered that she didn't need making over, she was wondering why Jed Stewart had asked Mrs. Gregory not to mention her signature; wondering if he suspected dishonesty? Why wonder?

Hadn't she been sure for weeks that the two men in Mark Trent's house were there for some other reason than sheer love of a New England village in winter?

The thump of Mrs. Gregory's cane brought her mind to attention.

"I've asked you twice, Brooke, if you thought Sam liked Daphne Field."

"He likes her, Mrs. Gregory, but Sam won't allow himself to go sentimental over anyone at present."

"Allow himself! Then he isn't in love. We may be living in a profoundly changing society, but love hasn't changed. It still strikes like lightning, burns, and if it's the real thing, settles into a steady flame. But I'm glad he doesn't care for the Field girl."

"I'm sure he doesn't, Mrs. Gregory."

"I knew that boy had sense. She's no helpmeet. She's one of those moody by day and twinkly by night creatures. They say that tomorrow is in the hands of youth. Some of the hands — notably the Daphne Field type — seem tragically inadequate. So many of the young talking the same rubbish, so many of them incapable of enduring struggle and disillusion, so many of them running to Reno at the first obstacle in the matrimonial path. Well, whatever they do, I hope they'll cut out some of the rancor and narrowness and animosities which inhibited my generation. They've begun by turning under the silly idea of exclusiveness; it's what a person is that counts now, not the family behind him, nor his money."

She rose and drew her sable cape about her shoulders. "If you are going to town tonight you ought to be dressing. What are you wearing?"

"An adorable silver frock. It does things to my hair, brings out the copper glints in it."

Mrs. Gregory lingered on the threshold. "Be nice to Mark, Brooke. He's a wonderful boy, don't you think so?"

"I'd hardly call him a boy — he's too dictator-minded, but that's the trend. *Chacun à son goût* — I've joined a French class — I prefer Jerry Field's type."

Mrs. Gregory expressed her reaction by a denatured snort.

"You prefer Jerry Field! I'd like to take you over my knee and spank sense into you! Good-night!"

Brooke laughed.

"Good-night, Mrs. Gregory. Even if you don't approve of me, I hope you'll come again soon."

She was still smiling as she returned to the living-room window for a last lingering look at the colorful west. The sun had left a rosy glow on the horizon. Above it a wash of crocus yellow blended with the blue sky to make a young leaf green. High up floated clouds of mauve and gold and crimson, like tattered banners flung to the breeze. She crossed to the window which faced the ocean. How she loved it, loved its ever-changing values. Some days there were only blues, all tints and shades; sometimes just green with nothing else but sparkle; and sometimes it was a study in gray, sullen and menacing with not a suggestion of color.

She pressed a wall button and set softly shaded lamps glowing like huge illuminated flowers; the light turned to velvet the scarlet petals and green leaves of the poinsettias in the conservatory. She poked the fire till the logs stuck out saucy orange and blue and crimson tongues.

"It is unbelievable that all this comfort really is mine," she told herself. "Only a year ago, Brooke Reyburn, you were driving a shabby sedan and counting every penny and —"

Memory slashed into her self-congratulation. Mrs. Gregory had witnessed a will a week before Mrs. Dane had died. Where was it? Should she go to Jed Stewart at once and tell him what she had heard? But he knew. He had asked Mrs. Gregory to say nothing about it. Why hadn't he told her? What did it all mean? It gave her a panicky feeling, as if she were wandering blindly in the dark on the edge of a precipice. She poked the fire vigorously. It was a physical outlet to her turmoil of mind.

"Take care, Miss, or you'll set the chimney afire," Henri warned from the threshold.

"I think not. It was thoroughly cleaned when I came here to live."

Why was he puttering? He was drawing the hangings over the windows, pulling a rug in place, refolding the morning newspaper on the desk, fussing about the parrot's cage, a parrot who had lost half of his tail and all his self-assurance since his excursion into the outer world. Mr. Micawber sulked and dozed most of the time, like an old person who had lost the desire to live. Was Henri making an opportunity to ask a favor? Except to give orders, she had not talked with him since the night the police had removed him from Lookout House kitchen for questioning.

He cleared his throat and drew long

bony fingers over his slack mouth.

"I — I've been wanting a chance to talk with you since — since we — we found the parrot, Miss."

He was avoiding mention of the tragedy at the filling station. Why? Hadn't that occurred the night Mr. Micawber had taken an evening out? Were Henri and Clotilde preparing to leave? She wouldn't cry over that. They would have to give a week's notice and that would keep them here until after the production of Sam's play. Nothing must stop that. It would make a hit, it was bound to, there was not a dull moment in it, no play with dull moments could survive. The foundation of his career as a playwright would be laid. She pulled her thoughts, which had begun to climb the ladder of golden possibilities, back to earth. Henri would think she was wool gathering instead of play-royalty gathering. She asked:

"What have you to say to me?"

He drew his fingers across his mouth. "It's about that — what happened at the filling station. You know I went to the movies that evening, came home and went to bed. Miss Lucette and the others saw me when I came down to find out what the noise was I heard. You know that after that

I dressed and went out to hunt for the parrot, that I brought him in with me, but the police want to check up on me every minute. You can help me very much, Miss."

"How?"

"By swearing that I was in this house at the time of the — the robbery at the filling station."

"But, as I remember it, you weren't, Henri. You said that you were hunting for the parrot."

The butler emitted a sound like the snarl of a savage beast at bay.

"You'd better say I was, Miss, or — or I'll tell how I found this in your desk." He drew a folded paper from his pocket.

Brooke felt as if all the blood in her body had crowded into her heart, as if her head were lighter than air. She laid her hand on the back of a gay chintz chair. She bit her lips hard. Why should that paper in the man's hand seem an ugly, menacing thing? As if flashed on a screen, his threat sprang into her mind:

"You'd better like Clotilde and me. We could put you out of this house if we wanted to."

She said:

"Mr. Sam has overlooked grand dramatic material right here, Henri. You would steal the show as the villain in his comedy. Just what is 'this'?" Her voice was tinged with amused unbelief.

"Take it, Miss."

Brooke thought of the fangs of a wolf as he smiled his secretive smile. She unfolded the paper and noticed that a tiny corner of the sheet was missing. Mary Amanda Dane's writing! Mrs. Gregory's signature! Henri's. Clotilde's. Was it the will of which Mrs. Gregory had spoken only a few moments ago? How had it come in Henri's possession?

"You say you found this in my desk?"

The butler's greedy eyes glittered like black beads. "Yes, Miss. I'm prepared to swear to that in court unless we can come to terms."

"Why didn't you take it directly to Mr. Trent or Mr. Stewart?" Was her voice as icy as her body felt?

"I thought it was too bad to do that until I found out if you and I couldn't work together. Mr. Mark tried to get me in wrong with the old madame." Hatred flamed in his eyes and voice. "Why should I help him?"

"Will this — this — help him?"

"Read it, Miss."

"I'll wait until I'm alone. The paper is torn. Did you tear it when you — pulled it from my desk?"

Henri's teeth showed between suddenly pallid lips.

"I — I — didn't pull it, Miss. I — I took it careful."

The last word was a whisper. What was there about a torn corner of a sheet of paper to terrify him?

"I'll talk with you about it later, Henri; perhaps — perhaps, as you suggest, we may be able to work together."

"I thought you might see it that way, Miss, but — don't take too long." There was a threat in his smug voice.

"If it is so valuable, how do you dare leave it with me? Perhaps you have a photostat copy?"

He made a Gallic gesture. Curious how the French came out in crises, Brooke thought in the midst of her mental turmoil.

"I don't need a copy. With me and Clotilde testifying that we witnessed a paper in this house a week before the old madame died — and with Mrs. Gregory swearing she did too — and me telling where I saw it next, you won't dare do much to it, will you, Miss?"

XVI

Brooke stood rigid, listening until she heard the door to the china closet swing. Curious how she had come to know every sound in this house which had been hers for so short a time. Hers! Was it hers? What was in the paper which Henri would swear he had found in her desk? She had pretended to consider his proposition that they work together merely to get time to decide what she should do. When Inspector Harrison had questioned her about the man who had slipped through her room, he had impressed upon her also the necessity of making Henri and his wife feel that they were not suspected of a hand in the filling station hold-up.

She raced up the stairs, switched on the light in her boudoir, locked the door behind her. She leaned against it. If only her heart would stop pounding. What a silly she was to be taken in for an instant by Henri's lies. He never had liked her. The feeling had been mutual. Hadn't she loathed his Uriah Heep personality and his fat wife? As if he could get hold of Mrs.

Dane's will! Wouldn't she have sent it to her lawyer? But there had been another will. Mrs. Gregory had said so. She had said also that Jed Stewart knew of it. Why, why was she backed against the door thinking, fearing, instead of finding out what it was all about?

She spread out the paper on her desk, shut her eyes hard, drew a long breath before she looked. There was not much on the page, but what there was, was in Mrs. Dane's fine writing. The date was that of a week before she died. The words burned into Brooke's mind as if written with a red-hot poker:

"I don't know how to word a formal will, but I hereby give and bequeath all my property real and personal, — which I left in a previous will to Brooke Reyburn — except the amount as stated in said will to be given to my faithful servants, Henri and Clotilde Jacques, to my nephew Mark Trent, to have and to hold during his life and to dispose of as he wishes. I know now that my ideas of right and wrong should not deprive him of his rightful inheritance. He was a wonderful son. He has been a devoted nephew. I make him sole executor without bonds of my estate. I ask him to provide an income sufficient for frills and fun for my dear young friend, Brooke Reyburn."

Brooke studied the signature. Mary Amanda Dane's without a doubt, unless it was a clever forgery, Anne Gregory's name sprawling under it, and Henri's and Clotilde's tight, foreign writing.

Elbows on the desk, chin in her palms, she stared down at the document. Life was curious. A woman's signature had dropped a fortune into her lap; another turn of her wrist, another writing of her name, and the scene was shifted: Brooke Reyburn was given her cue for an exit; she and Lucette and Sam would walk off stage together.

Suppose she destroyed this paper which would deprive her of a fortune? A lighted match under it and it would go up in smoke. Who would know? Who would believe Henri against her? Wasn't he already under suspicion in the filling station hold-up? Suppose he did try blackmail? He wouldn't get far with it.

What terrible thing was she thinking? The eyes of the white faced girl who stared back at her from the mirror were big with horror. Was she two persons? Had her other self turned craven? Had that thought changed her face? For an instant she had been a criminal at heart. She, Brooke

Reyburn, who considered her personal standards of honor and decency of the highest. After this she would understand temptation as she never had understood it before.

A car! Lucette and Sam. She must hurry and dress. Sometime during the evening she would give the paper to Mark Trent. That would be her answer to Henri. Where could she put it meanwhile? She would tuck it inside her frock.

She was fastening the corsage of green orchids Mark Trent had sent her to the front of her gleaming silver frock when she met her brown eyes in the mirror. She dropped the flowers as if they had burned her fingers. She couldn't wear his gift until she was sure that he believed that she had not known until this evening of his aunt's change of mind. Why hadn't he come directly to her when he had heard Mrs. Gregory's story? Because he believed she knew where the will was, that she was dishonest, that was why. Perhaps he was right. What would he think of her if he suspected that for a split second she had thought of burning it?

She would wear Jerry's gardenias; she had chosen Mark the Magnificent's orchids first, simply because he was her host, she assured herself.

She added more color to her white cheeks, to her lips, dusted her face with powder, anything to switch her mind from that nightmare instant of terrifying suggestion.

She waited until she heard her brother's and her sister's doors close before she opened hers. Sam popped his head out and called:

"White tie tonight, Brooke?"

"Of course, Sam. Our promising young playwright must be swanky. I've had your top hat ironed and there's a gardenia in a box on your dresser."

She heard his groan of resignation as she started down the stairs.

She stopped on the threshold of the living-room she loved. Now it would be torn up by the roots, all her father's treasures would go back to storage. And her gorgeous flower-windows would be but a dream.

"What of it?" she asked herself. "You're not the only person whose fortune has started down the toboggan slide these last few years."

She turned on the radio; that might help steady her mind which had gone merry-go-round. A man's "golden voice" sang tenderly:

" 'Won't you come over to my house
And play that you're my little girl?' "

A foolish little song but it quieted her
throbbing pulses. She crossed her arms on
the mantel, rested her forehead on them,
and gazed unseeingly down at the flames,
wondering what she would do when she
left Lookout House, resenting it that she
had been given this fragment of ease,
luxury, and security from the menace of
the big, bad wolf of poverty. Now it would
go.

"People are right, there is no Santa
Claus," she confided to the fire. "I feel as if
I had pulled the works of a watch apart
and hadn't an idea how to put them together again."

All that she had which was really her
own was five hundred dollars in the bank
she had saved while working. Would she be
obliged to return the money she had spent?
That would mean dragging a ball and
chain of debt the rest of her life. Cheerful
prospect. Could Mary Amanda Dane's
"little friend, Brooke Reyburn," see herself
accepting from Mark the Magnificent an
income sufficient for "frills and fun"?
Never. She would have to hunt for a job.
But she wouldn't have to hunt — she

wouldn't! The Palm Beach offer! Had the position been filled? She would send a night letter. Better do it now before Sam and Lucette came down.

As she waited for the telephone call to go through, she told herself that she had learned one inestimable lesson: she had learned that for every person the gateway to success was in himself; that achievement was a matter of keeping on keeping on, of giving one's best and trying, everlastingly trying to make that best better. She was returning to business equipped with that knowledge.

She gave her message and turned to the fire. She didn't really mind going back to work, she had loved it, but she had planned to do so much for her mother, for Lucette, for Sam.

Sam! Nothing must happen to distract his mind from the production of the play. If she were to produce that will now, the neighborhood, to say nothing of the cast, would palpitate with excitement, the Reyburns would have to leave Lookout House at once. She knew nothing of law except that it was as relentless as a juggernaut. What the Court decreed had to be done. A producer from New York was coming to see Sam's comedy. The Boston manager wouldn't bring him down unless he thought Sam had talent. The performance was only forty-eight hours away. Could she keep Henri quiet until then? If she couldn't she was the world's worst actress, and Sam had said that she was good. After the play Mark Trent was to keep open house for cast and audience. She would stay until the last guest had departed, then she would give this will, burning against her skin, to him and fade gracefully from the picture. Better lock it up in her desk until then. It wouldn't be safe to carry it around with her.

As she ran up the stairs to her boudoir she planned. Stealthily, during the next two days, she would pack up the personal belongings of the family. She would engage the women who had helped her open the house to come and clean it thoroughly and close it. She would ask Mark Trent if the furnishings might stay where they were until her mother's return from England. She hated to ask even that favor but she would have to swallow her pride. She would know tomorrow if the Palm Beach position were still open. Accepting it would mean leaving Lucette in town, but Sam would look after her. She must begin to earn, pronto.

She locked the paper in an inside drawer of her desk and slipped the key into her bag of silver sequins. Back in the living-room she looked at the portrait above the mantel. Said very low:

"This all means that you and I will be on the move again. On the move, but with banners, Duchess! With banners!" She threw a kiss to the woman in green satin and emeralds who looked back at her gravely.

"Hey, Brooke, what are you mumbling about? This crime wave hasn't struck in on your little brain, has it?" Sam demanded anxiously from the threshold.

Brooke's laugh sent the elixir of courage surging through her veins. If she could make that sound after the blow she had received, she could impose on Henri for two days. Surprisingly she realized that as the shock wore off, she began to feel as Christian in Pilgrim's Progress must have felt when the load slipped from his shoulders. She knew now that beneath the excitement and joy of using the unexpected fortune had pricked the conviction that the money did not belong to her rightfully, that it was Mark Trent's. The voice in which she answered Sam's question held a tinge of buoyancy.

"My brain is all right. It is doing its sixteen hours a day without a hitch. I was having a heart-to-heart with the Duchess. It's a habit. We are great pals. Sam, you're a knock-out. I adore men in evening clothes. I hope sometime I'll live where they always dress for dinner."

"You're not so grubby yourself in that silver thing. You'd better move in next door, if you want to live with dinner clothes. Trent and Stewart have the habit."

The reference to Mark Trent brought memory flooding back. Brooke quickly changed the subject.

"Have you heard any more particulars about — about what you call the crime wave?"

She perched on the arm of a big chair and looked up at Sam standing with one elbow on the mantel.

"Nope, nothing except the usual lot of wild yarns which roll up like snow-balls at a time like this. Have you ever thought that one of her ex-lovers might have bumped off the fair Lola?"

"Sam! Where did you hear that?"

"Sit down! Sit down! Didn't hear it. That ex-lover motif is a plot, a little thing of my own. It's my conception of what should have occurred to put claws, tearing,

285

digging, ravening claws into the Filling Station Mystery. May use the idea sometime; that's why I asked you to clip all the accounts of the police activities and confessions, if there were any. Have you done it?"

"I have, from every paper I could get hold of. When you want them they are in a Manilla envelope in the lower right-hand drawer of my desk. I haven't said anything to you about it but I was afraid that after what had happened, Mark Trent might feel that he could not go on with the play."

"Afraid! That's putting it mildly. I nearly had heart failure till he assured me that he would keep his part. He'll make 'Islands Arise.' He does more than play the lead, he puts glamour into the comedy and warmth and strength and vitality. I told him he was a fighting lover. He looked queer for a minute; perhaps he was thinking that he didn't put up much of a battle for that wife of his who walked off with the French Count. Why should he change his plans for a woman like that? The shock of the tragedy has practically worn off. Spirits are picking up and by day after tomorrow everyone will be keen to make whoopee, to get the thing out of their minds. Two days! Boy, but I get cold feet when I think of all that night means to me."

He frowned at his younger sister who, in a diaphanous white evening frock sprinkled with gold leaves, appeared in the doorway.

"Lucette, when Jerry Field quotes 'Islands Arise,' look as if he were saying something serious, not as if he were inviting:

" 'How about a little stepping, gal?' "

"I've followed exactly the business in my sides, Master Reyburn."

"Don't apologize."

"I'm not apologizing. I'm explaining."

Brooke laughed and linked her arm within her sister's.

"Attagirl! Sam has caught the dictator germ. We two must stand together against the savage male."

Was that really Brooke Reyburn gaily defying her brother, she asked herself, the same girl who not an hour before had felt her secure, lovely world crashing about her ears?

"You're riding on the top of the world this minute, aren't you, Brooke?" Sam grinned approval, but his brows knit as he looked at Lucette.

"Remember, kiddo, that tomorrow night will be the last rehearsal."

"For which blessing, praise be to Allah!"

"Stop wise-cracking and get this. You've got the habit when you go up stage of stopping at the door and looking back at Trent. Don't hold up your exit. You distract the attention of the people out front from the lead. Just go."

"S'all right by me, Master Reyburn, I'll go. I'm glad you'll be behind tomorrow night at rehearsal, Brooke. If Sam starts to put in a whole new scene, strangle him. He has rewritten the play three times since we began rehearsing."

Sam reddened.

"That isn't true, Lucette, and you know it. I changed one scene, and didn't I make it tremendously more forceful, dramatic, and colorful? Didn't it build to a surprise climax?"

"And how did you get your effect? By slashing at the leading woman till she rushed from the stage in tears."

"Perhaps I was raw, but did you notice what she did with her lines the next night? They were so furiously alive they gripped my throat."

"Treat 'em rough stuff! I'll tell you now, Sam Reyburn, you'll never get me in another play of yours."

"Boy, I won't want you! 'Islands Arise'

will be a smash hit! I'll have the best actors in New York camping on my trail for a chance in it! I'll —" He looked at his sisters watching him with fascinated eyes. Dark color surged to his hair. "I suppose you two girls think I'm a darn fool."

Lucette made a little dash toward him and patted his arm.

"Not a darn fool, but a best-seller, darling. I'll bet publishers will be after you in droves for the printing rights, including the Scandinavian."

"Don't let old inferiority complex get you, Sammy," Brooke warned. "Lucette and I know that this play of yours will be box-office, that it will set your name in lights on Broadway. Can't you just see Mother flying across the ocean — if necessary — for the premiere? We'll all have ravishing costumes and —"

Memory side-tracked her voice. She and Lucette couldn't go to New York for the opening. Suppose she didn't get the Palm Beach job? She would have no money. She shook herself mentally. To dwell on that was to admit defeat, to mismanage her life. She wouldn't permit mismanagement in her life any more than she would in business.

"What an emotional gal you are, Brooke.

You've gone white with excitement over what may never happen. 'Tisn't likely a break like that will come my way," Sam prophesied gloomily.

Brooke swallowed the lump in her throat. Sam mustn't suspect why she had gone white. She said in a voice drenched with mystery:

"Listen, you two, I'm getting fed-up with country life. The day after the play we'll open the apartment."

"That'll make a big hit with me, but first, unless we want to be late for Trent's party, folks, we'd better start with a hey-nonny-nonny for the big city." Sam added, "You two certainly have the million-dollar look, girls, if you are my sisters."

XVII

Mark Trent glanced at Brooke Reyburn seated at his right in the dim Mirror Room of the recently opened Supper Club. Light from the illuminated table-top brought out the copper glints in her hair, the glow in her radiant eyes, and laid a pinkish sheen over the gleaming silver of her frock. She was eager, young, appealing. He loved her laugh, he loved everything about her, her devotion to her family and her loyalty to inherited ideals, her gay spirit, her beauty, and above all, her ardent mouth. One couldn't believe to look at her now that she had carried the financial burden of a family. Why wasn't she wearing his orchids? Doubtless the answer to that was that she preferred gardenias. Had Field sent them?

What chance had he, a man whose life had been twisted and tangled by a tragic marriage, against gay, debonair Jerry Field? None, he answered promptly, and as promptly told himself that Brooke must love him. That marriage was years behind him. Why allow the memory of it to creep back tonight when for the first time in days his mind had been free of the haunting vision of Lola as he had seen her last?

He forced his thoughts from the past to observe his guests. The rhinestone straps of Daphne Field's blossom-pink satin frock scintillated with rainbow sparks with every novement of her body. Lucette was adorable in a fluffy white and gold thing which accentuated her rich brunette coloring. Sam was observing the crowd through narrowed eyes; Jerry Field was talking in a low voice to Lucette. Jed Stewart was on the other side of Brooke.

Through the haze of smoke from countless cigarettes, Mark Trent could see what seemed to be disembodied faces, faces dotted with two points of light which were eyes, some of them beautiful, some of them brilliant, many of them dull, a few pairs furtive, and a few pairs greedy. The air was heavy with perfume. Corks were popping, women were laughing, and, in the midst of a spot of light which gave a curiously white effect to her face, a girl in a gown of sequins as golden as her hair was perched on a piano, crooning in a husky voice which held no note of music. Aside, in the dusk, the orchestra leader accompanied her song with the music of his violin. His small black mustache and glittering dark eyes in a swarthy skin contributed to a Spanish caballero effect.

The singer slipped from the piano. Her sweeping obeisance set every sequin on her frock a-glitter. The audience applauded. The lights went up. People stopped at tables to chat. The hum of conversation mounted. Silver tinkled against china. The leader stepped to the microphone:

"We're on the air, lads," he reminded, and raised his baton.

The orchestra glided into a rhythmic invitation. The diners sprang to their feet. Old men slipped an arm about women who snuggled. Young men slipped an arm about women who laughed; tough men planted well-groomed hands on the enameled backs of women who stumbled. One couple kissed lingeringly as they passed. Lover's eyes sought lover's eyes; white hands clung; hushed voices questioned.

Jerry Field and Lucette left the table. Sam groaned and held out his hand to Daphne.

"Come on, let's get it over. I suppose you'd like to step?"

"Of course I would, martyr!" She slipped a white arm about his neck.

"Nothing unsteady about her tonight," Mark thought. He pushed into the background the memory of the night he had had to steady her to the car. He had liked her, she had been amusing, but he had not invited her out after that. She had taken little wine tonight, Lucette had barely touched hers, Brooke had refused it. Now her eyes were following her brother. Was she worried about Daphne's influence on Sam?

He watched her, watched the throbbing pulse in her throat which made him think of the beat of tiny wings against bars. Did she love Jerry Field? When he had danced with her tonight he had felt as if he never could let her go. Why should he? He was free, really free to tell her that he loved her.

As if she felt his intense concentration on her, Brooke looked at him with questioning eyes. Mark smiled in response.

"Did you know that I was thinking of you? I was hoping that you were not worrying about Sam and Daphne. If you are, don't."

"Thanks, I'm not. If that were all I had on my mind, my heart would be so light that it would be bumping against the ceiling like a run-away balloon."

"What is troubling you? Can't I help?"

"No, thanks. No!"

"That was emphatic, almost as if you

were afraid of me. Care to dance?"

Brooke motioned toward the couples packed in so close they could barely move.

"You don't call that dancing, do you? But do dance yourself. You must know every attractive girl here. You have risen to bow at two minute intervals ever since we arrived at this table. Does he know every one in the world, Jed?"

"I wouldn't go so far as that, but he has friends in every part of the world. If Mark and I were to trek to Labrador, I'd bet someone would step out of an igloo — if they have igloos in Labrador — clap him on the shoulder and say:

" 'How are you, Trent?'

"As for New York and points south, those regions swarm with his buddies. Just caught a wireless from a girl I know. See you later."

As Jed Stewart left the table, Mark Trent took his chair.

"If I sit back to the dancers I shan't appear so like a jumping-jack."

"That jumping-jack idea is all yours. I was being noble, setting you free to dance with someone else."

"Thanks for the consideration, but the only girl with whom I care to dance is sitting at this table. You wouldn't encourage a host to leave his guest of honor, would you?"

He glanced at the gardenias on her shoulder.

"Don't you care for orchids? I should have sent violets, I know you like them. You wore them the first time we met; no, it was the second time."

"The orchids were beautiful." Brooke traced a pattern on the illuminated table-top. "Sometime I'll tell you why I didn't wear them tonight."

"Are you engaged to Field?"

She shrugged lovely shoulders and glanced up provocatively.

"You fairly gnashed that question. You are miscast in 'Islands Arise'; Sam ought to write something for you in which you could play an ogre. You've just the voice for it."

"All right. I'm an ogre. Meanwhile, how about answering that question?"

"I said that sometime I would tell you why I didn't wear the orchids; that doesn't mean tonight; it means after the play and your party. However, had I been a perfect lady, I would have said, 'Thank you billions' for the flowers long before this. Curious how accustomed we have become to thinking in billions, isn't it?"

"I don't want your thanks, I want —"
Mark disciplined his stormy voice. "Remember that afternoon in Jed's office?"

"The afternoon you refused to marry me?"

"Haven't you forgotten that?"

"There are some things one doesn't forget."

"Then here is something to put beside it in your memory book. Will you marry me, Brooke?"

She looked up with startled eyes, then laughed.

"That proposal — if it is a proposal?"

"It is."

"Has all the fire and ardor of a silent policeman."

"Shall I give a demonstration of fire and ardor?"

"No! Of course not! Don't look at me as if you were trying to see the wheels of my mind go round."

"I hadn't gone much deeper than your eyes. Have you never been told that you have beautiful eyes? You haven't answered my question. Will you marry me?"

The orchestra was playing a soft swaying accompaniment to a baritone voice singing before the microphone:

"I only love one and that one is you,
And that one is you."

There was a burst of applause from the dancers.

Mark reminded:

"You haven't answered my question, Brooke."

Her eyes were brilliant with anger as they met his.

"I answered it the second time you refused to marry me. Perhaps you have forgotten that. I haven't."

Mark crushed back a mad impulse to kiss her contemptuous lips until she went limp in his arms. Repression sent the dark color to his face.

"No, I haven't forgotten that you said that you wouldn't marry me if I were the only man in the world, that divorced men left you cold."

She laid her hand on his sleeve.

"I was sorry the moment I said that. Really I was. Please forget it."

"Do I seem such a cold fish that you don't realize that it is fuse to dynamite when you look at me like that?"

She snatched her fingers from his arm. He laughed.

"Don't be frightened. You are safe. This

is a changing world but my New England sense of propriety still holds." He glanced at her hands. "Don't you care for rings? You never wear them."

"I'm mad about rings, but I like them very choice, very big, very gorgeous. Lucette has a carload of costume jewelry. Sometimes she persuades me to put on one of the huge rings, but I don't really enjoy wearing it."

"Why don't you make yourself a present of one that is very choice, very big, very gorgeous?"

Her cool, laughing eyes met his. "That is another question I will answer after the play and your party."

The *maitre d'hotel* stopped at the table. He glistened from the top of his sleek black head to his patent leather shoes. He looked Italian with a streak of Turk; he spoke American with a French accent.

"Good evening, Mr. Trent. Glad to see you here, sir."

"How are you, Franchot? This crowd looks like prosperity back to stay."

"Business has been good ever since we opened. We had so many reservations for this evening we had to reinforce the staff of waiters and bus-boys. I don't like strange help in a jam like this, but what else could we do?"

As he walked away, Mark Trent said to Brooke:

"We were talking about rings. Aunt Mary Amanda had several which were quite gorgeous. They are yours, remember."

"Oh no! They are not! They — I'm terribly thirsty. Do you suppose this Club would serve anything so small-townish as sparkling white grape juice? I love it."

Mark Trent gave the hovering waiter an order.

"I noticed that you didn't touch the wine, Brooke. Why didn't you ask for what you wanted?"

"Because it makes one so conspicuous in this age and generation to be a total abstainer; isn't that the pre-war term for it? You see, alcohol blurs one's skin, plays the dickens with the size sixteen figure. If I lost that I might not be a hit as a model. I —"

What thought had sent that quick tide of color to her face?

"Is that the real reason?"

Sparks of laughter pricked through the gravity of her eyes.

"You have missed your vocation. Instead of going into insurance you should have studied law. You could have specialized on wills. It would be a cagey criminal who wouldn't crumple when you put him through the third degree."

"Is it the real reason?" Mark persisted, even as he asked himself what was back of her mocking reference to wills.

"Inquisitor! If you must know, there is another. A remote tribal reason. Once upon a time, generations ago, a black sheep in Mother's family drank himself to poverty and death. She was brought up on the 'lips that touch liquor shall never touch mine,' code. To respect her prejudices and convictions seems a very little thing for me to do for her after her years of devotion to me. Mother! What wouldn't I give to talk with her tonight!"

Mark noted the quick glitter of tears.

"You are troubled about something, Brooke. You have kept this party on the crest of the wave with your gaiety and charm, but I've sensed an undercurrent. Let me help."

Her eyes were on her rosy-nailed fingers as they adjusted a gardenia at her shoulder. The violins sang, the saxophones wailed, the leader crooned. She shook her head:

"Nothing you can do, thanks. I have a feeling that I'd like to talk with my mother, that's all. Silly, isn't it?"

"Phone her."

Her radiant eyes flashed up to his.

"I could do that, couldn't I?" She shook her head. "No, no, I couldn't. I had forgotten. I can't phone to England."

The lights in the room dimmed. The dancers returned to their tables. The singer in her glittering sequins stepped to the stage. The orchestra leader nestled his violin under his chin, laid his fingers on the strings and drew his bow with a flourishing sweep. The spotlight traveled about the room, whitening faces, setting rhinestones on a shoulder-strap agleam, brightening already too bright eyes, striking rainbow fire from the jewels on the breast of a *grande dame*. It lingered at a table.

Brooke gripped Mark's arm. She leaned close, whispered:

"Quick! Where the light is! The waiter! He's the man who ran through my room!"

XVIII

Behind the scenes in the Club House Theatre, Brooke, as property woman, checked her list for the last time. Every article which the characters would need to take to the stage was present and accounted for. It didn't seem possible that the hour for which the Reyburns had been preparing eagerly for weeks had arrived. In front the orchestra, violins, piccolos, and a drum, was playing with rhythmic throb, with exuberant verve. The music, what could be heard of it above the murmur of voices in the hall, was stimulating; it should inspire the actors to do their best, she thought. Almost time for the curtain. If only her heart wouldn't pound so. It shook her body. But hadn't her body shaken with excitement whenever she had seen Sam act? He was coming. He was almost as white as the shirt front of his evening clothes, his eyes were like flames as he stopped beside her.

"Just had a cable from Mother wishing me luck. It's zero hour, Brooke. Locate the producer and manager out front. Watch 'em. If they go out after the first act and

303

don't come back, the play's washed up; if they sit through the second, it's got a chance; if they come back for the third, boy!" He turned to Jerry Field who was like a stranger in his make-up.

"Go on to that stage, Jerry, and whang the ball!"

Field nodded to Brooke before he disappeared into the wings. Should she wish Sam luck, his sister wondered? Better not. The hand which gripped his blue-covered, dog-eared script, lined and criss-crossed with cuts and changes, was white-knuckled.

The stage was cleared. Lucette, Daphne and Jerry Field went on and took their places. Sam was in the wings! Jed was at the switch-board! The curtain man was waiting for his signal! Sam raised his hand. The house dimmed. He wig-wagged with two fingers. Jed brought up his lights. The orchestra stopped playing. Another motion of Sam's hand and the curtain rose slowly. Brooke's heart parked in her throat, running on high.

Lucette waited for the greeting of applause to quiet before, without a trace of nervousness, she spoke her first line. Sam nodded approval, frowned as Daphne answered shakily. Brooke couldn't see the stage, but she could hear the voices. Jed

Stewart was red and perspiring under the responsibility of getting the actors on and off. Once as he passed her he whispered:

"Get a peek at Mrs. Gregory out front, third row, centre. She's blazing with jools."

"Has the New York producer come?"

He nodded. "Second row, centre. Sleek blond fella, with a grand marcelle." He caught Sam's eyes glaring at them and disappeared.

Every sentence moved the play forward, unfalteringly. Jerry Field had been on and off before Mark Trent, in his blue lounge coat, appeared to make his first entrance. As he approached the wings, his eyes, smiling, disconcertingly intent, met and held Brooke's and set the blood tingling in her cheeks.

The rehearsal last night had been so hectic that he had had time only to tell her that Jed Stewart had left the Supper Club to report about the waiter to Inspector Harrison. In the morning paper she had seen a statement that the bandit in the Hunt filling station case was being trailed to Canada. Of course she hoped that he would be caught, but it was a relief to know that he was far away from what newspapers would call the scene of his crime.

She handed Daphne Field a letter as she made her exit. She would go on again in a few moments.

"Don't put it down or you may forget it," Brooke warned.

Her thought reverted to her own affairs. What had Mark really meant when he had asked her to marry him? Of course he couldn't know that his accomplished love making had opened her heart wide, had let the love for him which she had refused to acknowledge, out into the sunlight. Love making! That was funny. Not once had he mentioned the word. She had gone gayly on her way, not knowing that she cared, knowing only that when she forgot that he had called her a schemer, she loved being with him. He was so companionable, life and ideas and the world seemed more vivid when she was with him. Why hadn't she realized where she was drifting? What had he meant by that look as he had taken his entrance? It was as if he had flung a chain about her, had challenged her to escape. What would he think when he knew of that paper concealed in her desk? She had almost betrayed herself at the Club when she had so hastily retracted about telephoning her mother. He couldn't know, of course, that her old-time bogey, Expense, had wig-wagged the Stop signal.

She must keep her mind on her job. She held up her hand to stop snapping-eyed Kowa who, with a dinner jacket dangling on a hanger, was about to follow his employer on to the stage. She whispered:

"Wait! Wait! Mr. Trent will change here when he comes off."

"Thank you, much obliged, most made mistake," Kowa murmured.

She could hear Mark Trent's voice, faintly ironic. It was her cue to start the phonograph which was to produce a song as if sung in the street below.

   " 'In the gloaming, oh my darling,
   Think not bitterly of me.' "

The sweetness and fervor of the man's voice brought a terrifying ache to Brooke's throat, a burning beneath her eyelids, as with the small machine in her hands she walked away to give the effect of music fading in the distance.

   " 'It was best to leave you thus, dear,
   Best for you and best for me.' "

The last word thinned into silence. Mark Trent's cue.

"That song is old stuff, but sure fire. Believe it, Madge?"

The laughing tenderness of his voice
twisted Brooke's heart unbearably. She
tore her thoughts from him and watched
her brother. She could see his lips move in
unison with the lines spoken on the stage.

The curtain fell slowly on the minor
climax of the first act. The setting and
theme had been established and the characters presented. The audience applauded
enthusiastically. From a hole in the curtain
Brooke saw the New York producer go up
the aisle. Would he return?

"Don't you dare go away, don't you
dare!" she flung at his straight back.

The orchestra swung into a fox trot. The
leader had been instructed to keep the
music gay, to counteract the taint of tragedy which still lingered in the community.
Sam, white with excitement, had pulled off
collar, tie, and coat. Brooke could see the
beat of the pulse in his firm brown throat
as she joined him in the small room in
which the members of the cast assembled
to listen for their cues. They were changing
while the scene was being shifted to the
forest back-drop.

"How did it go?" His voice was hoarse.

"It's wonderful, Sam. Not an unneces-

308

sary word; every line was 'Forward march!' for your story. The acting is the best I've ever seen in an amateur performance."

"So what? Does it prove anything? They're all good except Daphne; she isn't getting her lines over. I hold my breath every time she opens her mouth. Isn't Trent great? He's the spark-plug of the cast. Wait till you see him in the crucial moment in the next act, when he thinks the girl he loves has double-crossed him. Hi there! Not that way! Not that way!"

Brooke's eyes followed him as he dashed into the wings to direct the setting of a flat. How deeply he felt this production of his play. He was suffering the labor pains of creation. He would be exhausted when it was over — no, not if it were a success — success didn't exhaust, it revitalized — and it would be, the second act was stronger than the first, the pace quickened, and the third mounted steadily to a smashing climax.

For the first time she was conscious of the world outside the theatre. She raised the shade and peered out. Snow fell like a Fifth Avenue shower of confetti on the head of a returned hero, lightly splashed against the glass, lazily swirled before the headlights of parked automobiles. Not much of a storm yet. Lucky that even this had held off until the New York producer and Boston manager had been personally conducted to their seats. Had they come back? At the risk of being caught on the stage as the curtain rose, she applied her eye to the peep-hole. They were in their places. She offered a fervent little prayer of thanks and dashed from the stage.

Jerry Field appeared beside her dressed in leather jacket and knickers, with a gun in his hand.

"How's it going, Brooke?"

"I can't see the stage, but from the response of those out front I'd say it was a hit. You're grand in that sports costume. You've made every point, Jerry."

"Thanks. That's because when I say a word of love to Lucette I'm saying it to you." He caught her hand and pressed his lips to it fervently.

"Please — don't, Jerry."

"You've said that too many times, sweet thing. After the play we'll have a reckoning — get me?"

"After the play." Brooke repeated the words to herself. So much was to happen that would change lives, after the play.

"Hey! Field! Field, come on!"

Sam's whisper. Sam's beckoning hand.

Brooke followed Jerry as far as the wings from which she could see him drop to a log on the stage, left centre.

"Why don't you turn thumbs up and end the poor boy's torment?" asked a low voice behind her.

She turned quickly. Something in Mark Trent's voice made her furiously angry.

"That's quite a suggestion that I end 'the poor boy's torment.' I will. Tonight."

"Don't do it until I change after the show. I want to drive you home, Brooke. There is something I must say to you."

Brooke felt the blood rush to her face and recede. Had Henri double-crossed her and told him about the will? Did Mark Trent think she intended to hide it? She wouldn't give him a chance to accuse her before she produced that paper locked in her desk. She said as steadily as she could with his eyes boring into her soul:

"Sorry. The minute the curtain falls, I shall dash to Lookout House to change into something snappy for the grand celebration. You wouldn't have me come to your grand party in this green knit, would you? Quick! Sam wants the wings cleared."

She backed out, conscious of Mark Trent's disturbing presence close beside her.

"The music has stopped! There go the foots!" She caught his sleeve, looked up and begged in an unsteady whisper:

"Do your best, Mark. This act will kill or make the play."

His lips were on hers so quickly that she had no chance to protest. He kissed her passionately, thoroughly; said in a husky whisper:

"Credit that to the silent policeman. Now, I'll play that part to the hilt."

Brooke tried to ignore her racing pulses. She mocked:

"I seem to be in the path of an emotional cyclone: first, Jerry Field; now you. I suppose Jed will be the next. Your cue! Quick! Quick!"

In an instant he was on the stage. She heard his voice, jubilant, a trifle unsteady, call out:

"You beat me to it, didn't you, stout fella? I stopped to help a broken-down buckboard over the world's worst bit of corduroy road."

Brooke shut her eyes tight in an effort to steady a whirling world. Mark Trent's lips on hers had been like an electric current through her body. Every pulse, every nerve responded. Making allowance for the fact that he was keyed to the nth pitch of excitement because of the play, why had he done it? He didn't trust her. He thought her a schemer. Was it part of his and Jed Stewart's espionage plan? Thank heaven, it was only a matter of a few hours now before she would have that will out of her desk and in the hands of the two men who had been on her trail for weeks. She had been happy, even since she had known that Mary Amanda Dane's fortune no longer belonged to her, she was not afraid to tackle the business world again — hadn't Carston's Inc. talked with her for an hour yesterday arranging details of her trip to Palm Beach? But since Mark had kissed her, she was not unlike one of those meteors she had seen the other night, torn from its orbit and flung into a new world.

She listened. It was very still in front, a sort of hypnotized stillness. She could hear the voices on the stage, but she couldn't keep her mind on what they were saying. Even as she supplied properties, even as the actors made their entrances and exits she was thinking of Mark Trent's eyes as he had looked down into hers, was wondering what he wanted to tell her on the way home? She thought of her plan to hand the paper to him after the last guest had left his house tonight, to dramatically restore the fortune he had lost.

How Reyburnish! The incurable dramatic streak in the Reyburn temperament had been in the saddle when she had planned that. As if Mark Trent and Jed Stewart would be surprised. Hadn't they settled in the Other House for the sole purpose of finding that missing will of Mary Amanda Dane's? Would they believe her when she said that Henri had produced the paper only two days ago? Henri would come back with the lie that he had found it in her desk. Her desk! As if he could get into her desk. She hadn't looked at it since she had put it away. She couldn't. It gave her a sense of nausea every time she remembered that she was holding it back; perhaps she would be put in jail for not producing the will at once. That thought didn't help much.

Why was Sam leaving his post? He was stumbling toward her. His face was chalky. His eyes were black with fury. There was a suspicion of froth about his lips. She caught his arm, terrified. Whispered:

"What is it, Sam? Fire?"

"Fire! Fire! Nothing so simple! That darnfool Daphne has skipped two pages of dialogue and they've gone on from there!"

XIX

Brooke felt as if she were turning to stone. Two pages of dialogue dropped from the very heart of the play! It was cruel. She bit her lips savagely to steady them. Whispered:

"Go back to your place, quick, Sam! Mark Trent is on, isn't he? He'll put it back. He'll give them the right cue. Watch him; he'll put it back."

She had no thought for her own problems after that; they were submerged in concern for Sam's play. The part which had been dropped conveyed implications upon which the denouement depended. She had braced Sam with the assurance that Mark Trent would restore it. Could he? Two pages lost. It was too much to expect.

The seemingly impossible was accomplished. The missing dialogue was restored and expertly restored, Brooke realized, as she saw the color creep slowly back to Sam's face, saw his hands unclinch. At the close of the second act the deafening applause was punctuated by calls for the author. But Sam was adamant.

"No! No! Keep that curtain down! I won't have the continuity of the story broken by the actors bowing and scraping behind the footlights. After the show, folks, after the show."

As the curtain fell with dramatic slowness for the last time, the audience stood clapping and calling. As it rose again, Brooke saw the blond marcelle, second row centre, make its way up the aisle followed by a man with sleek black hair. The producer and the manager! She had seen them go out after the second act. They had come back for the third. That must mean something. Were they leaving before speaking to Sam? He was on the stage now in the midst of the cast who had taken their bows; the arms of the women were heaped with flowers. He had put on coat and collar and tie but the white bow had gone rakish. He looked very young as he stood grinning boyishly and waiting for a chance to speak. His voice shook as he said:

"Thanks lots! Glad you liked it. Couldn't have put it across without their help." He indicated the men and girls around him on the stage, and the audience broke into thunderous applause. The curtain fell slowly.

Brooke's eyes were blinded by happy

tears as she started for the dressing-room. She must get back to Lookout House to change for the party. The girls of the cast were going to Mark Trent's in the evening frocks they had worn in the last act. Leaving the wings, she collided with the marcelled blond. The New York producer! He was unaware of her murmured apology as he gesticulated and talked to his sleek-haired companion. She listened unashamedly and heard him say:

"It's got everything. Humor, suspense, moving simplicity, fidelity to ideals, and unfaltering movement."

"But has it got box-office?"

"I'll gamble my last dollar on it. It's the old recipe for play-writing carried to perfection:

" 'Make 'em laugh; make 'em weep; make 'em wait.' Where'd you say that boy got his start?"

"He kicked off as playwright for his fraternity. You'll have to hand it to that male lead for putting his part across. He's got magnetism. I'm hard-boiled in this business, but when in the second act he accused that girl of faithlessness, I could feel the air vibrate."

Brooke's cheeks were hot as she slipped away. She remembered Mark Trent's eyes before he had gone on for that scene, his voice as he had said:

"Credit that to the silent policeman."

Why think of herself now? She should be on her knees giving thanks for Sam's success, for "Islands Arise" had been a success. No matter how friendly its intention, an audience couldn't force such enthusiasm; it had been spontaneous, genuine.

She dodged acquaintances and strangers in evening clothes who were crowding on to the stage to greet the actors. In the dressing-room she slipped into her fur coat and ran downstairs to her town car parked near the rear entrance.

The snow was falling half-heartedly as if it had not quite decided if it were worth while to come down at all. She drove swiftly toward home. Mark Trent had asked her to plan his party, had told her to go the limit in preparations to make it a success. That was a dangerous commission to give Brooke Reyburn; once her imagination as to color and attractiveness were given free rein, it was apt to take the bit in its teeth. She had ordered gigantic pale yellow snapdragon for the library, it would be perfect with the crimson hangings; masses of pink carnations for the dining room, and poinsettias to be banked in the hall. She had selected Templar roses for the print room under the stairs. She had given the caterer orders. Mark Trent had said:

"Go as far as you like with everything, only be sure that there is enough to eat and sufficient help. To have plenty is an obsession of mine."

There would be plenty and then some. Just before she left Lookout House for the Club Theatre, the caterer had arrived with his van and a horde of waiters. They had sounded like an army making camp.

Not such a bad night. How lovely the lights were. They had the sheen and iridescence of great opals. How quiet the streets under the spell of a night-world buried in snow.

As she entered the drive she looked at the two rambling houses of frost-bleached stones snuggled side by side. Their roofs sparkled with snow. Every window was lighted, every window was broadcasting a welcome. The convolutions of the iron balconies had been picked out in white till they looked like marble railings. She blinked her lashes. Anyone would think from the tightness of her throat and the wetness of her eyes that she wasn't glad that that pesky will had been found before she had been plunged deeper into debt to Mary Amanda Dane's estate.

Trent's Japanese cook came forward to open the door of the car. Snow powdered his shoulders and cap. His eyes glittered in his swarthy face. His teeth gleamed as he ducked his head in a funny little bow. Brooke let down the window.

"I won't get out here, Taku. I'll run into our garage. All the space outside will be needed for the cars of the guests."

"You right, Mees. Thank you. Much big party, Kowa say."

Would there be room for Sam's coupe? Brooke wondered, as she drove into the garage. One corner had been filled with ice cream tubs. He could leave it outside, she decided. She shut off her engine and partially closed the door as she went out.

As she reached the dark hemlock behind the Other House, she lingered for an instant in its deep shadow. How still the world was. Snow fell as softly as if someone above had slit open a pillow and shaken down its feathers. There was no near sound of surf tonight.

"This is the last time I shall see it like this." Brooke swallowed something that was half laugh, half sob; then jeered at herself:

"Girl driven from home watching its windows through the driving snow. You would dramatize this, wouldn't you, Brooke Reyburn? You —"

She shrank deeper into the purple gloom under the tree as two men came down the back steps from the kitchen — waiters, she knew by their clothing. Not more than five feet from her one of them stopped to light a cigarette. He growled:

"The boss can wait for them ice cream tubs till I get a smoke."

"Sure he can. Light up again and take a look at this."

A hand held a scrap of paper within the light of a match. The same voice said:

"It's the picture of the dame who said: 'He was a swell-dressed fella.' Guess I'll have to date her up!"

The other man closed his hand over the match.

"You an' your dames! Forget 'em for tonight, or you'll crack up on this job. Come on!"

As Brooke dressed in her room, the words and suggestive laugh of the man who had produced the picture kept boiling up through her jubilation over Sam's success, through the inescapable memory of Mark Trent's eyes and voice as he had caught her in his arms.

Who was he? Her mind proposed and rejected possibilities as she dressed to the faint rhythm of the orchestra from the Other House, to the beat and throb of a Strauss waltz which was as natural, as unforced as the music of a woodland brook dancing its sparkling way to the sea.

She was adjusting a rhinestone and synthetic emerald clip to the shoulder of her white satin frock when a thought forked through her mind like lightning. The amber and brown eyes of the looking-glass girl frowning back at her widened with amazement; her red lips moved.

"He said — he said — 'I'll have to date her up!' "

In an instant she was on the floor beside her desk with a big Manilla envelope in her lap. She pulled out a bunch of clippings. She had it! The picture of a girl, Maggie Cassidy, and under it the caption:

"She said that the man she saw in
the garage was a swell-dressed fella."

The waiter who had shown the other man the clipping was the Bath Crystal Bandit, the man she had recognized at the Supper Club! He was the man who had tied up Hunt in the garage! Was he also the murderer of Lola Hunt?

The question turned her fingers to ice as she tucked the picture of the girl inside her frock. Rigidly she disciplined a sense of panic which set her pulses galloping. She must keep her head. She must think. She forced herself to restore carefully the clippings to the Manilla envelope, the envelope to the drawer. Was that really her colorless face in the mirror, were those her eyes burning like flames?

Why was the man in Mark Trent's house tonight? His pal had said: "Forget 'em, or you'll crack up on this job." What job? Something big must have tempted him to come so near the scene of his last hold-up, or had that newspaper headline stating that he was being followed to Canada made him feel secure? What was he after? More jewels?

"Get a peek at Mrs. Gregory out front, third row, centre. She's blazing with jools."

Jed Stewart's words answered Brooke's question as clearly as if whispered in her ear. The man had come for Mrs. Gregory's diamonds.

She must notify the police! The waiter who had lighted the cigarette doubtless was an accomplice. Of course there would

323

be more than one working. They might escape! She snatched her hand from the telephone in its cradle on the desk. Not that. Wires had ears. She would go herself. Across the causeway. To Inspector Harrison at headquarters. She could go and be back before she was missed. Suppose she were stopped on the way! Where was Henri? Was he in on this? She must locate him before she left the house.

She caught up a green velvet wrap, stuffed some bills into her emerald satin bag. Pelted down the stairs, into the living-room toward the bell. Stopped. Where was the parrot? He was not in his cage! Had he made another break for freedom? She looked between the gilded bars. What seemed to be merely a bunch of green feathers lay stiffly on the bottom.

"Well, if this isn't just one of those days!" she said aloud.

"Oh, Brooke!" Jerry Field called from the hall.

As she appeared in the doorway, he exclaimed:

"Of all the gorgeous creatures! You look like a million!"

"Jerry, drive me across the causeway, will you? Quick!"

"What's the matter?"

"I must go. Is your roadster here?"

"Left it by your garage."

"By the garage!"

Brooke's blood congealed. Suppose as they stepped into the car the two crook waiters should appear for a tub of ice cream? Would the men suspect her errand? Into her mind flashed her reply to Mark Trent:

"That's quite a suggestion that I end the poor boy's torment. I will. Tonight."

What a thought for this crisis! What a thought!

"Wait a minute, Jerry! While I'm upstairs, set the parrot's cage in the back hall, please. I — I can't bear to have it here. You'll see why."

She raced up the stairs, charged into her bedroom, pulled a suitcase from the shelf. On the way down, she took the two lowest stairs in a jump. She thrust the case into Field's hand.

"What's the big idea?"

"Don't — ask — questions! Let's go!"

"You can't walk in the snow in those white satin sandals, you'll ruin the green heels."

She pushed him toward the door. "Get going! Get going!"

"Well, I'll be darned! Come on."

Brooke felt the dampness between the straps of her sandals. It seemed miles to the garage. There was Jerry's roadster! A waiter was coming down the back steps. It might be the Bath Crystal Bandit! She called in a guarded voice to the Japanese who was directing parking, but loud enough for the man on the steps to hear:

"Taku! Put this suitcase in the rumble. And, Taku, if you see my brother, tell him — tell him," she raised her voice, "that Mr. Field and I have run away to be married."

XX

"So we're off to be married! That's all right with me," Jerry Field approved fervently.

Brooke, whose face was pressed against the back window of the roadster, twisted round in her seat.

"Don't be foolish, Jerry. Of course we're not. That was a red herring drawn across our trail."

"Just why the red herring?"

The ironic note in his voice gave her a chill tremor of dismay; she didn't care for the way in which his eyes narrowed as they peered through the wind shield. She protested:

"Don't speak like that, it makes me shivery, and goodness knows my teeth are fairly chattering now." She turned to peer from the rear window. "No car in sight yet. Can you go a little faster?"

"Not without a risk of skidding off the causeway and breaking our necks. Can't you see how the snow is plastering the wind shield. The squeegee barely moves. Why the haste?"

"While I'm telling you I'll keep watch.

The excitement began upon my return from the play."

She told him of leaving her town car in the garage, of stopping in the purple gloom under the hemlock to look at the lighted windows of the stone houses crouched on the ledge; her breath quickened as she repeated the words of the man who had produced the newspaper clipping:

" 'It's the picture of the dame who said: "He was a swell-dressed fella!" I'll have to date her up.' "

"That was what the Cassidy girl said about the man they suspect robbed Mrs. Hunt!"

Field's voice was sharp, his personal problem was submerged in a mounting tide of excitement. The car shot ahead like a whippet unleashed.

"I know that now. The certainty as to who he was flashed through my mind while I was dressing, and the suspicion that he might be at the Other House tonight to lift — that's the technical term, isn't it — Mrs. Gregory's gorgeous diamonds."

"Why didn't you phone the police?"

"With Henri in the house? I may be a slow thinker but I'm not absolutely dumb. I'm trying to do my part, in answer to those glaring headlines:

" 'WOMEN, WHAT ARE YOU, SITTING BEFORE YOUR FIRES, DOING ABOUT THE CRIMES BEING COMMITTED?'

This is what I'm doing about it. I was going to headquarters alone, and then you called to me and I knew it would be surer and safer if two went."

"And the suitcase?"

"A touch of theatre. I thought if one of the gang saw us starting, he might suspect he had been discovered, but if he heard what I told Taku he would feel secure. Elopements happen every day."

"Not in my young life," Jerry Field retorted crisply.

The storm had settled into its stride. Visibility was about zero. The northeast wind blew the snow in blinding sheets, shrieking and moaning as it passed.

"So this is New England! What a night!" Brooke had her face pressed against the back window. "We won't have much competition on the road."

"What's that roaring? Doesn't sound like the wind."

"It must be the surf on the distant

ledges. A flare! I can barely see it! Another! A ship in distress!"

" 'God pity the poor sailor on a night like this,' " Field quoted grimly, and bent forward to peer through the wind shield.

They maintained a breathless, alert silence until the roadster turned a corner into a street which had an air of lonely spaciousness. Buildings looked like the iced masterpieces of confectioners. Street lights paled in contrast. Just ahead bulked the combination jail and police headquarters, gloomy and ponderous. Above the roof a tower loomed against a snow-filled sky; from it stretched aerials, frail as a spider's thread, potent as a winged mercury on business of the gods. Dark as a dungeon, silent as a tomb were the woods behind it.

"Shall I come in with you?" Field asked, as he stopped the roadster before a heavy iron door and cut off his engine.

"Yes. I may need you to corroborate my story. When I burst in upon them in this gown, they may think I'm crazy. Hurry! We don't know what is going on at the Other House."

Field slipped his arm within hers as they mounted the snowy steps.

"I'll stick around and wait till you call me. Don't shiver, sweet thing. You're not afraid of the Inspector, are you?"

"Afraid! No. Haven't I been cross-examined by him almost every day since what Sam calls 'our late unpleasantness'? It's just the Reyburn temperament."

Her satin sandals skidded treacherously in the corridor as she confronted a policeman whose nose, criss-crossed with a network of fine veins, had the effect of a red "stop" signal.

"Where's the Inspector? I must see him. Matter of life and death," she confided breathlessly. In her excitement she caught the man's arm and shook it. He scowled at her, looked beyond her at Jerry Field; his expression mellowed.

"Inspector's just come in. He's in the Radio Division. Go through those swinging doors up them stairs to the tower."

Brooke was through the doors before the man had finished speaking. Three or four men leaning over a great U-shaped table looked up as she entered the room. With a muttered exclamation, the Inspector left them and came forward.

A man sitting at a telephone said something in a low voice to an officer before a microphone. Tubes in the broadcasting apparatus crackled into life. He said slowly and distinctly into the mike:

"Calling car 3131. Car 3131. Car 3131. Go to K and Tenth Street."

Brooke commanded breathlessly:

"Listen to me, Inspector. The man who robbed Lola Hunt is serving sup-per at the Trent h-house on the Point!"

Maddening to have her voice break like that. How strangely he looked at her, almost as if she were a criminal. He had always seemed friendly. Didn't he believe her? Didn't one of the three men frowning at her believe her?

Inspector Bill Harrison smiled, a curious smile.

"Wish I'd known this before, Miss Reyburn. I've just come from the Point, following a tip I had. What's the dope on this bandit? Is it the same guy you saw at the Supper Club?"

"It must be, Inspector. Tonight —"
Before she had finished telling of the alleged waiter's remark about Maggie Cassidy's picture, machinery was crackling again and the man at the microphone was broadcasting distinctly:

"Calling car 1942. Car 1942. Car 1942. Go to Trent house on Point. Inspector will meet you. Calling car 6784. Car 6784. Car 6784. Go to Trent house on Point. Inspector will meet you."

Inspector Bill Harrison was out of the room before the man at the microphone had completed the call. One of the officers turned over two discs on the U-table; the other frowned at her with the bluest, most Irish eyes she ever had seen as he answered her unspoken question:

"We don't dare be more explicit over the mike, Miss. The thugs pick up the messages."

"Will they — will they get there in time, Sergeant?"

"Time for what, Miss?"

"I think — I think he's there to get Mrs. Gregory's diamonds — she's — she's simply plastered with them tonight."

With the last word the stiffening departed from Brooke's knees. She clutched at the nearest woodwork. Said shakily:

"Do you know, I've just realized that I haven't eaten since breakfast. Silly of me, isn't it?" She couldn't explain that she had been too busy packing to leave Lookout House and with preparations for the play, to eat.

She slipped into the chair the blue-eyed officer pushed behind her.

"Sit down, Miss. I'll bring you coffee. Like a hot dog?"

Brooke's stomach literally turned over at

the suggestion. "No! No! Please don't bother. I must go. Mr. Field is waiting for me downstairs. I'll have something when we get home."

"Don't move. Stay where you are. Guess you don't like hot dogs. You turned kinder green. I'll bring the coffee and some crackers and I'll get Mr. Field, too."

As Brooke waited in the quiet room, snow beat a soft tattoo against the windows of the tower. Would the police cars get to the Other House in time? Would the storm delay them?

She looked down at her white satin sandals as she wriggled icy toes; the green heels were stained beyond repair. Ruined, but in a good cause, she told herself, they could be replaced. Replaced! She had forgotten! She no longer had the Dane money to spend. This was the night she was to give the will to Mark Trent and Jed Stewart. She hadn't thought of it since she had looked at the picture of Maggie Cassidy. She must get back! What time was it?

"Calling car 406. Car 406. Car 406. Watchman at First National Bank reports three men in auto lingering at corner. Suspects hold-up."

Only for an instant did the voice at the microphone switch Brooke's thoughts from the promise she had made to herself. She looked at the clock. Twelve. Only midnight? She had thought it must be morning. She wouldn't wait for the coffee. At the risk of upsetting the steaming contents of the cup he carried, she caught the blue-eyed officer's arm as he approached.

"I've just thought of something, Sergeant. I must get home. Mr. Field is waiting downstairs —"

"He'll wait, Miss. Drink this, and here's some cake."

His cajoling voice brought a flash of laughter to Brooke's eyes.

"Thanks. The coffee smells marvelous."

The man at the telephone spoke to the man at the microphone. The man at the mike called steadily, distinctly:

"Calling car 45. Car 45. Car 45. House behind Cassidy's garage on Point. Woman's screams heard by motorist passing."

The man at the U-table turned down another disc.

"That's the last car we have to send. Trouble's on the loose in this part of the U.S. tonight. I'll bet those big shots up at Trent's have planted these other acts so they'd have the police scootin' round and they could make their getaway."

"Will they make it? Can they make it?"

"Not unless they're smarter than I think they are, Miss Reyburn," the sergeant reassured. "No guy burning up with brains would have showed that girl's picture an' said what that one said, no matter if he was in the midst of the Atlantic ocean alone on a raft. Two detective cars are on the job and they've got machine guns, pistols, and tear-gas bombs." He stopped speaking to listen. "Who's coming now? One of those press boys poking his nose in, I'll bet."

"Don't let him see me, please."

"Go out that other door and downstairs. This guy won't stay long. We don't allow visitors here."

In the moment that she waited to listen to the sound of approaching feet, the room was indelibly stamped on Brooke's mind. The blue-suited man at the U-table, with the overhead light turning his gray hair to silver, was frowning at the door, one hand was on the holster hanging from his belt; the uniformed man at the telephone, the man at the microphone looked as if crouched to spring. The blue-eyed sergeant had dropped the plate; it lay in halves on the floor at his feet. Except for the spatting of snow against the window, the room was eerily still.

Jerry Field was pacing the lower corridor when she reached it.

"It's about time you appeared, Brooke! I was just coming up to look for you. What do we do next?"

"Back to the party of course."

The wind swirled her short hair, clutched at her satin skirts, tugged at her velvet wrap as they went down the jail steps. As Jerry Field tucked the robe about her wet feet he looked up. Snow had settled in the brim of his soft hat, whitened his shoulders.

"Let's make a break for town, sweet thing, and make that yarn you told Taku the truth."

The expression in his eyes, the break in his voice hurt her. She said unsteadily:

"Please, Jerry! I can't care for you that way. Take me back quickly, will you? We mustn't miss Sam's party."

"Oh Sam! Sam is your white-haired boy. He's all that you Reyburn women think of or care about. I believe you'd sell your soul for him!" Having delivered which both definite and inferential statement, Jerry Field jumped into the car and started the engine.

After one look at his grim mouth and gloomy eyes, Brooke snuggled into her corner of the seat. There was something uncannily pertinent about the last sentence he had flung at her, almost as if he had known that she had mortgaged her conscience, if not her soul, by holding back Mary Amanda Dane's last will until Sam's play was over. It wouldn't be long now before she would have that haunting burden off her mind. Would the guests have left Mark Trent's before she reached the Other House? Had the officers seized the two waiters before they had stolen Mrs. Gregory's jewels? Perhaps they had no intention of stealing them. Perhaps that suspicion was a figment of her colorful imagination.

What had the after-the-play party meant to Sam? She had looked forward to it for days as being a triumphant hour in his life, with heaps of congratulations and perhaps an option. That was before she had known what she would have to do at midnight. Her heart flew to her throat now when she thought of it. What a mysteriously restless thing a heart was. Always seeking, always starting off on an adventure in loving or living, soaring with happiness and expectancy one minute, beating a tom-tom of warning the next, perhaps dropping to the depths at a word or a look.

Even though Mary Amanda Dane's money never had been hers, what a gorgeous time she had had spending it, all of which — cheering reminder — in some way she must pay back. She thought of the mimosa, acacia filled bay of the dining room at Lookout House, of the tiers of poinsettias with the light bringing out their scarlet perfection in the sun porch off the green living-room. And she thought, "No matter what comes, nothing can rob me of the colorful memory." Merely visualizing the beauty had braced her, warmed her.

Her thoughts raced on to the monotonous accompaniment of the purr of the motor and the squeaky overtone of the windshield scraper. Why had Mark kissed her? From his cool, cynical manner it was evident that he didn't love her. Didn't he? She had not been kissed many times in her life, but tonight a man's lips on hers had sent her blood surging through her veins; the mere remembrance set red-hot slivers pricking in her pulses, made her cheeks burn, and sent a tingle even to her icy toes.

She cleared her throat as if to rid her mind of the troublesome memory. She would better keep her attention on what she would say to him when she produced that will. Lucky she had this uninterrupted time in which to think. Toward the east the drab, heavy clouds were thinning before a spreading radiance.

"I believe the snow is letting up, Jerry. Look! The moon is trying to break through! Drive faster. I can't wait to know what has happened."

"Don't worry, you'll get to the party all right."

Brooke ignored his gruffness. "Of course I want to get to the party. Then I shan't feel guilty that I dragged you away from the fun and congratulations. Leave me at Lookout House. I must change these soaked sandals before I join the festivities. Here we are."

From the top of the steps she looked down at Field who was looking up at her.

"I'm sorry, Jerry," she whispered softly, before she entered the house and closed the door behind her.

"He doesn't really love me, he's a spoiled boy who wants what he can't have," she reassured herself, as in her boudoir she changed her wet stockings and sandals. The warmth and fragrance and color of the room transported her to another world from the snowy world outside her window.

She readjusted the rhinestone and emerald clip on her white frock, sprayed perfume on her hair, powdered her nose, accented her lips. She shook her head at the looking-glass girl.

"Stalling, aren't you, Brooke Reyburn? You dread to face Mark Trent with that will you've kept back for two days, don't you? Get going!"

She crossed to the desk, found the key where she had hidden it.

"Zero hour," she said aloud, and unlocked the drawer in which she had placed the will.

She looked down. Brushed her hand across her eyes and looked again.

The drawer was empty.

XXI

People coming, but not going; music never stopping. It was that kind of a party.

To the accompaniment of the hum of voices, the stimulating beat and throb of the orchestra, the distant faint tinkle of silver and glass, Sam Reyburn made slow progress through the gay, colorful crowd on the lower floor of the Other House, grinning at girls in lovely evening frocks who cooed over him; frowning at men who tried to detain him; shaking hands with attractive deference with elders who congratulated him.

From where he stood on the lowest step of the circular stairway, Mark Trent watched him. "All this praise is heady stuff for a boy," he thought, and then reminded himself that Sam wasn't a boy. Why wasn't Brooke with him to share the honors? She had been the first to leave the hall, the man in charge of the parked cars had told him. Where was Jerry Field? He hadn't appeared either.

A curious premonition turned him cold. Of course Brooke hadn't meant it when in answer to his sarcastic suggestion she had said she would end Field's torment. Hadn't she? There had been infinite determination in her crisp retort:

"I will. Tonight."

"Seen Brooke, Mark?" Sam Reyburn inquired as he approached. "I want her to be the first to know that I'm to get a contract; that I have an option in my pocket and a cheque. She's been grand, always on hand to help me keep my head above water when I thought I was sunk. We put the play over, m'lad! Gosh, I can't believe it, but we sure put it over."

Mark Trent laid his hand affectionately on his shoulder.

"Great stuff, Sam, great stuff. I was sure that the New York producer was hooked when he spoke to me."

Sam grinned. "Offered you the lead in a Broadway production, didn't he? He's a publicity hound. Think of the headlines:

'LEADING INSURANCE EXECUTIVE LEAVES LUCRATIVE BUSINESS FOR THE STAGE.'

Will you do it?"

"What do you think? How's the party going, Mrs. Gregory?"

Mark Trent smiled at the woman whose blazing tiara on her marcelled white hair, and plastron of diamonds on her purple velvet gown dimmed what sparkle life had left in her tired eyes. She answered crisply:

"Listen to the hubbub and you won't ask the question. Your party has brought out tails and white ties, Mark, that's a triumph in itself. I always know what guests think of my parties by the way they dress for them." She patted Sam's sleeve.

"My boy, your play is the sweetest, loveliest, most heart-wringing thing I've seen on the stage for years. Where's your sister? I want to tell her what I think of it."

"Lucette's dancing and —"

"I don't mean Lucette, though I'd like to tell her that she stole the show — I read theatrical news so I know that's the correct term — from the leading woman. There was a convincing touch of realism in young Field's love-making and I didn't wonder. Where's Brooke?"

Sam Reyburn's grin diminished in size and quality. A hint of anxiety clouded his eyes.

"That's what Mark and I were wondering. She left the hall before the rest of us; she told me before the first curtain was rung up that she would dash home to change for the party."

Mrs. Gregory's face grew a shade less colorful. "I don't like her not being here, I don't like it. I've been uneasy about that girl every moment since she testified at the inquest about the strange man who passed through her room the night of the filling station hold-up. The man hasn't been caught. She knows too much. They may try to put her out of the way."

The strong lenses in Sam's horn-rimmed spectacles magnified the horror in his eyes.

"What an awful suggestion, Mrs. Gregory! What a gosh-awful thought!"

It was an awful thought, but improbable, most improbable, Mark Trent assured himself. With difficulty he cleared his voice of hoarseness before he accused:

"You've been reading mystery stories, Empress, confess now, haven't you? Just the same, we'll start on Brooke's trail at once. What is it, Kowa?"

He spoke sharply to the servant who had wormed his way through the crowd of dancers who overflowed from the library to the hall.

"Much obliged. Madame Gregory's car here. Chauffeur say to tell her storm bad, very bad. She better get home. He know she not like to be out in storm."

"Tell him to wait. I won't go till I know where Brooke is," Mrs. Gregory snapped.

"Did you see Miss Reyburn come in, Kowa," Mark Trent inquired. Of course, the suggestion that she was in danger was absurd, but it was getting under his skin.

The Jap's slanting eyes narrowed to mere slits. He put his lips close to Mark Trent's ear and whispered:

"Miss Reyburn tell Taku she and Mr. Field go to marry, thank you. She carry suitcase, sir."

"What!"

Had he shouted the word? Mark's eyes flashed from Mrs. Gregory to Sam Reyburn. Both were regarding him anxiously, but apparently neither had caught the content of Kowa's whisper.

"Has anything happened to Brooke?" Mrs. Gregory's lips twitched, tears filled her eyes. Sam caught Trent's arm.

"What did Kowa say? What did he say?"

Mark Trent steadied his mind. He must reply to their questions. What should he say? He couldn't blurt out the truth here. Perhaps Brooke had flung that remark at Taku for dramatic effect. But the suitcase —

"Mark! Mark! Why don't you answer?"

He looked down into Mrs. Gregory's

eyes, terrified now.

"Brooke is perfectly safe. She — There's Field! Ask him where she is. He saw her last. Go get him, Sam! Go get him!"

"No need, he's coming as fast as he can push through the dancers, and Jed Stewart is at his heels. They are white as sheets. What's all the mystery? The air is full of it. My skin's turning to gooseflesh. For Pete's sake, where's Brooke, Jerry?"

Jerry Field was breathless from the effort of shaking off congratulatory hands which had tried to detain him.

"Changing her sandals at Lookout House. I've got to speak to you, Trent! Quick!"

Relief stopped the thumping of Mark Trent's heart. Had Brooke married Field, would he be here? He would not. He turned to Kowa still standing beside him and asked in a voice he had difficulty in keeping steady:

"Is anyone in the print room?"

The Jap disappeared and returned with incredible speed.

"No person there, sir."

Mark spoke in a low tone to Jerry Field:

"Slip into the room back of the stairs. Sam, tell the musicians to play something loud and gay; then join us. Now that we know Brooke is safe, Mrs. Gregory —"

"Mrs. Gregory is coming with us," Jed Stewart interrupted, and slipped his hand under her arm.

Even with the door of the room closed, the beat and rhythm of the music outside set the air within vibrating. A cheery fire crackled on the hearth. Incredibly long-stemmed Templar roses in a tall vase made a splash of gorgeous crimson against the neutral tinted walls hung with Japanese prints, scented the air with their spicy fragrance. Mrs. Gregory resisted the seductive depth of a large chair and sat erect on the edge.

"What's happened? What's happened?" she demanded testily.

"Wait a minute. Thought I heard something." Field pulled aside the hangings at the window and peered out; Jed Stewart on his toes looked over his shoulder. "Yep, there they go. Police are no respecters of supper parties."

"Police! Who go? Where? What?"

"Keep your shirt on, Sam. Everything's going to be all right."

Jerry Field drew the hangings close and returned to the mantel. The lighter he held to his cigarette was not quite steady. "Now, folks, listen to my bedtime story."

For an instant there was no sound in the still room save the purr of the fire and the tap of a snowy vine against a window. Then it seemed to Mark Trent that the woman in the deep chair, Sam Reyburn with his elbow resting on one corner of the low bookshelves, Jed Stewart backed against the door as if to barricade it, stopped breathing as Field told how Brooke had commandeered his roadster and himself to take her across the causeway, of the reason she had given for her going, of her suspicion that the man she called the Bath Crystal Bandit might be serving as waiter at the party because of interest in the jewels of one of the guests.

Mrs. Gregory instinctively put one hand to her tiara and one to the blazing plastron at her breast. Her mouth quivered uncontrollably.

"I suppose you mean mine. W-when did they in-intend to take them?" she quavered.

Mark Trent crossed the room. He sat on the arm of her chair and put his hand on her shoulder.

"Steady, Empress, they can't get them now. Go on, Field. Then you and Brooke are not married?"

"Married! No such luck. Didn't I make

that clear? Brooke told that yarn to avert suspicion from our get-away. Do you think I'd be here if we were married?" There was a glint of steel in his eyes as they met Mark Trent's.

"Where was I — oh yes. We made headquarters in record time. Brooke told her story. Your kitchen, Trent, was the scene of the neatest, quickest clean-up in the history of crime in this state, I'll bet. No, don't go. Inspector Harrison sent special instructions to you to keep things moving here so that the news of the arrests wouldn't get out until he had the men safely in jail. Sorry to report that you've lost your chauffeur, Mrs. Gregory."

"Dominique! Not Dominique? He's been with me for years. Why have I lost him?"

"He's been taken along for questioning. The Inspector didn't have time to go into it here. The Jacques at Lookout House also are being personally conducted to headquarters. Quite a party, if you ask me. I didn't hear much, but your man Dominique, Mrs. Gregory, was to have engine trouble on the way home. While he tinkered, you were to be relieved of your jewels."

Anne Gregory's face was gray; it

dropped into sagging lines, her mouth quivered childlishly. Suddenly she was an old defeated woman.

"Isn't there anyone in the world I can trust?" she whimpered.

Mark Trent tightened his arm about her shoulders.

"Of course there's someone you can trust, you have Brooke and Sam, Jed and me, and —"

"Don't forget me," Jerry Field interrupted. "Now, who's come?" he queried.

The low quick knocking at the door was repeated. Jed Stewart opened it cautiously and let in a drift of dance music and Lucette.

Her lips were startlingly red in contrast to the whiteness of her face. The rhinestone straps which held up what there was of the back of the bodice of her pale blue frock sent out a million or two iridescent sparks. She caught the lapel of Mark Trent's coat as he took a quick step toward her.

"They're whispering outside that Brooke and Jerry Field have eloped. It isn't so, is it? Brooke wouldn't —"

Mark Trent turned her by the shoulders that she might see Jerry Field standing by the mantel. He saw the look in the girl's eyes, saw something in the man's spring up to meet it. He felt the quiver that ran through her body, felt the effort she made to overcome it as she said flippantly:

"News flash! Eloping bridegroom returns without lovely bride. Where's Brooke, Jerry?"

"Changing her wet sandals at Lookout House."

"Wet sandals! Where has she been?"

"She'll be here in a minute and tell you herself, Lucette. Better go back to the party," Mark Trent suggested. "The New York producer and the Boston manager are still here, aren't they? We're depending on you to see that they have the time of their lives."

"Boy, when Brooke didn't appear, I forgot those bozos, forgot that we'd had a play." With his hand on the knob of the door, Sam stopped. "Come along, Lucette."

Lucette caught Field's arm.

"Come with us, Jerry, and stop the rumor that you and Brooke have eloped; also we'll let people tell us what hits we were in 'Islands Arise.' That producer told me that if I would come to New York at once he'd give me a small part in a comedy he's putting on."

Jerry Field hooted.

"A kid like you on the real stage! He's spoofing. Come on out and I'll tell him a thing or two, sister."

He put a proprietary hand on her shoulder.

She shrugged away from him.

"You're not my brother yet, Jerry Field, and I'll do my own telling. In fact, I've about decided to accept his offer and sign on the dotted line."

"Now listen to me, Lucette," Field commanded, as the door closed behind them.

"Suppose we go back to the party," Mark Trent suggested, and offered his arm to Mrs. Gregory. "Do you feel able?"

"Able!" The word was an absolute, contemptuous, sweeping denial of weakness. Mrs. Gregory laid her hand, which trembled slightly, on his arm; her faded eyes twinkled as she looked up at him.

"Don't try to make an old lady of me, Mark. I'm what is called nowadays an 'older woman,' a generic term which may include any female of the species over forty."

Jed Stewart held the door open.

"You're a grand sport, Mrs. Gregory," he acknowledged impulsively.

She stopped on the threshold. "A sport,

Stewart, because I refuse to shed tears over one more lost illusion? I haven't time to look back; I'm going forward, 'with banners,' to borrow Brooke's favorite phrase. When she says that in her buoyant voice, I hear a burst of martial music, the tramp of feet marching forward, see Colors waving. Come to dinner tomorrow evening, Stewart; I want to change my will. Let's go, Mark, I'd like to meet that New York producer. Who knows, he might want me to sign on the dotted line."

As Mark Trent stepped back that Mrs. Gregory might precede him into the hall, Jed Stewart caught his arm.

"Just a minute, fella!" He lowered his voice. "The Inspector wants us to wait up until he gets here, no matter if he doesn't come till daylight."

Mark nodded assent. The throb of a harp, the singing of the violins, the quaver of the horns, the brooding of the oboe were muted to a caressing minor, heartbreakingly sweet, as he piloted Mrs. Gregory to a throne-like chair in the hall. He left her and went in search of the New York producer. It required considerable finesse to evade clamorous friends. Even as he acknowledged praise of his acting, congratulations on the party, he was thinking what a queer, aching, vivid thing love was, with its ecstasy, its inevitable misunderstandings, its quarrels, and he wondered why he bruised his heart against Brooke's dislike, wondered if she would ever forgive him for that kiss. At least he —

"Mark! Mark!"

Before he had a chance to evade her, Daphne Field flung a bare arm about his neck.

"Dance with me, please! Mark! Mark! You must love me!" The girl's voice caught in a sob as she pressed against him.

Too annoyed to answer, he put his arm about her to guide her out of the room. As he turned he saw Brooke Reyburn standing directly behind her. There was a curious light in her eyes, a mocking smile on her lips.

XXII

Even as Brooke smiled and accepted congratulations on the success of her brother's play, did her best to entertain the New York producer who attached himself to her from the moment Sam presented him, she was asking herself impatiently:

"Will the party never end? Who stole that paper from my desk? Can I make Mark Trent understand why I held it back? If it is lost, will he ever forgive me?"

But all parties end. The last of the guests, with Mrs. Gregory carefully tucked into their limousine, drove off in a flood of moonlight which transformed the world into an enchanted land of dazzling purity. The producer and manager left in a powerful car after hearty handshakes with Sam and a backward look at Brooke as she stood between her brother and Mark Trent in the hall. The musicians tenderly stowed away their instruments, the leader pocketed a cheque before they coasted down the drive in the bus whose wheels churned up fountains of snow as they turned. The perturbed caterer packed up equipment and such waiters as the police had left him and departed in his van.

Except for the Reyburns, the Fields were the last to go. Had they lingered in the hope that they would be asked to stay and talk over the party? Brooke wondered. Sam had treated Daphne with a brusqueness bordering on brutality.

"It wasn't that dumbbell's fault that my play didn't bite the dust," he had growled when Brooke begged him in a whisper not to show resentment, to dance with the girl once. But he had stubbornly refused.

She drew an unsteady breath of relief when the front door had shut out the brother and sister. They were outlanders in the present situation. She couldn't have told her story before them, and she must tell it quickly; that will must be found. She wanted Lucette and Sam to hear what she had to tell Mark Trent and Jed Stewart; the sooner they knew of the change in her fortune, the better. Perhaps at this very moment Mark Trent was wishing that the Reyburns would leave and that Daphne was staying. What response had he made to her impassioned:

"Mark! Mark! You must love me!"

He had caught her quickly in his arms. Had he suspected that the girl standing behind her had overhead her wail? His face had gone dark red. Well, after tonight he might devote the rest of his life to Daphne Field. Who would care?

"I would. Horribly. Achingly." Brooke answered her own question and sunk her teeth into her lips to steady them.

Mark Trent linked his arm in Sam's.

"Don't wig-wag the let's-go signal at the girls, maestro. Jed and I can't let you off yet. Come into the library. Half the fun of a party is talking it over. I told Kowa to bring in some eats. I don't believe you Reyburns ate a mouthful of supper; you were too busy receiving congratulations. I'm starving myself."

Sam grinned.

"Now that you call the matter to my attention, I could toy with a little food. Come on, Brooke."

Lucette was curled up against the pillows in a corner of the library couch hugging her knees, when they entered. Stewart was backed up to the mantel. The girl's eyes were brilliant, her cheeks were pink, the voice in which she greeted them was bumpy from excitement:

"Come in, folks, and hear Jed tell me how good I was. He predicts that I would be an overnight sensation on Broadway."

"Snap out of that idea and snap out of it quick."

"Don't growl, Master Reyburn; he has been handing bouquets to the play too. I done you wrong, Sammy, when I crabbed about the last minute changes you made in the script; they were the high lights. Where's Jerry?"

The swift change from laughter to gravity in Lucette's eyes hurt Brooke. Why, why didn't Jerry Field love her instead of wasting his affection on a girl who cared for him as a friend only?

Mark Trent answered Lucette's question.

"He and Daphne have gone home. You put it all over the other women in the cast of 'Islands Arise,' Lucette."

"She was a knock-out and so was the leading woman," Sam agreed, "but, if you want to know who had the New York producer eating out of her hand, it was our little sister Brooke. After she arrived — trust a Reyburn to realize the dramatic value of a late entrance — I couldn't pry him away from her; lucky I got my option before she appeared. What were you saying to him, Brooke?"

"We talked theatre fast and furiously. It was a wonder that I could think of anything but the near escape the party had from a hold-up."

Kowa entered with his quick cat-like tread. His eyes sparkled like black diamonds as he set a Chinese teapoy of red and gold lacquer beside each chair.

"Thanks lots for helping out tonight, Kowa," Sam said, as the Jap stopped before him.

"No thanks need. I too, much obliged, Mr. Sam. You very nice young man. Write great show. Make the eyes to sting and the throat to laugh. Perhaps if boss go to act in big city, he take me along. I like it great to help back big stage."

"Something tells me that Kowa has picked up the theatre bug. I cabled Mother the news, Brooke. Won't she be pleased purple?" Sam rested his head against the chair back and closed his eyes.

"Boy, I'm tired! I feel all in."

"It's reaction, and I'll bet you haven't eaten for hours and hours." Mark Trent spoke to Kowa as he returned with a laden tray.

"Serve Mr. Sam first. Here you are, maestro. Chicken salad, escalloped oysters — who thought of those? I haven't seen that dish since I went to my last church supper. Try some of this hot coffee."

Sam's grin was swift and a trifle sheepish.

"I'm all right, m'lad; slumped for a minute, that's all."

"Don't apologize," Lucette mimicked.

"I'm not apologizing. I'm explain—" Sam broke off with a grimace at his sister. "Humorous, aren't you, kiddo? Fuss over Brooke, Mark, she needs it more than I. What with bracing me every time I got cold feet about 'Islands Arise' and getting dragged into the crime wave, she's had a hectic time since she came to Lookout House to live — I'll take another shot at those rolls, Kowa — I don't wonder she has decided to trek back to the town apartment. What will we do with the parrot when we go, Brooke?"

Brooke felt her color rise in response to the flash in Mark Trent's eyes as they met hers reflected in the great mirror. This was as good an opening as any she could bring about to tell the story of the paper Henri had produced. She rose and stood behind her chair. With her arms folded on the top, she had a sense of being entrenched, out of danger for a while.

"We won't have to consider the parrot, Sam. Mr. Micawber has gone."

"Gone!" Sam and Lucette chorused.

"Did he make another get-away, or has Henri kidnaped him?"

"Neither, Sam. He's in his cage, just a heap of green feathers."

"Poor old duffer. He hasn't had any pep since the night he took off in a hop for freedom. I liked that bird. Something's always taking the joy out of life."

"Cheerio, Master Reyburn, you still have your option," Lucette reminded. "Why can't we move to town tomorrow? No more commuting! What a break! I suppose you'll close Lookout House, Brooke?"

Her cue! It couldn't have been more neatly timed had Sam written the lines for her, nor could the stage setting have been improved upon, Brooke told herself. What could be better than this story-book library with firelight turning Lucette's frock to violet and casting a shimmering pattern of claret on the yellow snapdragons in a copper bowl on a couch-end table; with the great mirror reflecting Sam, still a trifle colorless, and Jed Stewart with a forkful of salad from the plate on the mantel poised half way to his mouth as he regarded her with startled attention? It reflected also Mark Trent's lean dark face, his intent gray eyes, his repressed sensitive mouth, and even the waxy perfection of the gardenia in his coat lapel; it gave back her own eyes big and brown and a little, just a little, frightened.

Frightened! Why should she be frightened? Wasn't she about to hand over a fortune to Mark Trent? She forced a gay note into her voice:

"I'll close Lookout House, Lucette, because I have accepted an offer —"

The sentence trailed off as Inspector Bill Harrison strode into the room. His eyes seemed to pierce to Brooke's brain. Why was the man looking at her like that? She felt as if her heart had been released from a steel trap when he turned to Mark Trent and Jed Stewart, now standing side by side before the mantel. When he spoke she couldn't believe that the eagle eyes and soft voice belonged to the same person.

"Well, Mark, I got it!"

"Got 'it'! You're too modest, Inspector, you got the whole gang, I understand."

"Cripes, I'm not talking about those dirty thugs, Mark. That isn't what I came for. I got the will you was telling me about."

Brooke's blood chilled at his quick change of voice, his sharp look at her. Lately she had had jubilant moments when she forgot her doubts and believed that

Mark Trent had come to live in his house because he, perhaps, because he rather liked her. Now she had proof that he had suspected her of knowing where his aunt's last will was, had even hired Inspector Harrison to watch her. Suspicion had been bad enough, but certainty was squeezing her heart to pulp.

The Inspector pulled a paper from his pocket. Mark Trent glowered at it as if it were a rattler with head raised to strike.

"Here it is. The real thing. Signatures and everything o. k. I found it —"

"You found it in my desk, didn't you, Inspector?" Brooke interrupted icily.

Mark Trent's eyes were stormy, his lips were white.

"That's enough. Don't go on with this, Brooke."

"But I am going on with it."

"Let her tell her story, Mark. It's only fair to her."

Sam joined the two men before the fire.

"Jed's right, m'lad. The Inspector found the paper in your desk. That's your cue, Brooke. Go on from there."

Brooke went on. Through the steady sound of her own voice her ear noted the purr of the fire, the ghostly tap of a vine against the window, the faint shudder of shutters as the wind trailed through them, and her eyes saw Lucette, a grave, breathless Lucette perched on the arm of the couch; saw also the three men standing before the fire, the fire itself a mass of blinking, smoldering coals, and the Inspector motionless as a man of stone with the folded paper in his hand.

She told of her suspicion the first time she had come into this very library that there was a reason other than a passion for the sea in winter which had brought two men from the city to live in Mark Trent's house; and she told of Mrs. Gregory's admission, the afternoon before the Supper Club party, that she had witnessed a will of Mary Amanda Dane's and that she had been warned by Jed Stewart not to speak of it. And how, almost before Mrs. Gregory's car was out of the drive, Henri Jacques had confronted her with a paper and the lie that he had found it in her desk.

"Don't speak! Don't!" She interrupted her story sharply as Mark Trent opened his lips. "Let me finish!

"I took it with the idea that if I didn't, he might make more trouble with it. I let him think that I was considering his proposition that I pay him for keeping quiet. Of course I wasn't, but I can't expect you two men who have been suspicious of me from the moment you learned of my friendship with Mrs. Dane, to believe that. I was coming directly to this house with it. First, locked in my room, I looked at it to be sure it wasn't a blackmailing scheme of Henri's. It wasn't. It was Mary Amanda Dane's will leaving all her property, except legacies to the Jacques, to her nephew, Mark Trent."

She looked at Mark. "This is what I had on my mind the other night at the Supper Club. I told you then that I would answer some questions you asked after the play and this party, didn't I? They are answered, aren't they?"

"Stop and get your breath, Brooke; you'll crack-up if you don't," Sam warned.

"I won't crack-up and I won't stop till I get this thing off my mind. It has been a hideous nightmare, holding back that paper, I mean. Of course the contents of that will were a shock for a minute; but I knew that Mrs. Dane had been just. Then I thought of the play, that the sudden appearance of a missing will — there's drama for you, Sam — might upset the performance; so I locked the thing in my desk. I had planned to bring it here this evening. When I got back from headquarters tonight, I went to my desk to get it. The drawer was empty. Now I know that Inspector Bill Harrison, your sleuth, had found it, Mr. Trent. I suppose nothing I can say will make you and Jed Stewart believe that I have not had that paper from the moment Mary Amanda Dane signed it."

"That's enough, Brooke." Mark Trent's voice was low and authoritative. "I don't believe that you have had that will. I know —"

"Wait a minute!" Inspector Bill Harrison cut in. "Come over here."

He spread out the paper on the desk. He drew a flat leather case from his breast pocket and removed from it a white scrap.

"Exhibit A. Watch!"

The scrap fitted into the torn corner. There was a glint in his eyes as they passed from face to face of the three men bending over to read the finely written lines.

"I don't know what the rest of you folks think," his voice was as soft as velvet, "but, in spite of the fact I found it in her desk, I'm sure Miss Reyburn hasn't had the will in her possession ever since it was signed, because —"

He laid the tip of a square-topped finger on the torn-off corner:

"Because I found this scrap caught in Mrs. Hunt's bag the night her diamonds were snitched."

XXIII

For the length of time it took the old clock in the hall to chime the quarter hour, there was silence in the library, a silence as tense as if the still body of a black-haired woman with the open bag gripped in one bruised hand lay in their midst. Inspector Harrison broke the spell.

"And that ain't all I've got to show you. Bring him in, Tim!"

Brooke's breath stopped as a tall policeman with huge ears pushed a cowering figure into the room. Henri! Henri here! Would he dare persist in the lie that he had found that will in her desk?

"Sit down, Brooke."

With hands on her shoulders Mark Trent drew her from behind the chair and forced her gently into the seat. She felt his presence behind her as he said sharply:

"It's your move, Inspector. Let's get this thing over with."

"It ain't my move, Mark. It's Henri Jacques'. He's going to tell you what's kept him the busiest butler in the U.S. You're on the air, Jacques. Spill it!"

369

The command held the crack of a lion-tamer's whip. Henri drew his fingers over his slack lips. He made two attempts to speak before he produced a voice.

"I'll tell the whole story, Mr. Mark, and it isn't so bad as the Inspector's trying to make out, I swear it isn't. I didn't kill —"

"Start at the beginning!"

"I will, Inspector, I will."

Brooke looked down at her clenched fingers. She couldn't keep her eyes on Henri. Once she had seen a dog being beaten who groveled as he groveled now. His voice shook as he went on:

"It was like this, Mr. Mark. Madame Dane sent for Clotilde and me to come to the living-room one afternoon. It was the nurse's day off. She was in the wheel chair and Madame Gregory was there. Your aunt said as how we were all to sign a paper in her presence and then she was to sign in our presence. She laughed kind of shaky and said:

" 'I don't know much law, Anne — Anne was Madame Gregory — but I've learned how a will has to be signed to make it legal.' "

"Did Mrs. Gregory say anything?"

"Yes, Mr. Mark. She said, 'Do you think you should do this without consulting your lawyer?' and your aunt said that Mr. Stewart was away and she didn't dare wait till he came home because she hadn't been feeling well. We wrote our names. Mrs. Gregory left, Clotilde went back to the kitchen, and then the old madame handed the paper to me and said:

" 'Put that in my safe upstairs, Henri. I'll give it to Mr. Stewart when he gets back, but first bring me a glass of sherry. I'm tired.'

"She looked so white I thought she was going to faint. I jammed the paper in my pocket and ran. When I came back with the wine, Miss Reyburn was standing by the mantel laughing; you remember that afternoon, don't you, Miss?"

"Yes."

Brooke contrasted his beseeching tone with the voice in which he had told her that he could put her out of Lookout House.

"Direct your questions to me, not to Miss Reyburn, Henri. What did you do with that paper?"

"I was coming to that, Mr. Mark. The old madame was taken very sick that night. Not until after she'd been gone a week or two did I think of it."

"Then of course you read it?"

"Yes, sir."

371

"You showed it to Clotilde?"

"Yes, sir."

"When did you and she decide to fasten the theft of it on Miss Reyburn?"

The voice which came from behind Brooke's chair set her a-shiver. A steadying hand rested on her shoulder.

"We — we didn't think of it, Mr. Mark. Mrs. Hunt suggested that."

"How did she know about it?"

Henri passed shaking fingers across his lips.

"Same way she found out that we were going to sell your aunt's silver. Clotilde and I thought we might as well have it as the strange girl she'd left it to. You were in South America and Miss Reyburn would never know the difference — might as well come clean, he's third-degreed it out of me."

The glance Henri Jacques cast at the Inspector was green with venom.

"Mrs. Hunt said, if I'd get the silver to the white cottage, she'd dispose of it; that it was rare and worth lots of money, that a dealer would believe that it was hers, that he might suspect me. That seemed reasonable. Mrs. Hunt knew of a man to help. She said she'd take care of that will, too, she'd get money out of you for it and we'd go fifty-fifty."

The fingers on Brooke's bare shoulder bit into the flesh.

"Go on, Henri!" Mark Trent's voice was hoarse.

"I gave it to her. The afternoon before the filling station mur— hold-up, I showed the man she sent where the silver was, forgot the keys and left them in the doors. I remembered them in the middle of a movie, came home, went upstairs very quiet and got them. The man who was to move the silver to the old limousine was waiting in my room. While you were all laughing and eating downstairs I let him through into the Other House by the upper connecting door. He took the stuff through your house — the Japs were out, and I pretended to go to bed. He was to make a cross on the white cover when he had it in the car. I drove it to the cottage. I went in to tell Mrs. Hunt the silver was outside, ready to take to the city. She — she was on the floor. I swear she was. I swear I didn't touch her." Henry steadied his twitching lips with his fingers.

"But you took that paper over there on the desk out of her bag, didn't you?"

"I told you once I did, Inspector. I felt it

belonged to me. But I swear I never touched her."

"After that you tried to get money from Miss Reyburn, didn't you?"

"I didn't intend to ask for much, Mr. Mark."

"Take him out, Tim."

Henri stopped to hurl defiance at Inspector Bill Harrison.

"You think you're smart, but you wouldn't have known anything about this till we were safe out of the country, Inspector, if that expert thief Mrs. Hunt brought into the game hadn't stopped to wash and shave in Mr. Stewart's bath-room. Pretty snappy guy he was. I suppose he had to dress up fine before he called on her. She paid for pulling him in. He got her jewels all right, and he was out to get Mrs. Gregory's tonight. I wasn't in on that deal, Mr. Mark."

"Take him away, Tim." Inspector Harrison's eagle eyes followed the two men from the room before they came back to Brooke.

"Sorry I had to touch your desk, Miss Reyburn, but a high falsetto voice phoned me you had the will — I know now that it was Henri Jacques — so I went through your room while you were all at the play. I guess you're glad the truth is out. The minute I heard of that bath stunt I knew who to look for. That guy has made a specialty of breaking into houses week-ends where the folks were away, of making himself at home in the tub and carrying off what he wanted when he left, mostly men's clothes. Maggie Cassidy was right when she said he was a swell dresser. He ought to be. He's had his pick of the best. It's kind of funny when you think of it, ain't it? When I accused him of killing Mrs. Hunt, he crumpled and spilled the whole story. He had seen her rings when she engaged him to move the silver. Wanted them. Knocked Hunt out first. He's a quick worker. He and his pals aren't killers. There wasn't a gun in the gangload. There's a joke to it, they don't one of them know yet that the coroner's verdict was 'heart failure from fright.' I've kept that under my hat so I could scare the truth out of them. Well, Mark, your silver's safe and you've got your aunt's money."

"Thanks, Inspector, I'll tell you how much I appreciate what you've done, later. Sam, get Brooke's wrap. I'll take her home. You and Lucette stay here and get the Inspector something to eat. Wait for me, Bill, there are a few points that need clearing up. I have something to talk over with Miss

Reyburn, then I'll come back."

"You are not going home with me and we have nothing to talk over." Did he think that he could wipe out the memory of his suspicion of her in this lordly manner? Brooke asked herself.

"Oh yes, we have."

Sam chuckled.

"One of the thirty-six dramatic situations. Snap into it, Brooke. It is apparent even to this boyish intelligence that Mark wants to talk to you alone. Fair enough. Why make him go on the air? Be kind to him, he deserves well of his countrymen. Here's your wrap. Get going, folks. I want another shot at the chicken salad."

"If all you care about is eating, Sam Reyburn, I'll go."

Tears menaced Brooke's voice and eyes. At the door she held up her dignified exit.

"Better come with me, Lucette. You have to make an early start for town, remember."

Lucette curled up against the couch cushions.

"Don't worry about me, darling. I'll be on hand to punch the time-clock. I'll stick around with Jed and Sam and the exciting Inspector. I'm hungry too."

She added with an impish laugh:

"Better play ball Mark's way. If you don't, something tells me he'll go completely cave-man and drag you off by your hair."

"Just wait until you and Sam want me to help you out!"

Brooke flung the threat over her shoulder. As she crossed the threshold she heard Sam's voice, very grave, very grownup now:

"Jed, does that paper the Inspector found mean that Brooke loses the money?"

Lose it! It never had been hers, Brooke thought, as she stepped from the warmth and fragrance of the house into the outdoor pageantry of a cold winter dawn, with Mark Trent beside her. The world glinted with splinters of crystal where a slanting moon sifted its light through snow laden branches; the indigo velvet of the sky was stencilled with starry patterns; cedar hedges were blanched to marble balustrades.

They crossed the terrace in silence. The snow had not been cleared from before the door of Lookout House. Mark Trent swept Brooke from her feet and carried her into the vestibule. He kept an arm about her as he opened the door. Something turning like the wings of an autogiro in her throat, cut off her protest. The green living-room awaited them, softly lighted, faintly fragrant. Above the mantel the Duchess looked down with grave eyes; below, coals, murmurous as purring kittens, gave out a gentle glow.

"Take off your wrap."

Brooke slipped from beneath the velvet and the hands tightening on her shoulders. She barricaded herself behind a high-back chair. With one arm on the mantel, Mark Trent faced her. His eyes, smiling a little, maddeningly cool, filled her with rage. She challenged:

"You would come. Why? Didn't you want to tell me before the others that you had known about that will all the time?"

"But I hadn't known."

"You suspected that there was one, didn't you? You and Jed Stewart came to live in the Other House to watch me, didn't you? Do you think I have forgotten that you called me a schemer?"

"This seems to be turning into a question and answer period. Suppose you let me tell my side of the story. Sit down, please."

She shook her head.

"I prefer to stay here. Go on. I hope it doesn't take long. I have a lot to do before

I leave in the morning — sorry to have to ask to let the furnishings stay here until Mother gets back, but —"

"Don't be so breathless, dearest."

"I'm not breathless, and I'm not your dearest. I wish you would say what you forced your way in here to say and — and go."

"All right, remember, you asked for it. I came to say that after I knew who you were that day in Jed's office, I didn't believe that you had used 'undue influence' with my aunt. I admit that for a while I tried to fool myself, but I couldn't keep it up. I didn't open my house because I wanted to 'watch' you. I decided to do it on Thanksgiving day, because I — liked you and your 'whole darn family.' As the weeks passed, Jed and I were sure that if the second will had not been destroyed, Henri knew where it was. Not knowing its contents hampered us."

"But you know now?"

"Yes. And it hurts infernally to think that you should have been drawn into this sordid mix-up."

"Why shouldn't I be? It's what might be called poetic justice, isn't it? Didn't I start the trouble when I went to Lookout House to see your aunt for the first time? I'd been warned that business and friendship won't mix any better than oil and water. Now I know it. You had suspected for weeks that I had no right to your aunt's money, and yet you and Jed Stewart let me keep on spending and spending. When I think of those two cars I bought I almost lose my mind. How can I ever pay it back?"

"Pay it back! Don't be foolish. There is no question of paying it back. Have you forgotten that Mary Amanda Dane left an income to you?"

Brooke came from behind the chair to perch nonchalantly on the arm. For an instant she watched the flame-color pattern the firelight cast on her white satin frock. She was quite steady now, she assured herself, quite self-possessed. She managed a smile as she looked up.

"You don't think for an instant, do you, that I would accept a cent of that money? Would you take any from me when I tried to divide with you? I'm surprised, I'm really surprised that you don't play the martyr and ask me to marry you."

"No. I shan't ask you to marry me. I've made a lot of mistakes in my life, but, believe me, I've learned enough not to make that one."

His cool denial hurt Brooke intolerably.

He hated her, she told herself. Why shouldn't he?

"In the library a while ago you told Lucette you were leaving here because you had accepted an offer. Are you engaged to Jerry Field?"

A gate in the wall! A way out without letting him know that she cared, how desperately she cared for him. She laughed.

"I — Here come Sam and Lucette. They are stamping snow from their feet outside as a warning that they are about to interrupt our conference. Amusing, isn't it?"

"Amusing to you, perhaps. It isn't to me."

Sam's face was as red as the fire as he and Lucette entered the room.

"Sorry to interrupt, but —"

"Don't apologize."

"I'm not apologizing." His face went from red to crimson. "I'm only trying to explain, Brooke, that the Inspector's walking the floor and gnashing his teeth and muttering something about keeping the Law waiting. Jed tried to start him on 'Sweet Adeline,' but it wouldn't work. He wants you, Mark, and he wants you quick."

"I'm going." Mark Trent paused on the threshold. "Good-night, Brooke. We'll finish our talk tomorrow."

XXIV

"We'll finish our talk tomorrow."

A month had passed since Mark Trent had flung those words at her, since she had left Lookout House. They had echoed to the accompaniment of the whir of the wings of the great plane in which she had flown south at the urgency and the expense of Carston's Inc.; they had intruded in business hours; they had flitted like wraiths through her dreams. She had not seen him, he hadn't even written, Brooke told herself bitterly. Hadn't he said that he had made a lot of mistakes, but that he had learned enough not to make the mistake of asking her to marry him? After that, why couldn't she forget? Why did his voice everlastingly echo through her memory? Easily answered. Had anyone reason to know better than she that he was a superb actor? Hadn't he made Sam's play? Hadn't those lines provided a perfect exit?

For days after her arrival at Palm Beach she had thought that he might come, had imagined him striding forward to meet her as she stepped into the patio of the house where she lived, had even visualized his wonderful smile; or perhaps she would meet him on the street and greet him with cool, sophisticated surprise while all the time her heart would be suffocating her with its beat.

The days had slid by with the rapidity of telegraph poles past an express train window. She was conscious of a sort of breathless urge to keep up with something which was escaping her.

Keep up with what, she asked herself, as in the flower scented dressing room of Carston's Inc. she slipped out of the green organza number she had been modeling and into a frock of cool yellow linen. She was looking out unseeingly at the palm bordered white street when Madame Céleste entered. Her thin white frock rested Brooke's eyes after the rainbow collection she had put on and off for the last two hours.

"You done noble, *cherie*," the woman approved heartily.

There was something in her nasal twang as refreshing as a breeze from a thousand New England hills blowing through this tropical paradise.

"That last customer is one of the richest girls in the country. She ordered all the gowns you modeled. You look kind of tired, you've a right to, *cherie,* after landing that whale of an order. Get some lunch here, go home and rest until four, then come back. You will dress here, the society models will dress at the Shaw's sports house. Sidoné will be there to help them. You'll be the only professional mannequin, but I wouldn't trust an amateur to show that wedding gown. The charity fête begins at five. The wedding party will be the last feature of the style show. Look your best. We expect that some prospective bride will snap up the whole outfit when she sees you walk up the ribbon and flower bordered aisle in that heavenly white satin veiled in a mist of tulle. You'll make a ravishing bride, *cherie;* it will be your last appearance, so knock their eyes out."

The words "last appearance" penetrated the turmoil in Brooke's mind.

"Last appearance! What do you mean?"

Madame Céleste twisted her amethyst beads. "*Cherie,* don't go white on me. You know business hasn't been too good, and I have my orders. After the fashion show I'm to hand you a cheque for your commissions and a month's pay and you're through."

"But — but I thought I had sold a lot of frocks since I came."

"You have, and you can search me for the boss's reasons. Never knew him to turn a trick like this before — but, I ask you, is any business being run as it ever was run before? I'll tell the world it isn't. I'm terribly sorry to lose you."

For an instant, emotion threatened damage to the enameled calm of the woman's face.

"And I'm sorry to leave you, Madame Céleste. You've been more than kind to me from the day I started to model sports clothes, that seems centuries ago instead of years, and I've loved working for you. I'll be on hand promptly this afternoon. If this is to be my Palm Beach swan-song, of course I want to knock their eyes out. *Au revoir,* madame!"

Brooke was still puzzling over her dismissal when she reached the small Bermuda-type house, with its white washed roof and walls built around two sides of a patio, in which she had been living since she had come to Palm Beach, and entered her room. It was a narrow room, cool and shadowy, with delicate green hangings. Green toile de jouey covered the chairs, draped the dressing table. Two long windows shaded with dark jalousies opened on a gallery floored with tiles.

She changed from the yellow cotton frock to white shantung pajamas. She picked up letters from a desk, pushed open a window, stepped out on the gallery and breathed deeply of the light thin air. The scent of drying tiles, wet earth, and orange blossoms rose from below; above, fluffs of cloud skittered across a limpidly azure sky. Far away, broad as a giant's sash, indigo as the heavens at midnight, the gulf stream girdled the horizon; on the sparkling blue sea between it and the shore a mammoth yacht swung at anchor.

She glanced down into the patio with its freshly scrubbed tiles, its one royal palm, its clump of coconut trees. Red and purple bougainvillea, a mass of barbaric color, swayed front slender trellises. An orange-color table and lemon chairs repeated to a tint the crest of a white cockatoo which blinked and preened in a gilded cage.

Brooke promptly shut out the flood of memories loosed by the sight of the bird. "Poor old Mr. Micawber," she said under her breath, and slit open a letter from Mrs. Gregory.

Reclining in a chaise longue, she began to read:

Dear Brooke —

I suppose you are fanning yourself in the shade of a palm in one of the garden spots of the world, while I am looking out on a driving snow storm and at the town plow piling up unscalable mountains of white at the sides of the road. The worst storm of the winter, and what a winter!

I drove by the Dane-Trent place yesterday. It didn't help my sense of isolation to see both houses shut tight as a drum. I've seen Mark several times. He's been conferring with Bill Harrison about our bandits. For the first time in its history this old Point has made the headlines. Hunt has been cleared of any connection with the crimes; he didn't know what Lola was doing. Mark has given him money and sent him to South America. He would do a thing like that. We'll never know how Lola came in touch with the man you call the Bath Crystal Bandit. He won't talk now. He and the Jacques have been sentenced. The Commonwealth is to have the privilege of housing and feeding them for several years. Pity it can't be for life.

This district will send Mark Trent's

name to the primaries in June as its candidate for senator to the Great and General Court. We've wanted him for years, but he wouldn't listen; probably thought that a political campaign would bring details of his domestic fiasco to the surface. Now that that's behind him, he's a different person, seems in high spirits. Hope that it isn't because he's in love with Daphne Field with whom he's everlastingly playing round.

Jed Stewart was here yesterday to make some changes in my will. My diamonds are to go to you. Didn't you save them? He sent his love. He said he missed you. So do I. He and I are going to New York for the première of Sam's play. I'm taking Lucette.

Jerry Field is tagging along. He has a prejudice against letting her out of his sight.

Affectionately yours,
ANNE GREGORY.

Birds twittered in the vines; the fronds of the royal palm in the corner of the patio grated against each other. Brooke's eyes were on the indigo horizon, her mind busy with the words:

"Seems in high spirits. Hope that it isn't

because he's in love with Daphne Field with whom he's everlastingly playing round."

"Oh, forget Mark Trent!" she said impatiently, and opened Lucette's letter.

For the first two pages the word "Jerry" monopolized space; to even a feebleminded person it would be evident that Jerry Field was leading in a long stag line.

Brooke was glad of that, but how did Lucette manage to take on all the festivities and be fit for her work in the morning? As if she had anticipated the question, Lucette wrote, with words heavily underlined for emphasis:

After this evening I'll cut out the night spots. There's *nothing* in them for me. It's an ill wind that blows nobody good. If you hadn't lost the Dane money you would still be hovering over me like a hen with one chicken. You and Mother were so afraid to let me be on my own; *I* know what you've been thinking from your letters. Trouble with you two is, you don't trust me enough. Did you think I would *like* having men make passes at me? That I would *want* to look and act like a silly fool from too many cocktails? That I would drive around the country after midnight with a man who was so *tight* that I'd find myself at dawn messed up round a telegraph pole? I've tried them all — except the pole; that night I told my muddled escort that I had never driven a car like his, would he let me try it? I asked sweetly. He would. Of course I drove with the dumbbell's head parked on my shoulder, but, in the words of our old friend Henry W. L.,

"Into each life some rain must fall,
Some days must be dark and dreary."

You know that I've always loathed cheapness, and if the pastimes above listed aren't cheap — cheap — *cheap,* I don't know what is.

So *stop* worrying about little sister, darling, and get *this:* I want to be like you, Brooke. *You* don't smoke, you don't drink, and yet I've never seen a man who, when introduced to you, didn't stand a little straighter, fuss with his tie, and get that I've-found-her-at-last look in his eyes; and you're grand fun and the life of the party.

There, you have the Inside Story of my life, so what? Never thought I would let you know how I *adored* you — bad for you — but here it is.

LUCETTE.

P. S. News flash! Sam's play may be produced any day. Its predecessor is folding up; it was a terrible flop.

Brooke shut her eyes to keep back tears. She had known that Lucette loved her, but that she set her on a pedestal was unbelieveable. As to that "I've-found-her-at-last" look in a man's eyes, she should have seen Mark Trent's when he had called her a "schemer" in Jed Stewart's office.

Why think of it? Hadn't she plenty of happier things to think of? She glanced at the clock. Sam's play might be produced any day. She had lost her job. She was free to go to New York! Could she afford it? Why did that grubby question have to pop up to take the joy out of life? Of course she would go. She had flown to Palm Beach at the expense of Carston's Inc. She would take a bus in return on her own. She would go tonight, go on to a new adventure in living.

Tingling with excitement, she telephoned for a reservation on the night bus; packed a small trunk to be sent by express;

folded her silver evening frock and accessories into the air luggage suit-case which Carston's Inc. had provided. She would want the gala clothes for the première — thrilling thought. She laid out an amethyst tweed suit with crimson scarf and beret, to wear on the journey. It would be cold when she reached New York.

All ready and somewhere to go! She glanced at the clock. There was time for a swim before she started for the style-show. It would set her up and refresh her. She must look her best for her positively last Palm Beach appearance.

She slipped into a white water-frock and caught up a beach coat. Life was gloriously worth while even if the man one loved did think one a "schemer," she told herself, as she ran down the steps which led to the patio.

She was humming a snatch of gay song as she crossed the strip of yellow sand steeping in golden sunlight which the march of fashion had left behind. Arms extended, she slid into the sparkling water. It parted. Buoyant, foamy, it closed over her. Marvelous feeling. This would stabilize her mind, drown haunting memories. She swam with quick strokes, turned, floated, came back arm over arm, and, dripping with coolness, waded out to the shore.

A man rose from the shadow of the dark hibiscus hedge outside the patio. Its scarlet flowers seemed to nod at her in amused derision as she stopped in surprise. Mark Trent! This was the cue for cool sophistication.

He held out the beach coat she had dropped on the sand.

"Put this on, Brooke. Let's sit here. I want to talk to you and we may be interrupted inside."

So, casually did he bridge the month since he had said in Lookout House livingroom:

"We'll finish our talk tomorrow."

The memory contracted her throat. Resting on one elbow, she glanced surreptitiously at him as he sat with arms around his gray flannel knees. Why had he come? She feigned interest in a line of surf breaking against a distant coral reef as she sifted shining particles of sand. She broke the silence which threatened to become permanent.

"How did you know where I was?"

"I've been playing round with Lucette, more or less. Saw Sam when I came through New York."

"Sam! How was he?"

"Nerves taut as violin strings, otherwise in great shape."

"When does his play open?"

"Day after tomorrow."

"So soon!"

"Why that sudden look of horror?"

"It wasn't horror, it was — I've lost my job and I had planned to leave here tonight by bus, but traveling that way I can't possibly make New York in time for the première of 'Islands Arise.' "

"I know that you've lost your job. I had a talk with your boss before I left the city. He agreed with me that you shouldn't miss the opening of Sam's play."

"You mean that you told him to fire me? What right have you to interfere in my life?"

"The right of a sort of guardian; didn't Aunt Mary Amanda so request in that last will?" Eyes on a pelican fishing in shallow water, he accused:

"You haven't answered Jed's letters notifying you that the amount of income you had been receiving from my aunt's estate would be deposited monthly to your account as usual. I had to come to find out if you had received them."

Brooke sprang to her feet. Her beach coat slipped off. Slim and golden-skinned in her white water-frock, she dug pink toes into the hot sand.

"I didn't answer because you both know without being told that I won't touch that money."

Mark Trent loomed over her.

"Put this on again," he commanded grimly. "Why won't you touch that money?"

Brooke thrust her arms into the beach coat he held and stuck her unsteady hands into the pockets.

"Would you take a cent of Mary Amanda Dane's when I thought it mine? Didn't you say in that snobby voice of yours the afternoon we met in Jed Stewart's office:

" 'Hope you'll enjoy the house and fortune, Miss Reyburn.' Now it's my turn:

" 'I hope you'll enjoy the house and fortune, Mr. Trent.' I'm sure Daphne Field will be crazy about it."

"Daphne!" He caught her wrist in a grip which hurt. "Where did you get that crazy idea?"

How crude, how unbelievably crude she had been to mention Daphne's name, Brooke accused herself hotly. But, having blundered, she'd better see it through with the light touch.

"From Mrs. Gregory's letter. It was full of news, all about the new candidate for senator to the Great and General Court and — and the current lady of his heart. She's a grand gossip."

Mark Trent's eyes drew Brooke's like a magnet. Was the light in his laughter?

"Anne Gregory is more than a gossip; she's a strategist. I haven't spoken to Daphne Field since the night of the play and she knows it." He loosened his hold on her wrist. "What are you doing this afternoon?"

"I'm — I'm modeling — for the last time."

"Can't you get out of it?"

"No."

"That's decisive. I have a present for you, but this doesn't seem to be just the moment to produce it. You seem to dislike me more than ever. I thought we might play round together. If you can't, or won't, I'll join a bunch of friends who wanted to date me up for some sort of fête this afternoon. They were all excited about a plan to surprise somebody about something. I didn't listen; I was anxious to locate you. I'll see you tonight before I leave, Brooke."

"Are you leaving tonight?"

"Yes. By plane. Come with me?"

"Certainly not." She imitated his voice and inflection to a note as she stopped at the gate of the patio.

"Hope you'll enjoy the trip, Mr. Trent. Happy landings!"

XXV

The sky was like a huge sapphire; the sunshine was rose-tinted; the ocean a tumbling
mass of emeralds. A fragrant breeze, a mere
suggestion of a breeze, ruffled the bright
orange flame-vine on top of the high Spanish wall which enclosed three sides of a
garden open to the sea, a garden filled with
tables set in gay borders which were filmy
frocks; there were faces above the tables,
faces under large hats and men's faces with
no hats at all.

From a Moorish gallery drifted male
voices singing to the accompaniment of
guitars as Brooke stepped from the automobile which had brought her to the charity fête. Carston's Inc. had staged the
wedding party of the style show with me-
ticulous attention to detail, even to sleek
shining cars to bring the bride and bridesmaids to the ornate grilles which were the
garden gates. Reporters were there and
camera men, hordes of them, all the frills
and appurtenances of a wedding except
groom and ushers.

Madame Céleste, chic in black and

pearls, was flushed with excitement under her make-up; her French accent was noticeable for its absence as she whispered last instructions:

"Wait until the singers stop, girls. The moment the orchestra strikes the first note of the wedding march, start. Don't get flustered. Don't get out of step. You're all lovely, your floppy hats are divine, and your bouquets of Transvaal daisies combining the shades of your frocks are perfect. Remember to smile when you turn in the space where the altar should be and isn't, to come down the three stairs to the aisle. Brooke, you are almost too white under that tulle; perhaps I should have put on more rouge. Too late now. Remember that you're giving an imitation of a radiantly happy bride, *cherie*. They've stopped. Ready! Listen!"

A violin sighed a soft note. Others joined until strings and harps and woodwinds swelled into the wedding march from Lohengrin.

Bridesmaids, their lips scarlet, their eyes shining between dark mascared lashes, passed between the iron grilles and moved slowly up the ribbon-outlined aisle, dragging their gold slippers a little in time to the rhythm of the music, and the swish of their taffeta slips. The first two were dressed in billowy rose-orange net; behind them at a short distance came two more in a lighter tint, then two in soft yellow, then a fourth pair in ivory, and then the bride in snowy satin so soft in texture that it trailed in ravishing folds. Slowly she came with head slightly bent, eyes presumably on the mass of white Transvaal daisies and stevia she carried, hair shining like burnished copper beneath the mist of her veil, but she could see, could feel the people who crowded the garden, people distinguished, powerful, chic: what the papers would headline as the cream of society.

Brooke felt the surge of motion as everyone stood up — a tribute to Madame Céleste's stagecraft — the wedding procession was so perfect that habit had brought the audience to its feet. She must keep her attention on the girls in front — why had Mark Trent come to Palm Beach — this heavenly music made one all trembly inside — drag her foot — she almost forgot it that time — did Mark love Daphne Field — would Mrs. Gregory write that if it were not true — would she never reach the spot where she was to turn — three stairs to mount before she reached it — this ought to be great fun, why was she taking it so seriously — a mass of faces — they seemed to be closing in — even out of doors the scent of exotic perfume and flowers was suffocating — almost there — step — drag — the vivid colors, the people seemed unreal — she might be standing in the wings looking on at a play — why couldn't she keep Mark Trent out of her mind — what had he brought her — why had she said such frantic and bitter things to him — was it love to be tormented with longing for the touch of his hand, the sight of his smile — why did love seem so simple for a man, why did it complicate life so for a woman — the orange-color bridesmaids were mounting the steps.

Something pulled at her eyes like a magnet. She looked up. A group of men was standing near the steps. All wore white suits with blue shirts and identical ties of Java print; each one had a boutonnière of deep blue bachelor buttons in the lapel of his coat; all were smiling broadly, she could feel their repressed excitement. Mark Trent was with them. His face went colorless with surprise as his eyes met hers in the instant before she bent her head again. Why was he here? Was this the fête a bunch of friends had urged him to attend? He hadn't expected to see her, that was evident. Why should he? Weren't all the other models girls whom Madame Céleste called socialites?

The stairs. One! Two! Three! She was up. The bridesmaids had deployed to face the audience — she had almost thought "congregation" — the orange-color frocks were at the ends of the semi-circle, the tints paled till they came to the snow-white bride. Her veil had been thrown back. Time for her to turn. The music swelled into a paean of triumph. It looked miles to the iron grilles beyond which stood Madame Céleste. She was safely down the steps! She must smile.

"Ready!"

She heard the whispered word, saw the men in white who had been standing beside the stairs hurdle the guarding ribbon. One offered his arm to her. Urged huskily:

"Quick! Let's put it through."

She looked up. Mark Trent! All the bitterness and pain went out of her heart. It was as if a great wall she had built between them had crumbled to a heap which she could cross. In a flare of gorgeous happiness she slipped her hand under his arm.

"It would be you," she said, and smiled in the second before they were in step with the music. Behind her she heard peals of laughter, girls' voices, men's voices. Then applause. A woman called:

"How priceless! The men are coming out with the bridesmaids!"

Brooke stopped at the intricate iron grille. She withdrew her hand from Trent's arm, walked back a step or two, tossed her bouquet among the bridesmaids, waited to see it scatter in four parts, turned, and ran out through the gateway to the limousine.

Reporters and camera men flocked after her. Machines clicked. Mark Trent fairly lifted her into the car. He blocked the door from curious eyes as he bent forward and kissed her on the lips. It was a tender kiss. There was reverence in it, there was a promise in his eyes, but laughter in his voice.

"That's an important part of the ceremony, isn't it? Hold out your left hand, Brooke." He pressed a ring on her finger. "This is what I had for you."

He turned away as Madame Céleste hurried up.

"Back to the salon!" She gave the order to the chauffeur with the air of a queen on location. She pushed aside billows of tulle, and sank into the seat beside Brooke who hid her left hand in the satin folds.

"Will our fashion show crash the front page, *cherie?* I'll say it will. I had a feeling something was in the air when I saw that bunch of swell men by the steps looking like a lot of kids with mischief sticking out all over them. They rate a thousand dollar bonus from Carston's Inc. What publicity! Handed to us on a silver platter! You should have seen the bridesmaids coming down the aisle. Each one with an escort who looked as if he had stepped off a fashion page of Vanity Fair. It was a riot. The man who played groom was the top-notch of a bunch of top-notchers. Hollywood is his home. He looks like a stout-hearted lad who'll get what he goes after every time. If I'm a judge of a man's eyes — believe it or not, *cherie,* I've seen 'em flame when they looked at me — you'll see friend groom again."

As she drove home from Carston's Inc. dressed in the tweeds in which she was to travel, Brooke kept looking at the ring on the third finger of her left hand. The cabochon emerald blinked back at her like a great, green eye, the diamond setting sent out innumerable sparks of light. Gorgeous thing. She wore it only because she was afraid that it might be lost if she took it off, she assured herself.

The soft flush of a tropical evening was stealing forward when she entered the patio, the glamour of night was settling over the dark mystery of the sea. The afterglow turned the masts of the distant yacht to red gold. Birds twittered sleepily. The fronds of the royal palm stirred gently. A man who was pacing back and forth came toward her quickly. Brooke's pulses which had been none too steady broke into a quickstep.

"I thought you would be flying through the air by this time, Mark," she tried to say indifferently.

"Did you think I would leave my bride?"

She avoided his disturbing eyes.

"Bride! The wedding party turned into a riot, didn't it? It was fun. Great theatre. Madame Céleste thinks that those men were divinely inspired to advertise Carston's Inc. They —"

"Just a minute, dearest. Stop and get your breath while I explain my part of it. I told you that I met some men I knew this morning. They were all excited over a plan to surprise a wedding party at a fashion show with groom and ushers; they were a lot of boys all set for a lark; made me feel young just to listen to their fooling. When I found you wouldn't play round with me I

405

joined them. I didn't know till the last minute that they'd picked me for the groom — not a tactful selection, and I refused the honor. But when I saw you coming up that aisle — well, they would have had to battle over my dead body to take my place. Forgive me, will you?" His caressing voice sent a ripple along Brooke's veins.

"There's nothing to forgive. I thought it was fun."

"Then we'll let that ride for the present. We've got to hustle. I have a message for you from your mother."

"From Mother! Where did you get it? How? I'm — I'm so surprised I feel as if my mouth were puckering up like a child's." Brooke blinked back a sudden rush of tears.

"You dear! I phoned her ten days ago."

"Phoned! Not to England."

"To England. It's being done some, you know."

"Of course I know. Don't, don't be so wooden."

"Wooden!" His laugh sent Brooke's hands behind her to clasp each other. "First I was a silent policeman, now I'm wooden. That also we will take up later. I didn't know what you had written your mother about the new will. I thought she should understand that your income was the same as when she left; otherwise she might not dare spend money to rush home for the première of Sam's play this week."

"It is not the same as when she went away."

"Your mistake. It is. She arrives in New York tomorrow."

"Tomorrow! I don't care what it costs. I'll fly."

"I thought you'd feel that way. I have reservations for us for the night plane." He glanced at his watch. "Throw some things into a suitcase, air-weight, remember. I have a car outside. We have just time to make the flying field."

Was she real, was anything real, Brooke asked herself, as the automobile burned up miles and the broad road flowed away from it. It was alive enough now; the Palm Beach world was hastening to eat, drink, and be merry. Above, through the warm black velvet dome, dripped a million or two stars. A magic night. Shining automobiles, gracefully long and low; others, silent, powerful, fast, provided glimpses of gay wraps, films of chiffon, glints of lamé, smooth heads, waved coiffures, sparkling jewels, the sombre black of evening clothes. Chairs propelled by boys with faces dark as chunks of obsidian held gayly appareled occupants. She glanced at Mark Trent beside her. Was he real? As if he had divined her question, he touched the ring on her left hand.

"Like it? Is it big enough, gorgeous enough?"

"It's perfect."

"Then you'll wear it always, won't you? You know that I love you, have loved you from the moment I caught you up from in front of that roadster, that I want you to marry me, don't you? You didn't think for a minute that I would leave you behind here, did you?" His hand tightened on hers.

"But you said — that last night at Lookout House — that you had made a lot of mistakes in your life but that you had learned enough not to make the mistake of asking me to marry you."

"Wouldn't it have been a mistake — then? You were so angry that you would have turned me down, wouldn't you? I couldn't afford to risk that. You're not angry now, are you, beautiful?"

His husky voice, his demanding eyes, the grip of his hand on hers rushed through Brooke like a tide of crystal water, sweeping away doubt and fear and heartbreak. He hadn't asked her to marry him because she had lost the fortune. He cared. She would never fail him, never. She tried to keep her voice light as she asked:

"Do you realize that this is the first time you've mentioned love, Mr. —"

"Come here!"

He caught her close. His eager, ardent lips on hers stopped her unsteady voice.

The car drew up with a jerk. The driver pulled open the door.

"We made it, boss —" He stopped. Put his full-moon face into reverse. Reminded over his shoulder:

"You've got three minutes. Boy waiting for your bags. If you've decided not to go —"

Mark Trent jumped out. Turned to Brooke.

"Coming?"

She put her hand in his, avoided his eyes as she stepped to the ground. Great twin motors purred beyond an open gate at the starting apron. A giant torchlight swept the sky. From a passing car drifted a man's voice singing:

" 'You may not be an angel
   But angels are so few,

That until the day one comes along
I'll trail along with you.' "

Brooke said breathlessly:
"Is it real? Will you trail along with me?
Do you love me, Mark?"

His hand tightened on hers. Something
in his eyes took hold of something deep in
her soul.

"Love you! That's a slight understate-
ment, but we'll let it pass — for the present. Are we going to New York in that
plane?"

"I'm sorry. I —"

Mark Trent's laugh was young and buoyant.

"Don't apologize."

"I'm not apologizing. I'm just explaining," Brooke retorted gayly, as hand in
hand they raced toward the great winged
gray monster already quivering into life.

The employees of Thorndike Press hope you have enjoyed this Large Print book. All our Large Print titles are designed for easy reading, and all our books are made to last. Other Thorndike Press Large Print books are available at your library, through selected bookstores, or directly from us.

For information about titles, please call:

(800) 223-2336

To share your comments, please write:

Publisher
Thorndike Press
P.O. Box 159
Thorndike, Maine 04986